WAKE THE PAST

SALLY RIGBY

Copyright © Sally Rigby, 2024

The moral right of the author has been asserted.

To request permissions, contact the publisher at rights@stormpublishing.co

Ebook ISBN: 978-1-80508-627-7
Paperback ISBN: 978-1-80508-628-4

Cover design: Stuart Bache Design
Cover images: Shutterstock

Published by Storm Publishing.
For further information, visit:
www.stormpublishing.co

ALSO BY SALLY RIGBY

Cavendish & Walker Series

Deadly Games

Fatal Justice

Death Track

Lethal Secret

Last Breath

Final Verdict

Ritual Demise

Mortal Remains

Silent Graves

Kill Shot

Dark Secrets

Broken Screams

Death's Shadow

Buried Fear

A Cornwall Murder Mystery

The Lost Girls of Penzance

The Hidden Graves of St Ives

Murder at Land's End

Detective Sebastian Clifford Series

Web of Lies

Speak No Evil

Never Too Late
Hidden From Sight
Fear the Truth

ONE

Private detective Sebastian Clifford glanced up at the magnificent glass and steel domed roof of the historic reading room in Wickham College library, where the fundraising event for the Harborough Literacy Trust was being held. He'd agreed to attend on behalf of his cousin Sarah, who was on the committee, and had been travelling overseas for many months.

A Christmas tree sat in one corner, the glittering decorations giving the large room an ambient glow reminding him the festive season was around the corner.

'Thank you again for coming tonight. As you can see, it's going very well,' the organiser, Muriel French, said while smoothing down the full skirt of her blue dress.

'Indeed, it is,' Sebastian Clifford agreed, looking down at the woman who was at least a foot shorter than his six feet five inches. 'It was delightful to see the children on the stage talking about their favourite books. It showed the real impact of your reading programme.'

The event had been a refreshing change when compared to

some of the stuffy functions he'd endured in the past... thanks to being a member of the aristocracy. His father was Viscount Worthington, and Seb had grown up in that world. But thankfully, it was his brother Hubert who was the heir to that title, which meant Seb could lead a more normal life.

'Thank you. We're very proud of what we've done. It's a pity Sarah isn't here, though. We do miss her at our monthly meetings. Have you heard from her recently?'

'We spoke last week. She's planning on remaining in India for a while and unsure where to go next. I'm looking forward to seeing her sons Benedict and Caspian when they return to Rendall Hall for the Christmas break,' Seb replied. As well as standing in for Sarah's charity obligations, he was also caring for his cousin's seventeenth-century house until she decided to return to England. He didn't mind because it was the perfect place for him to run his private detective agency – Clifford Investigation Services.

'Do give her my regards when you're next in touch,' Muriel said.

As Muriel spoke, her assistant silently appeared and whispered something in her ear. She sighed. 'No rest for the wicked. It looks like our MC has had one too many to drink and we still have the silent auction to go. Do excuse me, and don't forget to bid.'

'You can count on it.' Seb had already written a generous cheque but planned to bid on several items to support their good work.

A waiter approached, carefully balancing a tray of champagne-filled glasses, but Seb held up his hand to refuse. He was driving tonight and wasn't one to take any risks. Plus, with the busy caseload he and his partner, Lucinda Bird – aka Birdie – had been juggling, he planned to spend Sunday catching up on admin.

His phone pinged and he was about to take it from his

jacket pocket and check the message when he noticed a woman heading in his direction.

It was Lady Angelica Charing.

The older woman was in her late sixties with a pale complexion and striking blue eyes. She was an acquaintance of Seb's parents but they'd only had a few conversations in the past. She was also one of the Literacy Trust's patrons.

'Good evening, Lady Angelica. I hope you're well.'

'Ah, yes, all the better now that I've found you, Sebastian,' she declared, a tremor in her voice.

Seb refrained from reacting, but his curiosity was piqued since she had the reputation of being stoic and unflappable.

'Is there a problem?' he asked, scanning the room but not seeing anything amiss.

'No. Muriel has it all under control as always,' she assured him with a smile. But then she lowered her voice, although the elegant façade remained unbroken. 'I do indeed have a pressing problem, which is why I need to talk to you.'

A group of children darted behind them, and Lady Angelica's fingers visibly tightened around the stem of her champagne glass.

'Of course. Shall we go into the foyer where it's quieter?'

'Yes, that's a good idea. I usually love seeing how enthusiastic the children are, but tonight, I have too much on my mind to enjoy it.'

'I'll lead the way,' he said, holding out his arm and steering them through the mingling guests. As he walked, his HSAM – highly superior autobiographical memory – kicked in, heading directly to the last time he'd seen her. Four years ago, at a ball in Windsor, where they'd exchanged pleasantries about the weather before the next dance had started and Seb's girlfriend at the time, Annabelle, had claimed him.

The foyer wasn't quite as grand as the library but it was dotted with clusters of club chairs and low coffee tables that were stacked with various library books, for people to browse through. And though it was far from private, at least the chatter had fallen away somewhat.

He pulled out a chair for her and she sat down, though her blue eyes never left his face. He sat opposite. Whatever was bothering Lady Angelica was clearly important.

'Sorry for the dramatics,' she said, leaning in slightly and lowering her voice. 'But I need your help. On a personal matter.'

'You mean as an investigator?'

'Yes. That's correct. I have a very – how shall I put it? – *delicate* situation that requires a good deal of discretion. I didn't know who to approach, but because of our connections decided that you are one person I can trust. It concerns a missing person.'

Before he could answer, a group of men walked through the foyer back into the reading room, where the MC was testing out the microphone. If her issue was as sensitive as she was implying, this was hardly the time or place.

'I am more than happy to help. If you'd like to see me on Monday morning, we can discuss your issue in more detail. I'm currently living at Rendall Hall. I believe you've been there in the past.'

Lady Angelica gave him a grateful nod. 'I can see I've made the right choice. Monday morning it is. Is nine o'clock too early?'

'Not at all. My business partner and I will look forward to it,' he assured her.

Seb went to stand, but before he could, she reached over and placed her hand on his arm. 'Thank you, Sebastian. It really is of the utmost importance. It's about a missing person and is a matter of life and death.'

* * *

Monday, 4 December

'I told you that going to these fancy events of yours would pay off,' Seb's partner, Birdie, declared on Monday morning as she turned up the heat on the ancient radiator and grinned at him. Her eyes were bright, and instead of returning to her desk, she dragged a chair across to sit closer to him. 'So, what's the case?'

'I've no idea yet,' Seb replied as Elsa, his beloved yellow Labrador, nudged his leg with her nose, clearly after a pat. He obliged before turning back to Birdie. 'She was obviously distressed, and considering she wanted discretion, I suggested we meet here this morning.'

'What do you know about her family? Are they friends of yours?'

'Not close friends, although my parents are acquainted with them. I've had several exchanges with Lady Angelica over the years. She's a Montague by birth, an aristocratic family from outside Dunchurch in Warwickshire. Rolton Hall where they live goes back to Elizabeth I.'

'I bet there are plenty of secrets to discover then.' Birdie smirked.

'I can't answer that. Angelica married into another very old family. The Charings. Lord Edgar Charing comes from Leicestershire and his country estate is Fleckney House. You might know of it.'

Birdie's eyes widened. 'If it's the place I'm thinking of, I went there on a school trip. The place is massive. It looked like something out of a Jane Austen book. I remember there were peacocks in the garden. So, what else do you know about her?'

'Angelica and Edgar married in 1980. It was a huge affair and covered in all the media.'

'Were you there?' She gave him an innocent smile.

'As you well know, I wasn't born in 1980. But my parents attended. Lord and Lady Charing have three children who are around my age. Leo's the oldest, Charles is in the middle, and Devon's the youngest. We went to different schools, so our paths seldom crossed.'

'I wonder what she means by calling it a "matter of life and death". Sounds pretty dramatic if you ask me. How did she seem in herself? Panicked?'

'Outwardly she came across as calm. She's what my father would call *old school*. Very calm under pressure. But... there was definitely something.'

'I wonder who this missing person is. Do you think someone's got lost in the castle? Places like that always have secret rooms. Someone could have leant against the bookcase and disappeared from sight. They might not even know it exists, and they could be trapped in the wall, with only ghosts for company.' Birdie waved her hands excitedly.

'Considering the amount of work that's been carried out on the house over the years, they have probably accounted for all the secret rooms. And I've never heard any rumours of the building being haunted,' Seb pointed out, though it didn't appear to dampen her spirits at all.

'You're right. That's too easy, too obvious. But there's a large lake in the grounds. What if someone went for a midnight swim?' she mused before shaking her head. 'No. Scrap that – someone would have seen them, or at least gone looking. Hmm. Let me have a poke around the internet.'

She jumped to her feet and hurried back to her desk in her usual whirlwind of energy. Elsa gave an adoring wag of her tail from where she was curled on the floor by the desk, and then promptly fell back asleep, tired from her morning walk.

Birdie leant forward, her fingers flying across the keyboard as a strand of bright red hair fell across her face. Making an irritated noise, she pushed it away and continued to work. Seb waited. As wild as some of her ideas sounded, Birdie's ability to think outside the box and look at problems from a variety of angles was one of the things that made her such an exceptional detective.

On cue, she leant back in her chair and rubbed her chin.

'Here we are. It looks like your Lady Angelica is involved in running the estate and has been doing a lot of work to keep it going. It's only open to the public during the summer, and for the village fete, so there goes my theory of a stray tourist. But it does say here that she's involved in a lot of charities. Here's a photo of her with your cousin Sarah. Looks like it's for a similar fundraiser to the one you went to the other night. Which means, if we need more information on Lady Angelica, we could ask Sarah. Or your mother.'

'Or Lady Angelica herself,' Seb reminded her. Although he knew why Birdie was keen for them to discover what they could from other sources. One of their most recent cases had involved a television celebrity who'd withheld vital information from them. But that didn't mean Angelica Charing would be the same.

'True. But I'm dying to know who has gone missing. Maybe—'

Ding. Ding. Ding.

At the sound of the doorbell, Elsa opened one eye, and Seb got to his feet and crossed the room. 'Well, we can't have you dying on us, so it's lucky that we're about to find out exactly who has.'

TWO

Birdie followed Seb out into the grand hallway and tugged her favourite navy cardigan closer to her chest. While she loved Rendall Hall, she was starting to see the downside of owning such a big house. Especially when it came to keeping the place warm.

Not that Seb seemed to notice. Either he didn't feel the cold, or he was used to it from having grown up in a house that was even larger than this one. For once, Birdie was pleased she lived in a more modest detached house with her parents and brothers. It might not be as fancy, but at least it didn't feel like the Antarctic.

Seb opened the door, and another gust of cool December wind blew down the corridor as Lady Angelica Charing stepped in through the doorway. She was tall, with sleek silver hair and intense blue eyes that landed on Birdie before narrowing. In turn, Birdie immediately squared her shoulders. Seb didn't give any signs of noticing the atmosphere as he ushered in their guest and closed the door behind her.

'Lady Angelica, may I introduce my business partner, Birdie.'

'Nice to meet you,' Birdie said, with a slight dip of her head.

'Likewise.' Lady Angelica gave her a brisk nod, though her jaw was tight with tension.

Birdie glanced through the open door and saw a man sitting in the car.

'Would your driver like to come inside out of the cold?'

'Thank you, but no. He's fine there,' Lady Angelica said as she shrugged off a navy wool coat that had dog hair clinging to the bottom, and passed it to Seb, who was standing by the long row of hooks.

Elsa appeared from the office and gave the air a curious sniff before letting out a low bark, then disappearing through to the farmhouse-style kitchen.

'That was Elsa, who's hoping she'll get a second breakfast now you've arrived.' Seb laughed, and for a second, the worried look on their potential new client's face faded. She was obviously a dog person. Birdie made a mental note of it, though it still didn't endear her to the woman.

They followed Elsa to the kitchen, which had thankfully warmed up, and Seb boiled the kettle and poured it into the large teapot. Seb was usually happy to have a teabag in a mug but apparently, he'd decided Lady Angelica would prefer loose leaf.

Birdie gave him a questioning glance, which he managed to ignore. Sighing, she collected the tray with cups and a jug of milk on it and carried it to the table.

'Tea?' she asked.

'Thank you.' Lady Angelica gave a distracted wave of her hand as Seb placed the teapot in the middle of the old wooden table.

'While we're waiting for it to steep, why don't you explain why you're here?' Seb said kindly.

The woman frowned, looking in Birdie's direction. 'May we speak in private? It's confidential.'

Seriously? Birdie went to open her mouth, but Seb beat her to it.

'Birdie and I are partners, and we work together on all our cases.' His voice was as stern as she'd ever heard it. 'Whatever your problem is, you can explain it to Birdie as well. She's an excellent detective and I'm lucky to have her as my partner.'

Birdie caught her breath, not sure how the other woman would react. But to her surprise Lady Angelica held up her hands as if to acknowledge an error.

'And rightly so.' She turned to Birdie, and this time looked at her properly. 'My apologies. It's a difficult time right now, but that's no excuse for my bad manners. Please accept my apology.'

The tension in Birdie's neck loosened. Seb had said Lady Angelica was usually very straightforward, and that was something she admired in anyone.

'It's okay. And I can assure you that whatever you tell us will be treated as confidential. You told Seb that this is a missing person's case. Who's missing?' Birdie asked, not wanting to prevaricate any longer.

Lady Angelica closed her eyes, as if trying to summon the courage to speak. Then she looked up, her intense eyes bright with determination.

'My son.'

'Which one? Devon, Leo, or Charles?' Seb asked while Birdie reached for the notebook she'd already placed on the table. Seb, with his memory, didn't need to take notes because he forgot nothing. But Birdie didn't like to rely on him and preferred to make her own record. She found their clients relaxed more at this visual acknowledgement of what they had to say.

'No, no, the boys are all safe,' Lady Angelica said, colour rising in her pale cheeks, but she didn't turn away or avoid their gaze. 'I'm talking about... about... my *illegitimate* son.' She paused a moment and looked from Seb to Birdie. When they didn't comment, she continued. 'He was born on the third of May 1972. I had just turned sixteen when I found out I was pregnant, and of course, it would have been scandalous if it had become public knowledge. My parents sent me away to have him, and then...' Her voice faltered and she made a soft choking noise. 'Well... then he was given up for adoption.'

Birdie swallowed, her heart hammering in her chest. Memories of what she'd recently been through came to the forefront of her mind. She'd been given up for adoption and had only recently found her own birth mother. Hearing it from a birth mother's perspective was disconcerting.

'The adoption act wasn't changed until 1976, so as you gave him up for adoption four years earlier, it might make it difficult to find any records,' Birdie said. 'Not impossible, mind you.'

Lady Angelica gave her an approving nod. 'Quite correct. As you might have guessed, I tried to investigate it on my own, but immediately hit a brick wall.'

'And is this the first time you've tried searching for your son?' Seb asked.

Good question. 1972 was a long time ago. Why had she waited so long?

Again, there was a pause before Lady Angelica answered. 'As I've already mentioned, there would have been a huge scandal if it had come out. Also my parents didn't give me any details regarding what happened to the baby. At the time, I was persuaded that it was for the best. For the child, and for myself. But now...'

She trailed off and Birdie exchanged a look with Seb. They'd both interviewed enough people to know that Lady Angelica was struggling to tell them something and that the best thing they could do was give her time.

Seb leant forwards and poured the tea from the pot, and by

the time Lady Angelica had stirred in some milk, she seemed to have composed herself. When she looked up at them, her eyes were moist.

'My youngest son, Devon, has chronic kidney disease, and desperately needs a transplant. He's on a waiting list, but time's running out. No one in the family is a suitable match... but the doctors think a blood relation is still the best chance of finding a potential donor.'

'That's terrible.' Birdie widened her eyes, all too quickly appreciating what a challenging situation it must be for Lady Angelica. To save her son, she had to risk her darkest secret. 'Is he on dialysis?'

'No. He has PVD and dialysis could make his symptoms worse.'

'What's that?' Birdie asked.

'Peripheral vascular disease, which involves the narrowing of peripheral blood vessels,' Seb said. 'It's a circulation disorder often caused by diabetes or lifestyle.'

'You're right it usually is. Devon's one of those rare people who has it through no fault of his own,' Lady Angelica said, her voice breaking slightly.

'I'm sorry to hear about Devon. It must be very hard,' Seb added, his own eyes full of concern.

'Frustrating is what it is,' Lady Angelica said, some fire returning to her voice. 'I would willingly do it if I could. And so would Edgar, or the other boys, and yet we can't. Which is why I've decided to find my oldest son. Not that the rest of the family know about him, I hasten to add.'

'What else can you tell us about the birth?' Birdie asked, her mind already moving through the avenues they could go down. 'Who's the father?'

'Roy. I don't know his surname. He worked as a gardener on my parents' estate that summer and was very dashing... I suppose I got carried away.' She closed her eyes, as if remembering.

Scenes from *Lady Chatterley's Lover* sprang into Birdie's mind. She'd studied the book for GCSE and had loved it. But she quickly shook her head to push them aside. This wasn't the time.

'In which hospital did you give birth?' Seb asked quickly, clearly wanting to keep Lady Angelica focused. 'You said your parents sent you away somewhere; does that mean you didn't have the baby in Warwickshire?'

'That's correct. By the time I came home from school for Christmas, I had suspicions that I was pregnant. When I told my mother, she immediately sent me to Norfolk to stay with her younger sister, my aunt Edith. The hospital's only small, and is still open, but when I contacted them, I couldn't get anything out of them.'

Birdie wasn't surprised. Record keeping isn't always what it should be in these sorts of places, and even if they still had details of the birth, it didn't mean staff would hand them out. Not even to the birth mother.

'I know your parents are no longer with us,' Seb said. 'But did either of them tell you anything about it, or did you find anything in their papers?'

She immediately shook her head. 'No. Not a word. That's the way it was back then. No point talking about things that have already happened. My father used to say stirring up the past was asking for trouble. But....' She sighed.

'What?' Birdie asked.

'There were times when I regretted not asking them where my eldest son was.' She paused for a moment. 'Sorry. I'm not helping.'

'Don't apologise. It can't have been easy,' Birdie said. 'What about Aunt Edith? Is she still alive? Has she been able to tell you more?'

At this, Lady Angelica grimaced. 'I'm afraid I haven't seen Edith since the birth. There was a huge family falling-out, and while my mother never told me the details of what transpired, I long suspected it had something to do with me. She didn't attend my mother's funeral, although I do know she's still alive.'

Birdie chewed her lip. With Lady Angelica's parents dead, and the whole thing kept secret, Edith would be the most likely person to know more, but if the rift had been due to the pregnancy, it might be difficult to get anything out of her.

'Who else knew about you being pregnant? Did you tell Roy or any other friends or family?' she asked.

Lady Angelica shook her head. 'No. My parents were adamant that it was kept secret. Plus, as soon as I told them, I was sent away so I didn't have a chance, even if I wanted to. Oh... wait. There's Nanny. Not sure why I didn't think of her before. She was with our family for years and became a companion-come-secretary for my mother after I went to boarding school. She's in a care home in Bournemouth. She turned ninety last month, and her mind does tend to wander. And... I would hate to bring up old memories and then have it slip out when Edgar or the boys are around. We do visit her when we're down that way.'

Seb leant forward, his brow drawn. 'I take it Lord Edgar and your children don't know about any of this?'

'Absolutely not. And that's the way I'd like to keep it. At least until we find my son and know if he's a match.'

'What about Devon?' Birdie asked. 'Does he know?'

'All I've told him is that I'm trying to track down a distant relative.' At this, she paused and took a shaky breath. 'It's hard trying to balance giving him hope with being realistic... Will you take the case? Money's no object. My only concern is saving my son's life.'

Excitement bubbled in the pit of Birdie's stomach. New cases always did that to her. Except they were facing an almost impossible task and might not be successful. She didn't want them to let the woman down.

She glanced at Seb, who gave a slight nod of agreement. Was he thinking along the same lines? It was complicated, and even if they did find the missing son, it didn't mean everything would work out the way Lady Angelica hoped. The man might not be a match. But, if they didn't help her, then her chances of finding her eldest son were minimal. Or she might hire someone else who wasn't as discreet with her secret.

'Although we can't guarantee success,' Seb said, his voice measured and calm, 'we are willing to try. And while I appreciate your need for privacy, we will need to speak with Devon and his doctors. Do we have your permission?'

Lady Angelica got to her feet and gave a decisive nod. 'Of course. Dr Desai is Devon's consultant nephrologist. I'll let her know you'll be in touch. Thank you, Sebastian. And you, too, Birdie. You've given me hope, when before there was none.'

THREE

After walking with Lady Angelica to the front door and watching while she was driven down the drive, they headed to the office.

'There's certainly a lot on the line with this case,' Birdie said, her mouth set in a concerned line.

Seb rubbed the back of his neck. 'Yes. It's not only complicated, but we mustn't forget there are ethical considerations. First we should contact Devon's doctor to find out what's involved in a kidney transplant.'

'Yes,' Birdie agreed, drumming her fingers on her desk. 'There's no point visiting Aunt Edith or following up on any leads until we have the full picture. Potentially, we'll be asking someone to give up a kidney for a family member they never even knew existed. Assuming they're compatible, which they might not be. That's a massive ask.'

Lady Angelica had given them the number for Devon's doctor, and Seb pulled out his phone and called it while Birdie settled down at her desk, opened up the laptop, and stared at him from over the screen.

'Dr Indira Desai's office,' a chirpy-sounding female voice answered on the third ring. 'How can I help you?'

'Good morning, my name's Sebastian Clifford. I'd like to speak to Dr Desai if she's available. It's regarding one of her patients, Devon Charing.'

'Ah, yes. Lady Charing has just called to say you'd be in touch. Dr Desai's next appointment isn't for another twenty minutes, so you're in luck. I'll put you through.'

'Thank you.' He lifted an eyebrow to let Birdie know he'd been successful, and she gave him a thumbs up in response.

'Hello, Mr Clifford, I'm pleased you called,' Dr Desai said when she answered. She had a warm reassuring voice, which Seb assumed would be necessary in her field.

'Thank you for taking the time to speak to me, Dr Desai. I'm in the room with my partner, Lucinda Bird. I'd like to put you on speaker if you don't object.'

'Of course, please do. Good morning, Lucinda.'

Birdie grimaced at the sound of her real name being used, which she hated.

'Hello, Dr Desai. Please call me Birdie,' she said, glaring at Seb, who shrugged an apology.

'Under normal circumstances we'd have contacted you first before agreeing to find this distant relative but Lady Angelica implied that time is of the essence,' Seb said. 'Is that correct?'

'I'm afraid it is. Devon has been assessed and although currently he's still eligible for a transplant, in terms of his health, without a donor, he'll be lucky to last six months. Unfortunately, none of his family are suitable. A kidney did come available for him through the HLA scheme, but it wasn't a match. It was devastating for the family, who had pinned all their hopes on it.'

Across from him, Birdie's eyes widened and Seb let out a grim sigh.

'I see. What are the odds of finding a donor in time?'

'I don't believe in sugar-coating the issue. Devon's blood group is O, which means he can only receive a kidney from someone with that same type. The trouble is, it's not just about the blood type. We need a tissue match as well. There are around five thousand people on the register at any one time, all needing a kidney transplant, and most of them will only have the option of receiving a kidney from someone who has recently died. Receiving an organ from a living donor not only improves the chances of it working, but that the recipient will have a better likelihood of living longer. It's certainly the preferred option for anyone in this situation.'

'Does the kidney have to be donated by a family member?' Birdie asked.

'Not at all. But because there's up to a fifty per cent chance of a family member, especially a sibling, being a match, it's the best place to start. Also, due to the seriousness of the operation and the risks, it's more often than not a family member who's willing to do it. Currently, much work is being done to encourage people to consider becoming living donors.'

'Could you talk us through the risks for donors?' Seb asked.

'Certainly. The reason we undertake living donations is that it's possible for the body to function perfectly well with one kidney. But, like all surgeries, there's a small risk of the donor not surviving.'

'How small?' Birdie asked, frowning.

'Very. It's a common operation and most of the complications are minor and can be treated,' Dr Desai said in a reassuring tone.

'Can the kidney be rejected?' Birdie asked.

'Yes. There's a chance the kidney will be rejected by the

recipient, which can take a huge mental toll on everyone involved, including the donor. I will send you more detailed information on this, if you would like.'

'Yes, please,' Seb said. 'What's the recovery period for the donor?'

'Anything from one to three months. As you can see, it's a big commitment and there's a lot for the potential donor to consider.'

'There is. Thank you for explaining it so succinctly. You've given us an excellent overview,' Seb acknowledged.

'You're welcome. I hope you can find this distant relative as quickly as possible. It could be Devon's last chance.'

Seb ended the call and drummed his fingers on the desk. 'Thoughts?' he asked Birdie, who had risen from her chair and was pacing the office.

Birdie stopped and ran a hand through her red curls. 'Lady Angelica didn't exaggerate about Devon's condition, which means we really do have our work cut out for us. While Dr Desai was talking, I pulled up a number of articles on the procedure and what's involved for the donor. I've forwarded them to you, so your super brain can get to work.'

'Thank you.' Seb ignored the joke about his HSAM. 'However, it's all moot if we can't find the adopted son, which will be no easy task.'

'Agreed. It really is an elephant situation.'

'An elephant situation?' Seb blinked, and Birdie gave him an amused grin.

'I can't believe you haven't heard that one. It's the old joke of how do you eat an elephant?'

'Is this something I want to hear?' Seb raised a brow, knowing her humour could be a bit over the top at times.

'Relax. It's not gory. The answer to how do you eat an elephant is simple. One bite at a time.' She sat back down at her desk, looking smug. 'Speaking of food. I'm starving. I'll make us some lunch, and while I'm in the kitchen, you can arrange a meeting for us with Devon Charing as soon as possible. It's glaringly obvious that time is most definitely not on our side.'

FOUR

'Whoa. Most things seem smaller when you go back and visit them as an adult, but not this place.' Birdie looked up at the imposing presence of Fleckney House that dominated the landscape. The dull grey sandstone and symmetrical windows gave the house an almost bleak appearance against the darkening sky. 'Do you think they use all the rooms?'

Seb gave her an amused smile as he turned his black BMW down a long private driveway that was flanked by trees on both sides.

'Originally, it was probably a lot smaller, but like many of these houses, it's been extended several times. What is now the front of the house was originally built as one of the wings in the 1780s, hence the Georgian architecture.'

He turned again and followed a smaller road around to the back of the property. It led to the double-fronted cottage where Devon and his wife, Celia, currently lived. When Seb had finally managed to reach them on the phone yesterday, Celia had explained they'd been at back-to-back hospital appointments. And while she'd been worried Devon might not be up to visitors, she'd agreed to let them visit, especially once Seb had emphasised how imperative it was.

Seb pulled up outside the cottage and they got out of the car. The entrance was flanked by two tubs of flowering cyclamens, and there was a small wreath hanging on the black wooden door. A woman answered it before either of them could ring the buzzer. She probably wasn't much older than Birdie, with dark hair pulled back off her face into a ponytail. There were grey smudges under her eyes, most likely from lack of sleep.

'You must be Birdie and Seb. I'm Celia. Please come in.'

'Thank you.' Birdie followed her inside, Seb close behind, through to a comfortable sitting room with white walls and two sofas at right angles to each other. On the walls were several blown-up black-and-white photographs of steam trains. On a recliner in the corner was a pale, skinny man. Devon Charing.

Even sitting down, it was clear that Devon was tall like his mother, with her same piercing blue eyes. But his complexion was waxy, as if he hadn't been outside much, and even from the doorway, Birdie could see the painful rise and fall of his chest as he tried to catch his breath.

Birdie swallowed. He was thirty-four, but there was a weariness to him that made him appear much older.

'Hello,' he said, trying to ease himself up into a more upright sitting position. Next to him was a small table with numerous pill bottles on it, while on the other side was a movable desk with a bright light shining over it. On the desk was a tray with a small model train on it and a collection of tiny cans of paint and brushes, along with a magnifying glass. 'Would either of you like a cup of tea or coffee?'

'No, thank you. We had one before we came here,' Birdie

quickly said, not wanting to make more work for an already exhausted-looking Celia. 'Are you feeling up to talking to us?'

'Yes. But probably best if you have a seat.' He glanced over at Seb, who was standing beside her. 'It's nice to meet you both. I know our paths never crossed, Clifford, but I believe we have a few rugby friends in common.'

'You played?' Seb settled down on the sofa closest to the man.

'Hooker.' Devon turned his head slightly to display his ear, which was covered in a multitude of lumps and bumps. It made Birdie pleased that she played cricket, which still had its own fair share of injuries but not like that. 'Still, I did manage to get the girl.'

'Only because you'd grown your hair long and I couldn't see,' Celia retorted, before walking over to him and kissing his cheek. 'And when I did, of course, I'd already fallen for you and your charming ways.'

'Did you meet at university?' Seb asked.

Birdie gave an approving smile at the way he was putting the pair of them at ease before approaching what surely was a very painful subject.

'We did. We were both at St Andrews. I was studying agriculture and Celia anthropology. After graduating, we returned to here and married eight years ago. Back then, the old kitchen garden was nothing more than a mass of weeds, but I began restoring it and it's now a working garden. At the time, Celia was working for a not-for-profit in Leicester. Things were going pretty well—' He broke off and shrugged. 'Well, you know what they say about the best laid plans. Everything's changed now.'

'Devon gave up work last year, and I resigned from my position six months ago to look after him full time.' Celia took over. She sat down on the sofa next to Devon's chair, but outstretched her hand so that they were still touching. 'We do have a nurse who comes in every day as well for medical help.'

Devon closed his eyes, though his shoulders were stiff. 'Not quite the romantic dream I'd promised her.'

'Better or worse.' She turned to him, as if wanting to make sure he heard her. Then she swallowed and looked directly at Birdie. 'Angelica said she'd hired you and Sebastian to look into a distant relative who might be a suitable donor. I hope this isn't going to be another wild goose chase. I don't think we can take any more disappointment.' Anguish shone from her eyes.

'That's correct.' Birdie brought out her notebook. 'We spoke to Dr Desai yesterday. But we wanted to chat to you both before moving forward. To see how you feel about it. It goes without saying that it's an ordeal.'

'At first I was in denial,' Devon said, his breathing still laboured. 'We had started trying for a family, but I constantly felt exhausted and rundown. I was concerned that I wouldn't have the energy to be a good father. At first, I figured I just needed to cut back on the beer and cakes and go for a few more runs. But the fatigue got worse. Once we received the diagnosis and were told I'd need a kidney transplant... well, it didn't seem real.'

'It was a shock.' Celia squeezed his hand in reassurance. 'But Devon's family were all willing to be tested as being potential donors, as was I. So, for a long time, while the testing was going on, we felt optimistic. But the last year has been hard. And then we got the call about a possible donor, only to find out it wasn't a match...'

This time she was the one to break off as she dabbed at her eyes.

'Believe it or not, the hardest part is seeing how upsetting it is for the rest of the family. Especially for Mummy.' Devon rubbed his eyes, his fingers showing smears of paint from his work. 'She's been working on the family tree over these last few years, but she's never mentioned this distant cousin before. I'm worried that she's grasping at straws, and that looking for him will end up making it harder. For all of us.'

After he spoke, he sank back in the recliner, clearly wiped out by the conversation. A prickle of worry rose in Birdie's chest. What if all they were doing was raising their hopes with little or no chance of success?

Seb seemed to share her concern and he leant forward.

'We're not here to give you false hope, Devon. But the information your mother has given us appears to be worth following up. If you are happy for us to continue, we'll do everything in our power to find him. But it has to be your decision.'

'And if you do find this cousin, then what will happen?' Celia asked.

'If we're successful in locating him, and if he's willing to be tested to see if he's compatible, Birdie and I will consider our part done.'

Devon was silent for several moments before nodding. 'Okay. But my one request is that you don't mention it to anyone else in the family. It's difficult enough, without having to manage their expectations as well.'

'You have our word,' Birdie promptly assured him.

'Thank you.' Devon's voice was faint, and it was clear he was totally wiped out.

'We should go.' Birdie got to her feet at the same time as Seb.

'I'll see you out,' Celia said, stopping only to put a knee rug over her husband. 'He gets worn out very easily.'

'It must be difficult,' Birdie said as they reached the door.

'As I told my stubborn husband, I said for better or worse.' Celia squared her shoulders and opened the door in time to see Lady Angelica striding down the path, followed by two black-and-white dogs. The blue coat from yesterday was gone and she was wearing a green quilted jacket. She held a long stick in her hand.

'I was hoping to catch you,' she said in a brisk voice before her face softened at the sight of Celia. 'How are you, my dear? Did you manage to sleep last night?'

'As much as I needed,' Celia assured her. 'Would you all like to come back inside? We can go into the dining room and leave Devon to rest.'

'Thank you, but no. You go inside and rest yourself. I'll pop around this afternoon after the nurse has been, if that's okay?'

'Of course,' Celia assured her just as a timer on her phone went off. 'Medication time. I'd better supervise because he's prone to forgetting to take them all.' She looked directly at Birdie and Seb. 'Thank you. It's been hard on Devon... well, for all of us. But... despite my initial reticence, I'd rather have some hope than none at all.'

Once Celia disappeared into the cottage, Lady Angelica nodded towards a large red-brick wall to the left of the cottage. 'The original kitchen garden is over there. Would you like to come for a walk and see it?'

'Of course. Devon told us how he'd restored it,' Birdie agreed, pleased she was wearing her boots and not her white trainers as they followed her down a muddy path. The two dogs led the way, their breath coming out in steamy columns from the cool air. They didn't speak until they reached the walled garden and Lady Angelica pushed open the wrought-iron gate.

'Jess. Jim. Heel,' she said. The dogs scampered to her side as they stepped through to the garden.

'Wow,' Birdie said, scanning the huge space with its numerous vegetable patches full of winter greens, all connected by wide gravel pathways. There was also a large greenhouse to one side and right in the middle was a fountain. Birdie hadn't been quite sure what a kitchen garden was but hadn't been expecting something on such a grand scale.

'Very impressive,' Seb said, nodding appreciatively. 'Devon

mentioned he'd done some work on it, but he really didn't do his efforts justice.'

'Yes, he's done a marvellous job. I've helped run the estate ever since Edgar and I married, but neither of us were interested in gardening. We have gardeners to take care of the grounds, which have been established for hundreds of years. But I'm afraid this walled garden was neglected. As a child, Devon would play in here, and as he got older, he started clearing out small sections, at first just to grow strawberries, but by the time he went to St Andrews, he'd already set up a much smaller version of what you see now. Although when he was away, it relapsed into its previously weedy state. It took him many months to turn it into the success it is today.'

'You must be proud,' Birdie said.

'Of course I am, though it's difficult to see him now, when he barely has the energy to paint his model trains. He's trying to finish the *Llantilio Castle* before...' She trailed off and stalked towards one of the garden beds. Seb, with his long legs, could easily keep pace with her, but Birdie found herself jogging to stop being left behind. 'What are your next steps?'

'We spoke to Dr Desai yesterday, and Devon is happy for us to go ahead with the search. So tomorrow, we'll drive to Norfolk to speak with Edith,' Birdie explained, withdrawing her notebook from her pocket. 'I'd like to get some more details from you regarding a timeline.'

'Such as?' Angelica asked, frowning.

'Do you remember the date you were sent to Norfolk?'

'I do. I'd gone home for the Christmas break and told my mother the night before Christmas Eve. The twenty-third of December. I was sent away the next day and arrived in Norfolk sometime in the afternoon on Christmas Eve.'

Birdie jotted it down. 'And your son was born on the third of May, as you've already told us.'

'Yes. I was admitted to hospital first thing in the morning.

The contractions had begun the previous night, although I hadn't realised that's what they were. I was kept in the maternity unit where I gave birth for what seemed like an eternity but was only two weeks.'

'Do you know the date the baby was given to his adoptive family?'

She swallowed and looked away, pain rippling across her face. 'I have no idea. It's a bit of a blur. The baby stayed with me for a few days and I fed him myself. Then, one day, I was informed that he'd gone to his new family and I didn't see him again. After that, I went into a fog and I can barely remember anything until I was discharged and my aunt collected me and took me back to her house. I stayed with her for a few weeks more, although that too is a bit of a blur. I was sent back home the day before my father's birthday on the twentieth of June. My parents wanted me to attend his birthday party.'

'Thank you.' Birdie shut her notebook and waited until Lady Angelica had composed herself. 'It must have been a painful time, but it might help with our enquiries.'

'Of course. I understand. I'm sorry I can't be more exact.'

'Sometimes our mind buries memories to help deal with pain and trauma,' Seb explained. 'But this is enough for us to go on. And Edith might be able to fill in some of the gaps.'

'You won't mention about Devon, will you?' Lady Angelica asked sharply.

'No,' Seb assured her. 'As discussed, we will be as discreet as possible. Though you will need to think about what to tell Devon if we are successful. He seemed dubious about the existence of this distant relative.'

'We'll cross one bridge at a time. First, find my son, and then we'll take it from there,' she said as a man dressed in overalls and a thick woollen jacket walked towards them holding a spade.

'We'll let you get on with your day and will be in touch with our findings,' Seb said.

'Please do. Now, Campbell. What's the problem? I hope it's not about those damned pigeons again.' She turned towards the man, leaving Birdie and Seb to make their way back through the stunning garden.

'So, what do you make of it all?' Birdie asked in a low voice.

Seb uncharacteristically ran a hand through his hair. 'We need to hope that whatever the rift is between Lady Angelica's family and Edith, it won't stop her from talking to us.'

FIVE

Seb stepped out of the car, only to be met by a huge gust of icy wind. There had been a frost when he'd collected Birdie from Market Harborough that morning, and the travel conditions had meant they'd passed several broken-down vehicles on the way. But the trip to Norfolk couldn't be delayed and thankfully, the conditions hadn't worsened. Nevertheless, he was still pleased when they'd arrived safely at Edith Godfrey's Georgian manor house on the outskirts of the small port town, Wells-next-the-Sea.

'I can't believe how cold it is here,' Birdie said, jogging on the spot and clapping her hands. 'Does she live here on her own? It's massive.'

'I imagine she'd have some live-in help,' Seb said, taking in the well-maintained garden and excellent condition of the two-storey building that showed none of the damage one would have expected from being so close to the harsh conditions of the North Sea.

'Let's just hope she'll see us. If Lady Angelica's right that the rift in the family was because of her pregnancy, we might not even get through the door.' They'd made the decision not to phone ahead in case they received an outright no to being allowed in. It was a risk, but on balance seemed worth it.

'It's a possibility. Though it happened a long time ago, and beliefs have changed since then.'

'Not for everyone. She might be more old-fashioned. I'll leave you to do the talking – you're more on her wavelength, being that much older.' She winked.

'I'll ignore that remark,' he said, well used to her teasing.

They reached the door and he pressed the bell.

There was a slight delay before it was answered by a woman in her mid sixties, who only cracked it open wide enough to peer out. 'If you're an estate agent, Mrs Godfrey isn't interested in selling.'

'We're not,' he assured her. 'My name's Sebastian Clifford, and this is my partner, Lucinda Bird – Birdie. We're private investigators and were hoping to talk with Mrs Godfrey about her niece, Lady Angelica Charing.'

'Now that's a name I haven't heard in a while. Mrs Godfrey's estranged from her sister's side of the family and has been for many years.'

'We're aware of that, but we would still like to see her.' Seb extracted a business card and passed it over. 'If you could please take this to her, we'd appreciate it. It's a matter of urgency. We promise not to take up too much of her time.'

The woman stared at it for several moments, as if trying to decide whether the proffered card was safe to touch. But finally she stretched out her hand and took it.

'You'll have to wait here.' She shut the door on them before Seb had time to respond.

Birdie let out a low whistle. 'I wouldn't want to get on her bad side. I thought she was going to flat-out refuse for a moment, which would mean we'd need to start door-knocking the neighbours to see if anyone remembered Lady Angelica from her time here. In this weather, it wouldn't be fun.'

'I agree,' Seb said, grimacing.

Although if that's what they needed to do, they would because there was no one else to undertake such an unpleasant task for them.

The housekeeper returned several minutes later, and this time she opened the door and nodded for them to come in. 'Mrs Godfrey has agreed to see you. Though please don't upset her. She's not been well.'

'Of course. That's the last thing we want,' Seb said.

They followed the housekeeper through to a sitting room at the rear of the house. A gas fire flickered in the tiled hearth, and the glass windows looked out to a stunning view of the North Sea. Clearly, this was why Edith still lived there. Next to him, Birdie let out a small gasp of appreciation.

A tiny woman with lively dark eyes and a shock of white curly hair was sitting on a sofa covered in a William Morris design, a cane at her side, which she clutched at with arthritic fingers.

'Please don't get up,' Seb said. 'And thank you for agreeing to seeing us.'

'You can thank the miserable weather for that. Otherwise I most likely would have had Mrs Jessop send you away. But if you've travelled in these conditions, I can only assume it's a matter of some importance.' She turned to the housekeeper and nodded. 'Mrs Jessop, please could you make a pot of tea and bring us some of the ginger biscuits if there are any left.'

'You know I always make a double batch.' Mrs Jessop gave the elderly woman a warm smile and bustled away.

'She's forever trying to fatten me up,' Edith explained and waved her hand at them both. 'Sit down, sit down. You're way too tall and I'll crick my neck if I have to look up at you for much longer.'

Seb bit back an amused smile and lowered himself onto one of the wingback chairs while Birdie sat at the other end of the sofa.

'This view is totally cool. I bet you never get tired of looking at it,' Birdie said.

Edith nodded in approval, seeming to like his partner's frank manner.

'I don't. The house belonged to my husband's family but I've lived here for sixty-seven years and no two days are the same. Now, what's this all about? There's only one reason I can think of, and that's to ask me about what happened when Angelica was last here.'

'That's correct. It was in 1972,' Seb said, which earned him a sharp look.

'I know what year it was. I might be old but my memory's intact. Who hired you? Is it Angelica, or have you been hired by the child? Who, of course, is now an adult.'

'We've been hired by your niece,' he said.

'I see. Why didn't she call me directly?' the older woman said as Mrs Jessop reappeared carrying a large tea tray, which she put on the low coffee table and began to serve. Seb took the cup of tea that was offered to him.

'Lady Angelica mentioned there was a rift in the family. She wasn't sure how she'd be received. Was it because of what happened?'

'Of course not. I always felt sorry for the poor girl, being shipped off here the way she was. But that was my sister – her mother – all over. Couldn't bear the thought of a scandal.'

'So what caused the rift then?' Birdie frowned.

The old woman closed her eyes, as if trying to recall a lost past event. Then she opened them again and sighed. 'Angelica's mother, Louisa, was my older sister, and after our father died, she took issue with the will and wanted to contest it but needed my consent. I wasn't interested – why should I be? I had a life here with Ernest. After that, she refused to have anything to do with me, which meant I lost contact with Angelica. Though, of course, I could hardly have missed all the fuss over her marriage to Lord Edgar Charing. I did intend to write to her, but Louisa was still alive and I thought better of it.'

'I'm sure she would have been delighted to have heard from you. Still would. We'd like to know about Angelica's time with you and the adoption.' Seb put down the teacup.

'Poor child. She was clearly terrified that her whole life would be over, and that her parents would never forgive her. I tried to reassure her' – Edith fished a handkerchief from the pocket of her cardigan and dabbed at her eyes – 'but it was difficult. Poor thing was so young. Only sixteen, and you know what it's like at that age. Everything is a matter of life and death. Plus, her parents didn't help. She settled down after a couple of months, though found it hard not going out and seeing anyone. She mainly stayed in the house and the garden, which, as you can see, is quite private.'

'What about her care? Did she have hospital appointments?'

'Her mother didn't want to draw attention to the fact Angelica was pregnant. But since I had no children of my own and really didn't know that much about pregnancy, it felt wrong for her not to have a regular check-up. A midwife from the town came throughout the pregnancy to make sure everything was as it should be.'

'Is this woman still alive?' Birdie tapped her pen against her notepad.

'I'm afraid not.'

'And what happened regarding the birth? Lady Angelica said she contacted the hospital but they had no records, or if they did, they weren't prepared to release them. Who arranged the adoption? Was it through an agency?'

'Louisa arranged the adoption through a solicitor they knew.

Angelica gave birth and after a few days, the baby was taken to his new parents. Angelica stayed here for a while to get her health back but didn't talk much. Clearly the whole thing had been distressing for her. I put her on the train back to Dunchurch in the June. Louisa wanted her home for Charles's birthday. And that was the last time I saw her.'

Across from him, Birdie's face had paled, as if she was trying to picture her own birth mother going through that. It was hard to imagine what it must have been like.

'Did you meet the family who adopted the baby?' Seb asked, giving Birdie time to recover.

'No, I didn't. The solicitor advised it was best not to know, because it might stop Angelica from moving on with her life.'

'Do you remember the name of the solicitor?'

'Yes. His name was Christopher Hambling from Hambling & Son in Rugby. Though he certainly wouldn't be practising anymore, if in fact he's still alive. After all, it was over fifty years ago.'

'Hopefully we can still find a record of the adoption,' Seb said, although it wasn't guaranteed. 'Did you visit Angelica while she was in the hospital?'

'Louisa told me I shouldn't go in to see her, in case anyone recognised me,' Edith said before poking her chin in up in a defiant gesture. 'But I did visit several times. I'm not sure she even knew I was there. She was exhausted but also completely distracted by the baby when she was allowed to be with him. It broke my heart. I remember the day he was taken, because when I arrived she'd just been told he'd been taken and she'd gone into some sort of trance. The nurse who was there said Angelica clearly didn't care about the baby, because if she had, she'd have been crying. It was absolutely nonsense. In those days we were all taught not to show our feelings and that's exactly what Angelica was doing.'

'Do you remember the exact date?'

'It was the twelfth of May. Nine days after the birth. It's ingrained in my mind because it was the same date King George was crowned. When we were young, our governess would make Louisa and I recite all the coronation dates by heart.'

'I'm impressed you remembered the exact date,' Birdie said, nodding in appreciation.

'I always believed mathematics far more useful to learn than a string of useless dates. I'm pleased it's finally paid off,' she said before her eyes narrowed. 'You still haven't told me why Angelica is suddenly looking for the child now after all this time? Has something happened?'

'I'm afraid she hasn't confided her reason in us. We've only been engaged to locate her son,' Seb said. He and Birdie had already agreed this was the best way to answer the question when it eventually came up.

They were interrupted by the appearance of Mrs Jessop, who began to gather the teacups, only stopping to look directly at Seb, her mouth set in a firm line. It was clear their time was up. Seb glanced at Edith. Her complexion had faded and there was a sadness in her dark eyes.

He rose from the chair. 'We'd better not take up any more of your time. Thank you for agreeing to see us. It's given us something to work with.'

'I'm pleased. And tell Angelica that if she would like to contact me, I'd be happy to hear from her.'

'We will,' he promised as they headed out of the room, following the housekeeper to the front door.

* * *

Back outside, the ice had begun to melt, but it was still cold and Seb turned on the engine to warm the car.

'Well, Mrs Jessop's a barrel of laughs,' Birdie said, rubbing her hands together to stave off the chill.

'She only has Edith's well-being at heart. What did you make of her story?'

'I think Lady Angelica's parents were more worried about the shame of an illegitimate birth than their daughter's welfare. But at least Edith tried to care for her as best she could.' There was an edge to Birdie's voice. 'We will need to let Lady Angelica know the family rift wasn't about the pregnancy at all, but about the inheritance. Do you think Lady Angelica will want to see her aunt once she finds out?'

'I don't see why not. I imagine it's not something she'd consider currently. There's too much on her mind.'

Seb pulled out of the driveway and headed back down the narrow road towards the centre of Wells-next-the-Sea.

'At least it was a useful visit. We know the date the child was given to the people who adopted, and the name of the solicitor who organised the adoption,' Birdie said, sounding more like her usual self as she retrieved her phone and tapped away at the screen. 'Good news. There's a Hambling & Son in Rugby, which means they're still in business. Whether they have any records of what happened is another story. It's too late to get to Rugby today before they close, and I'd like to do some more research into them first anyway. Is there anything else you want to follow up on while we're here in Norfolk?'

Seb shook his head as the stark but stunning landscape flashed past them. 'We already know that Lady Angelica has tried the hospital and hit a brick wall. I can't see why we'd have any more luck if we go there ourselves. Let's drive back home before this weather gets worse. Then we'll plan our next move.'

SIX

Thursday, 7 December

'I wonder if this will cost us a fortune?' Birdie said the following day as Seb drove down a tree-lined street in Rugby, looking for a place to park. Hambling & Son was based in one of the red-brick Victorian houses that had been turned into offices. Christopher Hambling was dead, but his son, Nicholas, and grandson, Felix, were now running the practice.

'The parking?' Seb asked, flicking on the indicator as an empty space came into view a few streets away from the office. 'I think we can stretch to that.'

'Not the parking,' Birdie said, rolling her eyes. 'I mean for the appointment.' She used the parking app she'd downloaded to pay for the spot and they got out of the car. 'Don't solicitors charge hundreds of pounds for a fifteen-minute conversation? And what if he talks a lot? It could be an expensive visit. Come to think of it, maybe we're in the wrong business? Think of how rich we'd be if we charged for every fifteen minutes of work we did.'

'You do realise that being a solicitor involves a lot of desk work, don't you? Not quite your thing, I'd say,' he pointed out. 'Not all of them are so expensive. We'll discuss it with the grandson. We're lucky he could see us today.'

'No thanks to the receptionist. She wasn't happy about it,' Birdie retorted, a flicker of irritation running through her. She'd called the office yesterday and had been told that both father and son were booked out until late January. But the woman's glacial tone had put Birdie's back up, and after explaining the urgency and that their client was a member of the aristocracy, the receptionist had reluctantly admitted that Felix did have cancellation in his calendar and could spare them fifteen minutes. The woman had tried to push for the aristocrat's name, but Birdie had refused to give it.

'Remember we're here on a case, so be nice,' he said as they reached the imposing building with a gleaming brass sign on the wall announcing the offices of Hambling & Son.

'I *am* nice,' Birdie corrected, then wrinkled her nose. 'Except when people are irritating. I reckon she just didn't like the sound of my voice. Maybe I didn't grovel enough for her.'

Seb studied her with a mixture of concern and curiosity. 'Is everything okay?' he asked, leaning in towards her, his eyes intent on her face. 'Are you finding the case hard because of the adoption? Because if this is too difficult—'

'Not difficult exactly,' she said, interrupting him. Why did she keep forgetting she couldn't get anything past Seb? She gave a small, wry smile, acknowledging his insight. 'It's strange looking at the whole situation from a different perspective. The whole time I was searching for Kim I was totally focused on me and not her. That's all.'

Seb nodded, his expression softening. 'As long as you're fine with working on the case.'

She waved a hand dismissively. 'Don't be daft. Of course I am. How much are we going to tell Hambling?'

'If necessary, we'll take him into our confidence,' Seb replied, his voice steady and confident.

She raised an eyebrow. 'And hope he doesn't decide to blab to the media,' she said, a hint of worry in her tone.

'We have to trust him.'

'Okay. How are we going to play this? Are you going to be good cop or bad cop?'

He gave an amused smile as he reached for the door handle. 'I suggest we see what happens before going down that route.'

'Just trying to be prepared. Now, watch me be nice.' She grinned at him and they both stepped inside.

What would have once been the square entrance hall to the house was now a reception area, though there was no sign of anyone working there. 'How can I be nice if there's no one here?'

'Maybe the receptionist you spoke to yesterday is hiding under the desk, trembling in fear?' Seb murmured.

'Haha, very funny,' Birdie retorted. There was a bell sitting on the counter but before they could reach it, a man in his mid thirties stepped into the room, slightly out of breath.

'Hello. You must be Birdie. I'm Felix Hambling.' He had a friendly smile and shook her hand. 'Brenda, our receptionist, is unexpectedly away today and it's impossible to get a temp at such short notice.'

'Nice to meet you. This is my partner, Sebastian Clifford,' Birdie introduced them both, ignoring the amused gleam in Seb's eye at the receptionist not being there.

'If you'd like to come through to our conference room, we can talk there,' Felix said. 'Although I'm not sure how I can help? Brenda mentioned it was regarding a matter from 1972.'

'That's right. We're private investigators, looking into a case on behalf of our client.' Birdie and Seb followed him down the hall to a small room. There was a table in the middle and six chairs were spread out around it. Dull winter light was beaming in from a side window. Felix sat down at one end and reached for a pad and pen.

'We've been led to believe your grandfather was the one who worked on the case in question,' Seb said.

Felix frowned. 'My grandfather is dead, and none of the records were computerised back then. It was all done by paper. Ten years ago, we contracted a company to convert the files onto microfiche to reduce storage. So, even if I wanted to look for them, it's not a simple case of putting in a name and hitting enter.'

'Microfiche? Isn't that a bit old-fashioned?' Birdie raised an eyebrow. While most of her own research was done online, she'd gone to the library several times in her time with the police to search through hundreds of the semi-transparent sheets that contained reduced-down articles and information to miniature versions, only readable with the large microfiche readers. But she had no idea they were still used by private businesses.

'It's becoming less and less common,' Seb said. 'But it does have some advantages.'

Felix nodded. 'At the time, we did consider getting everything put onto the computer, but it was a lot more expensive, and considering how often we refer to the older documents, it didn't seem worth it. That being said, it's not something we would routinely give access to, no matter how old the case.'

'That's completely understandable,' Seb agreed. 'However, we do have mitigating circumstances. Our client gave up a child for adoption in 1972, when she was sixteen. Your grandfather made the arrangements and brokered the process. Because it wasn't done through an adoption agency, it's a lot harder to trace. The way these cases are handled now is very different.'

Felix sucked in a breath, and the pen that he'd been holding dropped down onto the notepad. Clearly it was a surprise to him.

'I take it that brokering an adoption wasn't something he did regularly,' Birdie said.

'No, not at all. We mainly do conveyancing and wills. Though it was my great-grandfather who first started the business, and when my grandfather took over, there were some lean times, which might explain it. I don't believe my father was aware of this. He certainly hasn't ever mentioned it.' He rubbed his jaw, clearly conflicted about the case. 'Problem is, those records are still confidential. You must have other lines of enquiry you can go down.'

'Both the child's birth grandparents, who arranged the adoption, are dead and the only other person who knew about it is your grandfather, who's also dead,' Birdie persisted. 'Because it was done privately, the trail ends here.'

'I still need to respect confidentiality. There's a legal process that can be followed and with a court order, I'm sure something can be arranged.'

Birdie swallowed back her frustration. She knew Felix was just doing his job, but they couldn't afford to leave empty-handed. She glanced at Seb and gave a nod. They'd have to tell him.

'We need to respect our client's confidentiality, so I hope that what I'm about to tell you will remain private. Our client is Lady Angelica Charing,' Seb said.

It garnered an immediate response as Felix straightened his back.

'Do you know her?' Birdie asked.

'I know of her. We visited Fleckney Hall last summer. She was also born into an aristocratic family I believe. Did the adoption take place because of the social stigma at the time?'

Birdie nodded. 'You've got it. The pregnancy and adoption were covered up to avoid a scandal in the family, and she's now married and has three grown children of her own. One of them is gravely ill and, without a kidney transplant, might only live for another six months. The child she put up for adoption is their last hope of finding a donor, which means going through the court isn't something we have time for. Could you at least check the records and see if the family have specified anything about not being contacted?'

An uneasy silence fell over the room as Felix considered it. Birdie held her breath, knowing that everything hinged on him agreeing to at least look. Finally, he sighed.

'Okay. I'll check the files for you, but if they have requested no contact, then I'm afraid I won't be able to tell you anything.'

'That's great. Thank you,' Birdie said, sitting on her hands to force back the urge to do a fist pump.

'Please could you give me details of Lady Charing's parents.'

'Louisa and Charles Montague, and they lived in Rolton Hall, on the outskirts of Dunchurch. They would have contacted your grandfather sometime between January and May of 1972. Are you happy for us to wait here while you check, or should we come back to the office later?' Seb asked.

'Hopefully it shouldn't take too long, so I'm happy for you to stay here. But it will depend on what's in the case notes as to what I can tell you.'

With that, he disappeared back down the hallway. As soon as he was gone, Birdie leant back in her chair and groaned. 'That was tough. I was convinced he was going to say no.'

'He still might. Good job on picking up his surprise at Christopher Hambling's involvement in arranging the adoption. I hadn't noticed, but when you pushed, it was clear it didn't sit well with him. I think it's made him more sympathetic to our request.'

'Let's hope so.' Birdie spun around in the chair, trying to get rid of her nervous energy. While she loved the leg work of being a detective, the waiting could be draining. Not to mention the uncertainty.

Felix returned several minutes later, holding a piece of paper. And the smile had returned to his face. Did that mean it was good news? She jumped to her feet.

'So? Did you find the file? What did it say?'

'Most of it was regarding the legislation of the time, which, of course, is very different now. But there was no stipulation about contact or it being a closed adoption, which means I can give you their details.'

'That's fantastic.' Birdie let out a long breath, not taking her eyes off the piece of paper in his hand. It was always such a good feeling when things paid off. 'What do you have?'

'The child was adopted to Colin and Margaret Olsen, who lived in Lutterworth at 53 Halston Terrace.'

'What about the child?' Birdie asked. 'Was there any mention of his birth name, or the birth certificate?'

'Sorry. If my grandfather knew that information, he chose not to put it in the file. There is no mention of how he found the couple or their background. I don't even know whose name was used on the birth certificate. You might find the Olsens were listed as the birth parents. I have reason to believe that sometimes happened.'

'Far too often,' Birdie agreed, remembering some of the case studies she'd read while doing her own research. 'But this is still a good place to start.'

'Thank you for your help.' Seb shook Felix's hand and passed him a business card. 'Please send us your bill. We would appreciate you keeping this confidential. Lady Angelica doesn't want it to become public knowledge.'

'Of course.' Felix took the card. 'It was nice to meet you both. If I ever need a private investigator, I'll know who to call.'

'It would be our pleasure,' Seb said.

They both stepped back out onto the street and Birdie turned to Seb. 'Right. Let's head back and see what we can find out about Colin and Margaret Olsen.'

SEVEN

'I take it you've found something.' Seb stepped into the office with Elsa by his side. They'd just returned from a walk, only to see Birdie holding an imaginary cricket bat, which she was now swinging with quite a lot of force. It wasn't the first time it had happened – he had once caught her practising her spin bowling by running down the long hallway, her face a mask of intense focus and determination.

'Busted.' She turned to him, eyes gleaming. 'But you have to admit, invisible balls and bats do a lot less damage. Think of how many valuable antique thingies I've avoided breaking.'

Seb suppressed a smile, wondering what Sarah would think of her very expensive collection of Chinese porcelain being referred to as *thingies*.

'I'm not complaining. And there's been extensive research into how physical activity can assist thought processes. Is this in celebration of discovering where the Olsens now reside?'

'It is. And I didn't need a microfiche to do it!'

He followed her over to the large whiteboard set up in front of one of the bookcases that lined the wall. After leaving Felix Hambling yesterday, they'd driven to the address in Lutterworth on the off-chance that the family still lived here, or that their neighbours might know where they were.

The semi-detached house was in a pleasant area of the market town. However, it was mainly younger families who lived there and they'd hit a dead end. So they'd spent their time since then searching for them online. While Seb's speciality was going through accounts and numbers, it was Birdie who had a knack for research, and she wasn't just thorough, but also incredibly fast.

She'd managed to track the Olsens to Leicester and from there to Warwick. She'd also discovered their marriage certificate. The couple had both been in their late thirties at the time, therefore in their forties when they adopted the baby. They found no mention of them having a child, which meant, coupled with them not having the birth certificate, they still needed to locate the Olsens to have any luck in finding Lady Angelica's son.

'Do you care to share your discovery with me?' Seb scanned the whiteboard for updates, but they had yet to be written up.

'Keep your hair on,' Birdie joked. She reached for a marker and waved it in his direction. 'Unfortunately, Colin died ten years ago, but Margaret is still alive and well. She's moved back to Lutterworth and is living in a small care home there. She's ninety-two. From what I've found out, the couple lived comfortably, so it appears the boy was provided with a good home, even if it's nothing like the place where Lady Angelica grew up.'

'Nice work. Do you have the name and location of this care home?'

'What do you think?' Birdie reached over to her desk and picked up her laptop so he could see the screen. 'It's Bluebell Residential Care, and I've just got off the phone to them. Margaret goes by the name Maggie, and the nurse said we were

welcome to visit between twelve and two today, when she
would be in the day room and okay to see visitors.'

'Excellent work. I'll fetch my car keys and we can leave.'

Birdie dropped down to give Elsa a tickle and a quick kiss
goodbye. The dog let out a contented sigh and closed her eyes to
enjoy a nap.

Out in the hallway, Seb shrugged on his coat and they
walked out to where his car was parked. Lutterworth was only
twelve miles away, but he wanted to get there as quickly as
possible to give them ample time with the elderly woman.

Despite the cool weather, the day was bright and crisp, and
Sarah's garden was dotted with snowdrops and crocuses that
lined the driveway.

'We need to discuss on the way when to give Lady Angelica
an update,' Birdie said as they piled into Seb's car.

'Once we speak with Maggie, and find out the name of the
child, we'll have something more solid to go on,' Seb said. 'I
know Lady Angelica's being realistic about the process and
how tricky it could be, but I do worry about her being disap-
pointed.'

Birdie's expression turned sombre. 'Me, too. There is so
much riding on it. And with Devon's health the way it is, it must
be hard to stay pragmatic.'

Seb suspected that Lady Angelica, like so many of his
parents' acquaintances, had been brought up to be exactly that.
Pragmatic, reserved, and not easily swayed by emotions. But it
had been clear by the pain in her voice that she was struggling
to preserve that image.

'All we can focus on is doing our part.' Seb turned onto the
Harborough Road and headed west. The traffic was light, and it
didn't take long until they'd left the barren countryside behind
and reached their destination.

Bluebell Residential Care was a small purpose-built facility
set just outside of the town, overlooking widespread fields.

Inside was warm, and the woman at the desk smiled as they approached her.

'Hello, let me guess, you're Birdie and you must be Sebastian,' she said. Then as, if noticing their surprise, she wrinkled her nose. 'Don't worry, I don't have psychic powers, but poor Maggie doesn't get many visitors, so when you called earlier, it stuck in my mind.'

'It's still impressive of you to remember,' Birdie said in a friendly way before her mouth settled into a curious line. 'Though I'm surprised about visitors. I would have thought her son would visit regularly.'

At the mention of a son, the woman's smile faded.

'He used to visit more, but in the last couple of years, we've hardly seen him. Not that I'm judging. Unfortunately, it happens a lot. As the residents get older, it can be painful for their family to see them in that condition. Maggie's extremely frail now and she often drifts off. I had wondered if that's why Conrad stopped visiting her regularly.'

Seb resisted smiling. Finally, they had a name. Conrad Olsen.

'Such a pity,' Birdie continued, also showing no indication of the importance of what they'd uncovered, though he could imagine that inside, she was running around the cricket field, celebrating hitting a match-winning six. 'I was hoping he'd be here so we could meet with him as well. As I explained on the phone, we want to talk to Maggie about Conrad and his adoption. Would you be able to give me his contact details?'

The woman immediately shook her head. 'Sorry. I wish I could help, especially if you're trying to reunite him with his birth mother. Shocking the way those things used to be handled. But we're not allowed to give out any personal information. I'm sure you understand.'

'Of course,' Birdie agreed mildly, though she was obviously biting her tongue to stop herself from pushing further. Now that they weren't on the force, they had to be a lot more circumspect about the way they gathered information.

'Where can we find Maggie?' Seb quickly interjected, and the woman's smile reappeared.

'I'll take you. She's in the day room. Though, as I said, she does drift off from time to time, and we don't want her to get worn out or agitated.'

'We understand,' Seb said as they followed her through to a brightly lit room. In one corner was a group of residents playing cards, while several others were in small groups chatting, but they kept walking until they reached a small woman sitting on her own, staring out to the fields in the distance.

'Maggie. Here are the folks I was telling you about. They've come to say hello and have a chat. This is Birdie and Sebastian.'

'Oh, how lovely.' The elderly woman peered up at them. She was indeed frail, with watery blue eyes and tiny bird-like hands that clutched at the woollen blanket covering her lap. 'Have we met before?'

'No,' Seb assured her, quickly sitting down so that his height didn't intimidate her. The receptionist was still standing behind the sofa, as if to make sure they didn't upset her. 'But thank you for seeing us. We want to talk to you about your son, Conrad.'

At the mention of his name, Maggie's face lit up in a smile. 'Such a good boy. Never a bother, and his teachers were very impressed when he started school at how he already knew his alphabet. I'd taught him at home, you see.'

'Sounds like you did a great job,' Birdie said. 'We'd like to ask you about his adoption.'

'You know about that?' Maggie asked, confusion clouding her features.

'Yes, we're private investigators and have been hired by Conrad's birth mother to find him,' Birdie said, keeping her voice steady.

'Why?'

'She'd like to contact him. Is it okay if we ask you a few questions?' Birdie asked.

'Yes, okay.' Maggie smiled, which seemed to satisfy the receptionist, who left them alone and headed out of the day room. 'Colin and I couldn't have children of our own. We were school sweethearts, but lost touch when his family moved away. Neither of us ever married, and when he came back to Lutterworth for a school reunion, it was like no time had passed at all. Except...' Her voice started to waver and she looked out to the fields again.

Birdie exchanged a worried glance with Seb.

'So, after you married, you decided to adopt?' Seb quickly said.

Maggie blinked, her gaze once again coming into focus. 'That's right. Conrad was the centre of our lives. And such a good boy...'

Seb swallowed. It was hard to know whether their presence was going to affect Maggie negatively, or if it was just taking her back to the past and to pleasant memories.

'He's lucky to have grown up in such a loving family. Did you ever talk to him about his birth mother?' Birdie asked.

'No, dear. We didn't know who she was. But we often used to tell Conrad how lucky we were that she gave him to us. I do hope he'll visit me again soon and bring his wife and the two darling girls. But he's in Warwick, you see. Such a long way to come.'

'We could ask him if you'd like us to,' Birdie continued. 'And at the same time, we could chat to him about his birth mother. We know who she is and she'd love to meet him. We don't have his contact details. Do you have them? We could even call him now.'

At this, Maggie frowned and her bony fingers tightened around the rug in her lap. 'Oh, no. You can't do that. He'll be at work. I'd hate to get him in trouble. Best to wait until he comes to see me.'

Birdie visibly swallowed and Seb quickly took over. 'Of course. We understand. But we could phone him tonight, when he's at home. Or visit him in Warwick.'

'No, no, I don't want to be a bother. He's so busy, you see. But such a good boy.' Her eyes clouded over and she returned to looking out of the window.

She didn't move for several minutes, and he and Birdie gave a silent nod of agreement to leave. They didn't want to cause her any distress.

'Thank you for your time, Maggie. It's been lovely meeting you,' he said, but there was no answer.

'Any luck?' the receptionist asked once they'd reached the desk.

Seb shook his head. 'No, it was as you said. She kept drifting in and out and we didn't want to push her.'

The receptionist gave them a sad smile. 'I am sorry I can't help you more. But if you do find Conrad, please encourage him to visit. I know Maggie would be thrilled. She misses him a lot.'

'Of course,' Seb assured her before they left the building. Once outside, he turned to Birdie. 'It shouldn't be hard to find him now we know his name, date of birth, and location.'

'It makes sense that he's in Warwick, considering that's where his parents moved to when he was a teenager. He's obviously stayed there ever since. Now we know that he has two children he might be more sympathetic to Lady Angelica's plight.'

'Maybe,' Seb added as they got back into the car and he started the engine.

'Thank goodness Conrad's adoptive parents discussed the adoption with him. Can you imagine how difficult it would be if he wasn't aware of being adopted?' Birdie said with a sigh.

'True.'

'Although we mustn't forget that finding him is only half the problem. We still need to convince him to meet Lady Angelica and take the tests to see if he could be a potential donor. It feels a bit like climbing a mountain, only to realise we're not even half-way up.'

'A wise person once told me there is only one way to eat an elephant,' Seb reminded her.

Birdie laughed. 'You're right. We need to take it one step at a time. Right, it's Friday, and tonight I'm meeting the girls for drinks and a night of dancing. Care to join us?'

Seb refused to be baited. Birdie loved to tease him about his lack of social life. And while he definitely didn't go out as much up here as he had done in London, he wasn't a complete recluse.

'Believe it or not, I do have plans of my own. I'm going for dinner with an old friend. We went to university together and he's in Leicester on business. It will be nice to catch up.'

'Well done.' Birdie nodded at him in approval. 'Now, while you're driving, I'm going to start searching for Conrad Olsen.'

EIGHT

Birdie rushed out of the door and climbed into Seb's car, her head thumping, despite the mug of coffee she'd just downed in one.

'Ten minutes late,' he said, tapping his watch.

'You're lucky that's all,' she said with a grimace. 'We didn't leave the club until after two this morning. I might have to sleep all the way there.'

'Judging by your demeanour, I'd say that you had an enjoyable time last night. Yes?'

'It was brilliant. Though my feet are sore. They played nineties music all night. You'd have loved it.'

'Aren't you too young for that genre?'

'You must be kidding. I love it. How about you? Did you smoke cigars and drink single malt whisky while you discussed the good old days?'

'We had an excellent meal with an equally excellent bottle of wine,' Seb replied in his usual mild tone. 'It was minus cigars and whisky but we managed to muddle through as best we could.'

Birdie grinned. Despite their differences, she always managed to have a good laugh with him. As the caffeine got to work and pushed the last remnants of her headache away, she pulled out the research notes she'd made the previous afternoon.

Conrad Olsen hadn't been hard to find once they searched his name. Thankfully, the fifty-one-year-old still lived in Warwick; it meant he was within driving distance. He'd trained as an electrical engineer and worked for a large company, supervising their maintenance and inspection programmes. His wife was Tina and he had two teenage daughters.

More importantly, they had an address and a phone number. Fingers crossed he was home.

Once she'd read through her notes one more time, she closed her eyes and let the purring sound of the car's engine wash over her...

'Birdie. Wake up.'

'What...' She jumped and glanced at Seb, who was grinning in her direction.

'You've been fast asleep for most of the journey.'

'I've been resting my eyes, that's all,' she said, sitting upright in the seat.

'Hmmm... Do you always snore when your eyes are shut?'

'Okay, I might have dropped off for a few minutes. But at least now I feel more human.'

'A few minutes? I believe it's more like thirty. I'm pleased you're feeling better, though. Number six is further ahead on the corner. But I'll park here in case there isn't a space.' Seb pulled up outside a row of Victorian terraced houses.

The lack of drives and garages meant there was nose-to-tail parking on both sides of the street. They climbed out of the car and headed to the end of the row.

'What details are we going to give him? I know Lady Angelica is adamant she doesn't want him to know who she is, but we have to tell him something and give him a name.'

Seb nodded in agreement. 'You're right. We'll refer to her as Angie for now. At least until we know more about him and have reported back.'

'Angie it is,' Birdie agreed as they reached number six and she pressed the doorbell. 'Here goes nothing.'

There was a shuffling noise from inside the house and she let out her breath. Someone was home. Their trip hadn't been wasted.

'Can I help you?' A woman in a baggy grey tracksuit appeared in the door. Her blonde hair was tied back and her eyes were narrowed in suspicion. Was she Tina?

'Hello, my name is Birdie and this is my partner, Sebastian Clifford. We're private investigators and are here to speak to Conrad Olsen regarding an important matter that's come up during one of our investigations.'

At the mention of the word *important*, the woman's eyes widened. 'Private investigators? What is it exactly? Is it an inheritance? I'm his wife, Tina.'

'We'd prefer to discuss this with you and your husband inside,' Seb said as a couple of neighbours peered at them from behind lace curtains.

'Tell them to come inside, Tina,' a male voice called from the room on the left. 'Better than letting out all the heat. Not to mention giving the neighbours a show.'

Tina gave them a gruff nod. 'He's right. You'd better come in and tell us what this is all about.'

'Thank you.' Birdie and Seb stepped into the narrow hallway and closed the door behind them. They followed Tina into the front room, where a man was sitting on an easy chair. There were several folded newspapers at his feet, and another one in his lap. He put it aside and stood up as they entered the room.

He was of medium height with olive skin, dark eyes and black hair. His hands were clean with short nails. But there were several burn marks on his arms. They quickly made the introductions and he nodded for them to sit down on the sofa by the window. On the mantlepiece were several photos of Conrad, Tina and two dark-haired girls. There was another one of Conrad standing between an elderly Maggie and Colin Olsen, their fair skin and pale eyes in stark contrast to his own darker features.

He was nothing like them.

He was also nothing like Lady Angelica, who was also fair with blue eyes.

'So, what's this about?' he asked while Tina went into the kitchen to make coffee. 'You said you're private investigators. Does that mean someone hired you to find me?'

'That's correct. We visited your mother yesterday in Lutter-worth and that led us here.'

At the mention of his mother, his gruffness fell away and his eyes filled with concern. 'I've been meaning to visit her, but what with Tina, the girls, and my job, it's been hard to juggle. Not that you'd know we have two teenagers in the house. Both are still in bed asleep. And will probably stay like that until lunchtime. How is she? Ever since my father died, it's been diffi-cult watching her go downhill.'

The receptionist had been right about why Conrad hadn't visited much recently.

'She was in good spirits and talked about how proud she is of you and your family. It was kind of her to see us. We didn't want to wear her out and were only with her for a short time.'

'I'm glad to hear she's okay,' he said affectionately as Tina reappeared, balancing a tray of cups. 'So, let's cut to the chase. What's this about?'

'We were hired by your birth mother, to try and find you,' Birdie explained, 'and—'

'His *what*?' Tina's voice was high as she put down the tray, causing the cups to rattle. She turned to Conrad, her eyes full of questions. 'Birth mother? What does she mean by that?'

'Damned if I know.' His face drained of colour and his mouth was hanging open. *Hell*. Birdie swallowed. Their conversation with Maggie had led them to believe he knew about the adoption, but clearly that wasn't the case.

'Our apologies,' Seb said, concern shining from his eyes. 'We were under the impression that you knew about your birth, otherwise we wouldn't have brought it up in such a direct way.'

'Are you seriously saying that Maggie and Colin Olsen aren't Conrad's real parents?' Tina folded her arms and got to her feet. 'It makes no sense. Why didn't they tell him? They loved the socks off of him. It was almost smothering at times. Especially when he was trying to live up to his father's expectations.'

'Tina. Don't start with that. Not right now,' Conrad growled, though the colour had already returned, and he rubbed his chin. Birdie studied him as he turned to his wife. Despite the shock of it, he didn't seem surprised.

'Did you ever wonder about it?' she ventured to ask. He closed his eyes, at first not answering, but when he finally opened them again, he gave her a quick nod.

'I got teased through most of school for being so much darker than my parents. But my mother explained that it was because of all the vitamins she'd taken during the pregnancy. She was in her forties when she had me...' He broke off and rubbed his hand along the side of his face 'Hell. Adopted. I still can't believe they kept this from me.'

'Can't you just?' Tina arched an eyebrow at him before turning to Birdie. 'Don't get me wrong, Maggie's a sweet thing. But her and Colin were very old-fashioned. You should have seen their house. Lace doilies, knitted tea cosies and porcelain figures. It was like stepping back in time.'

'It's true. They would've thought it was for the best,' he agreed, though it was clear by the way he kept staring at his hands he was still coming to terms with the news. 'Except it wasn't the best for me. All this time I've been feeling bad that I never went to university like my father. He was an accountant and stayed at the one firm his entire life, even though they transferred him a few times. Got the gold watch and everything, and here's me, who barely managed to get through my apprenticeship. And even now trying to find a job that isn't...' He broke off again, as if recollecting where he was. 'You said my birth mother has paid you to find me. Why? Who is she, and what does she want? There's got to be a reason after all this time.'

His words rang out around the small room, and Birdie drummed her fingers against her leg. It was always going to be awkward, balancing Lady Angelica's request for secrecy and Conrad's right to know the truth.

'For the moment, we can't confirm her identity other than to say her name is Angie. But we have been in contact with the solicitor who brokered the adoption, and they checked their records. I'm sure if we make a call, we can arrange to get the information released to you. Although there's no mention of who your birth mother is in the records. They are about the adoption itself. Your parents would have been given their own copy of the paperwork. Because your father has passed away and your mother is in care, you might not have access to it, or it might have been thrown out at some stage.'

'Well, that's where you're wrong. There are three jam-packed boxes of papers in our loft,' Tina said. 'Colin made a big fuss about us keeping it all. We don't go up there much and haven't got around to looking through it all.'

'It might be a good idea to do that,' Birdie said, though Conrad's mouth was set in a stubborn line.

'Let me get this straight. After fifty-one years, my real mother decides to look for me, but doesn't want me to know who she is? So why did she hire you to find me? I'm guessing there's only one reason. She wants something. I bet Angie isn't even her real name.'

Tina turned to Conrad. 'You know, back then, it was a massive scandal if a girl got pregnant when they weren't married. Not like today. So, if this Angie woman still wants to keep it a secret, is it because she's famous? Or rich? Or both even?'

Birdie and Seb were quiet. It wasn't their job to agree or disagree with Tina's conjectures. However, Conrad was unmoved.

'I don't care who she is. She means nothing to me. Whatever she wants, she can forget it. I'm not interested.'

'Don't be ridiculous, Con. Think about it, if she's got money she might give some to you. This couldn't have come at a better time. You help her, she helps us. It could work out.'

Birdie took in the relief and hope in Tina's face and then noticed the stack of newspapers by Conrad's feet were all open at the jobs section. Had her research failed to uncover that he was now unemployed?

'Work out?' Conrad let out a snort. 'Out of the blue, she comes along and snaps her fingers and wants me to do something for her? Where was she when we almost lost our house five years ago? Or when you had to take that extra cleaning job so that Mattie could get braces?'

'You have every right to feel like that.' Birdie's throat tightened. She understood so much of what he was experiencing, because they were all emotions that she'd dealt with as well. But for Conrad, there was the shock of never knowing he'd been adopted in the first place.

'I still can't bloody believe this,' Tina muttered.

'I know there's a lot to take in, and we're not here to tell you what to do. We were hired to find you and ask if you'd consider taking a blood test. Someone in your birth family has a medical condition, and they're looking for someone with the same blood type.'

'Why? Do they want me to donate my blood?' Conrad asked.

'We're not sure what the medical procedure is,' Birdie said, hoping they'd believe her.

Conrad stared ahead unblinking and even Tina went silent as they both considered the request. Birdie felt the urge to keep drumming her fingers on her leg, but she shoved her hands into her jacket pockets instead. They needed to give him time to think and process what they were asking of him.

Finally, Conrad focused on them both. 'You can tell her that I'm not interested.'

Birdie stiffened, and next to her, Seb let out a soft breath.

There had always been the risk that finding Conrad wouldn't be enough to help save Devon. And even if they did want to tell him about his half-brother's health condition, now was clearly not the time.

'We'll leave now to give you some time to think about everything.' Birdie got to her feet and gave Conrad a supportive nod. 'Sorry that we were the ones to tell you this.'

'Don't worry. I'm not going to shoot the messenger,' he said, giving a shrug. 'But I meant what I said. For the last fifty-one years, I've had one set of parents. I don't see any reason to change that now.'

'Well then, you're more of a fool than I thought,' Tina broke in and dropped down to the floor next to where he was sitting. She picked up one of the newspapers and waved it at him. 'Con, think about it. You've been looking for a new job ever since you got booted out of TLM. And there's nothing here but minimum-wage crap. At your age, it's getting harder to even get interviews. Laura's Eric was looking for two years and ended up collecting trolleys at the supermarket wearing a high-vis vest and having to put up with seventeen-year-old kids who don't know their arse from their elbow. You'd hate it. This could be our chance.'

'I'll find something, I always do,' he growled, but his eyes had clouded over with fear, and upstairs there was a shuffling sound. One of his daughters must have just got out of bed. He closed his eyes and let out a weary sigh. 'This is a lot to take in.'

'I know it is, love.' Tina patted his knee before turning to stare up at Birdie, her eyes narrow. 'If this woman wants him to take a test, does that mean she'll pay him?'

Birdie turned to Seb. It wasn't something they'd considered and she suspected nor had Lady Angelica. But the fact that Conrad hadn't contradicted his wife meant that there was hope.

'We'll discuss it with her. If you could give me your number, I'll let you know what she says. In the meantime, if you have any questions, feel free to call or text me.' Birdie held out a card. Tina took it and plugged the number into her own phone. Birdie's phone pinged a moment later.

'There. I've just texted you. Call me after you've spoken to her, and if Conrad has any questions, I'll let you know. Is that alright, luv?'

Conrad looked up and nodded. 'Okay. But I'm not making any promises. Make sure you tell her that.'

'We will,' Birdie assured him, and after saying goodbye, they left.

As they walked back to the car, Tina stood in the doorway, probably wanting to make sure they were well away before she and her husband started talking about it. Birdie didn't blame her, and guilt jabbed at her as she climbed into the passenger side of Seb's BMW. Once the Olsens' door was closed, she leant back in the car set.

'What a mess.' She sighed. 'From our conversations with Maggie and the receptionist, I assumed that Conrad knew about his birth,' she said as they drove back through the old town, past the huge stone buildings and winding roads flanked with the evergreen hedgerows, on their way to the motorway.

'It's not your fault. Your own parents were so open with you, and it was an easy mistake to make based on our conversation. Neither of us took into account that Maggie's memory might have been playing tricks on her,' Seb reminded her. 'It was always going to be a difficult conversation to have. For better or worse, he now knows the truth about who he really is.'

'Only half of who he really is. I'm not surprised he wondered if he was adopted, considering how dark his hair and eyes are, and his olive skin. Maggie and Colin were nothing like that. Neither is Lady Angelica, or Devon.'

'He must get it from his father's side. Which may make it harder to accept Lady Angelica as his mother if they do meet.'

'What do you reckon about his wife asking for money? I couldn't believe it.'

'They have monetary problems. It's understandable.'

'Is it? Or could we say it was taking advantage of someone's dire situation.'

'Or simply a gut reaction. Whatever it is, Conrad has a lot to think about it.'

'Unfortunately, time isn't on our side. What shall we do now? Call Lady Angelica, or would it be better to visit?'

'I think she'd rather discuss this in person.' Seb slowed down as the traffic came to a crawl. 'Especially as there's now a question of payment. Buying and selling organs is illegal. However, Conrad is her child, which changes the dynamics. Plus, we know from our research and talking to Dr Desai that there's a convalescence period of six to twelve weeks, where he wouldn't be able to seek work. That might affect any benefit he's currently on. It's a lot for them all to consider.'

'I'll let her know we're on our way.' Birdie made the call and arranged for them to arrive at the hall within the hour. Then she rubbed at the bridge of her nose. Seb was right. There was a lot to consider, and no way of knowing how it would turn out.

NINE

It was raining by the time they reached Fleckney House. Behind the stone building was a large stable that had been converted into garages, and in front were several parking spaces. Seb reversed into a free spot and climbed out.

He pulled up the collar of his jacket and Birdie did the same as they jogged along the gravel path towards the large front door. Below them was the sweeping formal garden with a large fountain in the middle. But as another gust of rain swept past them, they didn't linger for long.

A butler appeared in the doorway almost as soon as Seb had pressed the bell. Seb suspected he'd watched their progress from one of the large floor-length windows that spanned the front of the hall.

'My name's Sebastian Clifford and this is Birdie. Lady Angelica is expecting us,' Seb said, keeping his calm voice, not wishing to alert the man that they were there to discuss something urgent.

'Of course. I will let Her Ladyship know you're here.' He

gave a slight nod and headed down one side of the wide marble-floored foyer.

'One day I might get used to being in these places, but today is not that day,' Birdie muttered next to Seb.

Her eyes were wide with curiosity as she peered around, before settling on a large oil painting. It was of the family and would have been painted at least thirty years ago, judging by how young Devon and his brothers looked. The boys were all seated on the floor, while Lady Angelica was perched regally on a chair with Lord Edgar standing slightly behind her, his hand resting on her shoulder.

As if on cue, Lord Edgar himself appeared from a doorway to the left, holding a tray with a broken teacup on it. He was tall and, despite being seventy-two, there was no hint of rounding shoulders or a bent spine, although his angular face was wrinkled and his grey hair had receded from his forehead. He frowned as he stared at the tray before looking up. His eyes widened in surprise. 'Oh, hello. It's Sebastian, isn't it? Worthington's boy. I heard you were living up this way. Nice to see you. One of the blasted dogs knocked this over with her tail. Lucky it wasn't the Meissen.'

'Hello, Lord Charing,' Sebastian said, returning the greeting. 'You're looking very well.'

'Eh, I do try my best. Still walk the entire property every morning. Best way to keep on top of things. How are your parents? Can't think when I saw them last.'

'They're very well. Mother is busy with her committees and my father is still involved in the estate alongside Hubert.'

'Good to hear. Personally, I never could abide by the day-to-day minutia of keeping this place ticking over. Thankfully, Angelica thrives on that side of things, leaving me to concentrate on making sure we can pay for it all.'

'Sounds like you make the perfect team. I'd like to introduce you to my business partner, Birdie,' he said, gesturing to her.

'Birdie? I had a friend called Birdie once. She married my best man. Lovely woman,' Lord Charing told her. 'Good to meet you.'

'You, too,' Birdie said, her eyes sparkling. Seb knew she hated having to explain her name, and he could see her warming to Lady Angelica's husband.

'I understand you're a detective of some sort. Am I correct?' Lord Edgar said, returning his gaze to Seb.

'That's correct, Edgar,' Lady Angelica answered for them as she appeared in the hallway followed by the butler. 'That's why they're here today. Hello, Sebastian, Birdie. Thank you for coming to see me.'

'Coming to see you, my dear?' her husband asked in a mild voice. 'Whatever for?'

'Let's go sit down and I'll explain.' She took the tray from his hand and passed it over to the butler, who wordlessly put it down on an antique side table. 'Could we have tea in the family room please, Gibbs?'

'Yes, madam.' He silently disappeared back down the hallway, and Lady Angelica led them through the wide hall into a smaller room towards the rear of the house. There was an open fire and while two leather chesterfields dominated the space, it was clear by the stack of books and the three dogs sprawled out on the floor by the hearth that it was often used by the family.

Lord Charing sat down in an armchair, not seeming at all put out by the fact his wife had hired detectives without discussing it with him first. Once they were settled, Lady Angelica turned to him.

'I've engaged Sebastian and Birdie to look into our immediate family tree to see if we could find a suitable donor for Devon.'

'Ah, I see,' he answered her, his face an impassive mask, making it hard to read his thoughts regarding his gravely ill son.

'Well, my father did have a roving eye by all accounts, so you might find he's left behind an illegitimate child.'

'You have no objection then?' Lady Angelica held her husband's gaze and didn't flinch at the mention of an illegitimate child. They were as stoic as each other.

'None at all. Whatever you think is best,' he said as Gibbs reappeared with a loaded tea tray.

As they drank tea and worked their way through delicious scones and sandwiches, the conversation moved to the problems with being able to locate tractor parts, before ending up in a discussion on the merits of installing a pump to help reduce damp in the cellar. Once they'd finished, Lord Edgar stood up and excused himself.

'I have a conference call with our lawyer. Years ago, we'd meet at the club and talk business over a whisky. Not so, nowadays. It's all a lot more formal.'

Lady Angelica waited until he had disappeared out of the room before getting up to close the open door. One of the dogs, who'd been asleep by the fire, opened his eyes before yawning widely and closing them again.

'You've met my son,' she said, her voice cool and blue eyes calm. But there was a tightness to her jaw, enough to suggest she wasn't as detached as she appeared. 'Please tell me everything.'

'We visited Edith to see if she'd met the family who adopted him or knew who they were,' Birdie said. 'But she hadn't met them, nor was she told their names. However, she did remember the name of the solicitor your parents engaged.' Birdie put down her plate and picked up her notepad. 'We visited and obtained the couple's names. From our research, it appears they were good people who loved the boy very much. The husband is now dead and his wife, who's in her nineties, is in a care home. But she gave us enough information to locate him.'

The room fell silent as Lady Angelica closed her eyes,

letting the information sink in. Then she swallowed and nodded.

'That is excellent news. And... and, uh, what's he like?'

'His name is Conrad, and he lives in Warwick with his wife and two teenage daughters,' Seb said, taking over and knowing it would be best to keep things brief. 'He's an electrical engineer, but is currently out of work. Unfortunately, he wasn't aware he was adopted, so the news came as a shock to him.'

'I take it not a positive one?'

'Like I said, it was a shock. His complexion is very different from his parents', and it had crossed his mind over the years.'

'Did you ask him about being tested?' Lady Angelica's hands were clasped tightly in her lap, as if she was trying to hold everything together, instead of letting the news of her oldest son and Devon's illness sweep over her.

'We did, and at first, he was reluctant to consider it,' Birdie said. 'But his wife is worried about money and asked if they would be paid for it. We were surprised, but they are in financial difficulties. They don't know what the test is for, or what would happen if he is compatible.'

'I'd be happy to pay for him to be tested, especially if it will help them. How much do they want?'

'We didn't discuss an amount. We thought it best to give him some time to get used to the idea and then go back once we'd discussed it with you.'

'A sensible idea,' Lady Angelica agreed. 'I will agree to any amount that you deem suitable. But it has to be on the condition my name isn't mentioned and that we don't meet. At least not at this stage. I would hate for the whole story to come out, only to find that it's still not enough to save...' She broke off and turned away, as if suddenly needing to inspect the wall.

'You don't need to worry about that,' Birdie quickly assured her. 'At this point, he has no inclination to meet you. Also, we do need to tell you that there's no guarantee he will agree to doing it. Even if there is money involved.'

Lady Angelica nodded. 'Thank you for being direct. What happens now?'

'We will contact him once we've returned to the office.' Seb got to his feet. 'When we have news, we'll contact you again.'

'How is Devon?' Birdie asked, standing up beside him. For a moment, their client's mask slipped and her mouth trembled. Then she briskly walked towards the door, the dogs all standing up to join her.

'He needs a miracle.' Her hand reached for the handle but didn't turn it. 'Please do your best to convince my son to help us. I have no right to ask him to and there's no reason for him to agree, but I'm asking all the same.'

TEN

'There's a good girl, Elsa,' Birdie said as she crossed the threshold back into the house with the dog, after they'd been out for a walk. Once inside, Birdie shrugged off her coat. The early start and her lack of sleep, along with meeting Conrad and then giving Lady Angelica an update, had taken its toll and she'd needed some fresh air to clear her head.

Seb had stayed inside to research into the ethics behind Conrad's request for payment, and, if it was possible, how it should proceed. He was still at his desk when she entered the office, which was pleasantly warm now that the heating had kicked in.

'What's the verdict?'

'I've spoken to an old colleague who sent me some guide-lines relating to the issue. I can forward them to you or, if you'd rather, I can give you the bullet points.'

'Bullet points suits me fine,' Birdie said. Unlike Seb, too many boring details made her eyes glaze over. She much preferred an overview.

'No problem,' he said, then gave her a concise summary.

'How much would be considered a reasonable amount for Lady Angelica to offer Conrad? Have you found that out?' Birdie asked.

'It's illegal for someone to be paid for donating an organ; however, someone can be reimbursed for travel expenses and any loss of income.'

'So if it takes three months to recover then he could be given three months' salary. Except he isn't working. Although I'm guessing we could use his old job.'

'Yes, that would be fine, I'm sure.'

'Can he be paid just for taking the test?'

'That's not illegal, providing it's not linked to being a donor.'

'Anyway, it's all hypothetical until we have Conrad's decision regarding the test and then his decision on being a donor.' She picked up her phone. 'I'll call him now and give him the news.'

Tina answered the call on the second ring. Had she been waiting by the phone ever since they'd left the house?

'Hello.'

'It's Birdie, I'm—'

'So, what did she say? Did she agree to pay him?' Conrad's wife demanded before Birdie had time to finish her sentence.

'There are a couple of things we need to discuss. Is Conrad there?' Birdie asked, not prepared to be sucked into giving her answers straight away. 'Also, my phone's on speaker because Seb's with me.'

Tina made a small snort of frustration before sighing. 'Sure. And don't worry, you're on speaker, too. Conrad can hear everything, can't you, luv?'

'Loud and clear. What happened? Did you tell Angie about me?' There was an edge to his voice. Was he testing them? Did he want to find out the kind of woman his mother was? Or, indeed, if he could trust any of them.

'We didn't give her any specific details about you. Considering she wants her identity protected for now, it's only right that we protect yours too.'

'How do I know you're telling me the truth? You could have given her a whole file on me, for all I know.'

Birdie glanced at Seb, who was frowning. 'You have every right to be concerned, Conrad,' he said. 'But I can assure you that your identity is safe, and if you don't wish it to be disclosed to your birth mother, then it will remain confidential.'

There was silence, as if he was considering Seb's comments. 'Okay. Thanks. What did she say when you told her you'd seen me?'

'She was relieved and happy to know you'd gone to a good family who loved you,' Birdie said, remembering Lady Angelica's unsuccessful attempt to hide the tears. 'How do you feel, now you've had time to give it some thought?'

'How the hell do you think?' Tina snapped. 'It's turned his life upside down.'

Conrad made a shushing noise. 'Sorry, but Tina's right. This whole thing's messing with my head. I can't even pretend that it's all one big mistake, because we looked at the boxes in the attic and found the adoption papers. Which means it's all true and my whole life has been one big lie.'

Birdie winced. Denial was a part of the acceptance process, but the fact he couldn't go through that stage now meant he'd probably moved straight on to the next: anger.

'Have you spoken to Maggie yet?' Birdie asked.

'No. I don't want to discuss it with her until things are a bit straighter in my head. I'm sure she had her reasons for keeping it from me and meant well, but right now, I might say something I'll later regret.'

'What about the money? Is this woman going to pay?' Tina asked, her voice sharp. Birdie folded her arms and tried to remind herself that Tina was only looking out for her husband and their family.

'She'll pay you, if you agree to be tested. Have you thought about how much money you'd like? We do have some guidelines and are happy to discuss them with you. It might help us to reach a figure that—'

'Actually,' Conrad's voice cut across her, and in the background, Tina made a grunting noise that sounded like she was swearing. 'Before we get to the money, there's something else I want. Now I've had time to think about it, I want to meet her for myself. To see what kind of person she is.'

'That could be a problem. As we explained, your birth mother is in a difficult position, and—'

'This "Angie" must be pretty damn desperate to pay you lot to look for me,' Conrad said, his voice as unemotional as Lady Charing's. 'I also want to meet my father.'

What?

Birdie had to slap her hand across her mouth to stop from swearing. But she was swearing on the inside as her mind tried to figure out all the steps something like that might involve. Or even if it could be done at all. As if this case wasn't hard enough already.

'That's a challenging request,' Seb said. 'Currently we have no information on your birth father. We have no idea if he's still alive. May I suggest we discuss this after you've had the blood test?'

'Nope. Ever since you and Birdie left, I've been doing nothing but think about it. I have no idea who these people are, so why should I do anything for them? I want to sit down with them both in the same room and face them.'

'Are you sure it has to be at the same time?' Birdie asked. 'Even if we can find your birth father, he and Angie haven't seen each other for fifty-one years. We've no idea if it's even possible.'

'It's what I want. Once I've seen them both, I'll be tested,' Conrad said firmly.

Birdie closed her eyes, trying to ignore the lump in her throat. She'd had years to get used to the fact she was adopted, but it had only been recently that she'd finally found her birth mother and talked to her face to face. Since her initial meeting with Kim, they'd met one other time when Kim had travelled to Northampton and they'd spent the day together. And while it had helped fill in some of the pieces of the puzzle for her, she only had to look at her own red hair that came from her birth father, Todd, to know at some stage she would need to find him as well.

It meant that she could totally understand Conrad's request. Even if he had no idea what the implications of it might be.

'Okay. We understand.' Seb steepled his fingers, a thoughtful expression crossing his face. She recognised it as meaning that he was already starting to work out a new strategy. 'We'll contact Angie with a view to gathering as much information as we can about your birth father. If we can arrange a meeting between you all, what kind of payment would you be looking at?'

'We want—' Tina started to say, but then it went all muffled as if someone had put their hand over the speaker. All they could hear was the muffled sound of an argument.

'I can't give you an answer yet,' Conrad said, coming back on the phone. 'I want to meet them first and then I'll let you know.'

'We understand. As soon as we have more information, we will be back in touch.' Seb leant forwards and picked up the phone and ended the call. He turned to Birdie, his eyes filled with concern. 'Are you okay? It looks like you got thrown by his request.'

'Yes. Sorry. It did catch me out,' she admitted as she began to pace the room. 'I know we're meant to be detached as investigators, but right now, I can see both sides of the story. Without the blood test and Conrad turning out to be a donor, Devon's life is at risk. But Conrad's world has been completely flipped, so much so that he can't process everything. I can see why he needs more answers.'

'It's impossible to remain detached all the time, Birdie. And I agree that it's not fair for us to put pressure on Conrad. But I am concerned we may run out of time. You know as well as I do how long these searches can take. According to Lady Angelica, she doesn't even know Roy's last name.'

Birdie stopped her pacing and gave him a grateful smile.

In the few years she'd known Seb, he'd gone from pain in the arse to colleague and now friend. He'd been with her throughout her search for Kim and he understood how complex cases like this would be. It gave her renewed energy, and she returned to his desk and picked up her phone.

'About that, I have a feeling that Lady C knows more than she's letting on; she—'

'Lady C?' Seb said, arching an eyebrow. 'Don't let her hear you call her that.'

'What? It rolls off the tongue a lot easier than *Lady Angelica*. But, anyway, to continue what I was saying. Did you notice when we first asked her about the father, she wouldn't look directly at us?'

'I did. Let's hope you're right and she was withholding information because everything hangs on us being able to find this man and him agreeing to see his son.'

'I suggest we pay our client another visit and give her an update,' Birdie said, leaning over and fishing Seb's car keys from the antique bowl on the desk where he always kept them. 'Then we can see exactly what she knows.'

ELEVEN

'I'll let Her Ladyship know that you're here,' Gibbs told them for the second time that day, before once again disappearing off to one side of the wide marble-floored foyer.

'Do you think he's really a robot who stands by the door on the off-chance someone arrives?' Birdie's eyes were bright with amusement. 'I mean, that was word for word what he said to us earlier.'

'Now who has a perfect memory?' Seb raised an eyebrow at her, and she grinned.

'I guess you're rubbing off on me. Next I'll be quoting pages and pages of legal documents.'

'Please, spare me,' he said, pleased to observe she was back to her normal self. Now all she had to do was comment on how much the door handles would have cost for him to be completely sure.

'Don't worry, I think you're safe,' she assured him before glancing to the side of the door. 'Check out that umbrella stand.

Do you think it's made of real gold?' She wrinkled her brows. 'What's so funny?'

'Nothing.' He bit back his smile just as the door to the family room opened and one of the dogs bounded out into the hallway, followed by Lord Edgar.

'Forget the robot theory. I think we've stepped into a time loop. This is exactly the same as last time,' Birdie whispered before the head of the house reached them.

'Clifford, Birdie. I wasn't expecting to see you again today. Does this mean you've found the missing relative?' His tone was polite and calm, almost as if he was referring to the weather, but Seb had been around his own father long enough to know that it didn't mean he was indifferent to what the success of their investigation could mean for his youngest son.

'I'm afraid we haven't yet, sir. But we'll be devoting all our time to the matter. We're here because we require more information regarding the donor issues that were discovered following testing of the family.'

'Ah, I see.' Lord Edgar bent down to pat the dog by his side. 'That's Angelica's bag. I'll leave you with her. She kept a record of everything. I'm off for a walk with the dog, before this weather turns again. Gone are the days when I can get drenched without it turning into a ghastly cold, or worse.'

With that, he disappeared towards the rear of the house.

Gibbs returned several minutes later and led Seb and Birdie into a study, where Lady Angelica was seated behind an open laptop on a wide desk. As they entered, she closed the computer and gestured for them to sit down on the other side of the desk.

'Thank you, Gibbs, that will be all,' Lady Angelica said, her voice not betraying anything. But once the door was closed, her calmness seemed to leave her and she rubbed the bridge of her nose. 'What did he say?'

'He has agreed but—'

'Oh my goodness,' Lady Angelica interrupted, her hand clutching at her chest. 'That's—'

'Wait,' Birdie called out. 'It's not that simple. Conrad has only agreed to the test if he can meet you and his father.'

Lady Angelica visibly shrank in the chair. 'Oh, I see... if that's what he wants we'll have to oblige.'

'If we can locate the father, he'll be informed about the child and your reasons for wanting to contact him. Your chances of stopping it from becoming public knowledge are slim at best,' Seb said, his face grim.

'I have no choice.' Lady Angelica dropped her head, fatigue caused by worry obviously weighing heavily. 'If we don't look for him, I'm risking Devon's life. I can't do that.'

'I understand this is difficult, but we need your help if we're to have any chance of finding the father,' Seb said.

'We need you to tell us everything you can about Roy,' Birdie added, notebook poised in her lap. 'We already know that you met him in the summer of 1971, and that he worked on your parents' estate in the garden.'

'That's right. I had just turned sixteen.' Lady Angelica swallowed, her face strained. 'Most of my friends from school were going to Europe or America for the summer, but my parents wanted me to stay in England and spend time with them. I'm an only child, so there was no one around of my age to keep me company. That's when I met Roy.'

'Did his family live locally?'

'I have no idea. Several of the young single gardeners lived in a boarding house in Dunchurch, because the properties on the estate were reserved for married workers, and they all travelled to work together. I don't know whether Roy lived there, or whether he simply had a lift in and out with them.'

'Is it possible to gain access to the estate's accounts from that time?' Seb asked, though he knew it was a long shot. Her parents were both dead and from what he remembered the estate, in the absence of a male heir, had gone from Lady Angelica's father to his brother, and then on to her cousin, Darcy, who now held the title.

She shook her head. 'No. In 1982, shortly after my uncle died and his son Darcy had moved in, there was a flood in the wing housing the estate offices. All paper records going back hundreds of years were lost. It was dreadful. So much family history destroyed.'

Birdie frowned and twirled her pen. 'I'm so sorry. Did Roy ever mention his family?'

A flicker of anxiety crossed Lady Angelica's face and she dipped her eyes.

Clearly the question had struck a nerve.

'He didn't talk about them, although I did overhear him telling one of the other gardeners that his father had been in prison. I'm ashamed to say that back then, it seemed almost exhilarating, because he was so very different from anyone else I knew.'

'Are you sure you have no idea of his surname?' Seb pushed, because even knowing Roy's father had been in prison, they were still left with the proverbial needle in a haystack.

What they needed was a last name.

'Of course I'm sure.'

Seb nodded. 'Okay. Is there anything else you can tell us? It might seem like an insignificant detail to you, but anything you remember could be useful.'

'No... Well... his friends did sometimes refer to him as El Greco.' She looked up at them, eyes clouded with uncertainty.

'Why? Was he artistic?' Seb gave her a curious look.

'Art?' Birdie swivelled to face him.

'El Greco is the name of a famous Greek artist, who inherited the title while living in Italy, although he's best known for his contribution to the Spanish Renaissance. The Museo del Greco in Toledo is dedicated to his work,' Seb explained.

'That's correct. An extraordinary gallery,' Lady Angelica agreed before pursing her lips together. 'But I think the nickname was more to do with his family. He didn't tell me where they were from, but on reflection, when considering his complexion, they could have been Greek or Greek Cypriot. It wasn't something we discussed.'

'It's still helpful,' Seb said.

'What else can you tell us about your relationship?' Birdie asked. 'Did you go out much locally? Or meet any of his friends?'

'Oh, no, it wasn't like that. We only spent time together. Alone.' Lady Angelica answered a little too quickly, and her gaze, once again, dropped down to her hands.

Interesting.

Birdie had commented that she believed their client could be hiding something from them. This confirmed it.

'Where did you meet then?' Birdie asked.

'In the old gardening shed at the far end of the grounds. No one was ever around and I could be myself. It was all so different from the balls and parties I attended with my friends. No make-up or constricting dresses, or worrying about getting caught smoking. It was only the two of us.'

'I see.' Birdie jotted down some notes. 'When was the last time you saw Roy, and what happened when you found out you were pregnant? Did you talk to him or stay in contact?'

'Once the summer holidays were over, I returned to school. There were no mobile phones or emails back then, and he didn't give me his address. So I couldn't write to him. By the time I came home for the Christmas holidays, I was four months pregnant. Thankfully, I wasn't showing much and managed to hide it. But I knew it would only be a matter of time, and so I confessed to my mother.'

'Did your mother ask who the father was?' Birdie asked.

'I told her I was drunk at a party and couldn't remember.'

'What did she say to that?' Birdie asked, her eyes wide. 'She must have been very cross.'

'She didn't waste her time admonishing me,' Lady Angelica said, with a flick of her hand. 'She accepted what had happened and her concern was dealing with it.'

'Did you see Roy before you were sent to Norfolk?' Seb asked.

'No. I didn't want my parents to discover the truth. It was one thing to believe the father was someone I'd encountered at a party. But knowing that he worked on the estate... I couldn't risk it in case they did something to harm him.'

Seb frowned. Something didn't add up. Would her parents really have harmed the boy? He put his thoughts to one side. There were more important considerations.

'How did your mother explain your absence to the school?' Birdie tilted her head, mouth set in a thoughtful line.

'My boarding school was full of students whose parents were ex-pats, living in different areas around the world. My mother informed them that I was going overseas on an extended trip and I'd have a personal tutor. That part was actually true, though the tutor was in Norfolk and would visit three times a week.'

Birdie opened her mouth, as if to ask another question, but a knock at the door interrupted her.

'Excuse me, madam.' Gibbs appeared in the doorway. 'You asked me to let you know when it's time for you to get dressed for the dinner you're attending this evening. His Lordship has already gone up to his room.'

'Thank you, Gibbs. I will be there shortly.' Lady Angelica rose from the chair and gave them a weary smile. The interview had clearly taken a toll on her. 'I hope that's enough for you to go on. I'm sorry not to be able to help further. Please do what you can to find Roy.'

'We will,' Seb promised.

They didn't speak until they were on the road back to Market Harborough and Birdie turned to him. 'I take it you noticed this time that she wasn't telling us everything.'

'I did.'

'I don't get it. Why is she holding out on us? After all, it's Devon's life that's at stake. Surely she'd want to give us the best chance of finding Roy?'

'The only reason I can come up with is that she's held this secret for so long she's reluctant to let it go because of what might happen if it becomes common knowledge. Unfortunately, it's something I've seen first-hand. My parents are part of the same generation. Reputation is more important than anything else. Several of their acquaintances have resorted to blackmail and bribery to stop their particular skeletons from coming out of the closest.'

'Then they need to have their heads checked,' Birdie retorted as her stomach growled. 'And now, unless you have other plans, I think we should stop at a pub on the way home for dinner. It's been a long day, and I get the feeling that tomorrow will be even longer.'

'There's a pub on the outskirts of Saddington. We'll try there,' Seb said. 'It will give us a chance to go over what we know and plan our next steps.'

TWELVE

Sunday, 10 December

Another day, another stately home.

Birdie climbed out of the car and stared up at the imposing red-brick building of Rolton Hall, which looked out over an extensive park and gardens, dotted with clumps of trees and a large lake in the middle. She had to admit it was jaw-dropping. If she had time, she'd research into all these buildings. Then again, there was always Seb. She arched an eyebrow at him.

'Go on, tell me about the Doric columns and why the windows would have cost a fortune after the window tax was introduced?'

'I think you're doing fine on your own,' he assured her before glancing to something past her shoulder. 'And you probably noticed that the garden was designed by Capability Brown.'

'Of course it was.' She gave an exaggerated sigh before grinning. 'Actually, I did know that, because I looked it up last night. Plus, despite the fact my mother can kill just about any plant imaginable, she is addicted to watching the Chelsea Flower Show coverage each year on the TV.'

'I thought the plan was to catch up on sleep last night?'

Birdie gave him a guilty grin. 'You know I like to be prepared. I'd been wondering why Lady Angelica mentioned a whole team of gardeners working on the estate at the time. No point having gardeners if you don't have massive grounds.'

'Homes like this are high-maintenance. Let's go. I wonder what reception we'll receive?'

'We'll soon find out,' she said, grinning, before smoothing down her jacket and following him to the imposing entrance. 'I still think you should name drop who you are.'

'For the sake of expediency, I believe you're right.'

After their meal the previous night, they'd discussed the case and decided to speak directly to Darcy Montague in the hope someone on the staff would remember Roy. It was risky, given their client's need for secrecy, but it was by far the quickest way.

'Can I help you?' A look-a-like Gibbs answered the door, using an equally robotic voice. Was there a school that taught them how to act like that?

Seb held out his business card and gave the man a calm smile. 'My name's Sebastian Clifford, and I'd appreciate if Lord Montague could spare me a few minutes.'

'That may not be possible. His Lordship is busy this morning.'

'My father, Viscount Worthington, suggested that His Lordship might be able to help.'

At the mention of his name, the butler's countenance defrosted and he gave a slight nod. Birdie winced. She knew Seb hated trading on his family name – along with the white lie – but accepted that it was sometimes a necessary evil.

'Of course. I'll go and enquire. Please wait here.'

'Now do you believe me about the robot theory?' Birdie

demanded once the butler disappeared into the bowels of the house.

'You do raise a compelling argument,' Seb said as the butler reappeared, followed by a tall man with blonde hair and the same blue eyes as his cousin. Birdie knew this to be Darcy Montague, who, now sixty-two, had taken over the title and estate after his father's death several years ago.

'Clifford? I don't believe we've ever met, but I have bumped into Hubert at a few events over the years.'

'My brother speaks very highly of you,' Seb said and made the introductions. 'We're sorry to interrupt your Sunday morning.'

'Between you, me, and the wall, you've saved me from having to watch my grandson sleep. Both my girls moved out years ago, of course, but the youngest has produced our first grandchild. I'm not sure I need to spend an hour on a Zoom call watching naptime. In my day, children were seen for an hour at teatime. The rest of the time, Nanny took care of them. Nowadays, it's hands-on for both parents.' He shook his head.

'Congratulations on the birth. Hopefully he will wake up by the time we've finished talking,' Seb said, eyes twinkling. 'Birdie and I are working on a rather routine missing person's case. Our client is the missing man's sister, and she hasn't seen her brother for over fifty years. But we've managed to trace him back to being employed here.'

'Fifty years ago?' Lord Montague let out a long whistle. 'As you know that's well before my time here, or even my father. Back then it was my Uncle Charles's.'

'Yes, I believe he was friends with my grandfather,' Seb said, again showing no hint of his dislike of name dropping, or the fact they knew Lady Angelica. 'We're hoping there might be a member of staff working here who was there then. A long shot, I'm aware.'

'That's a jolly good idea. I believe that Jim, our head

gardener, has been with us for about that time. I'll check if
he's working today.' He disappeared back towards the rear of
the large hall and could be heard having a quiet conversation
with the butler before rejoining them. 'You're in luck. He's
working in the kitchen garden, overseeing the leeks. I'll take
you over.'

The walled garden was at the side of the house, and while
not as imposing as the one at Fleckney, it was still several times
larger than the entire house Birdie had grown up in. And it was
full of vegetables. She wrinkled her nose. If you asked her, that
was way too many vegetables for one family to eat.

A group of gardeners were bent over what looked like
spinach. On seeing them, a lean man waved and ambled over to
where they were standing.

He was probably in his early seventies with weathered skin
and fine windblown hair that was streaked with grey.

'Good morning, Your Lordship.' Jim's voice was a slow
drawl that seemed to have been refined by years of practice, and
after the introductions were made and the purpose of the visit
explained, he took several minutes to consider it before finally
looking at them. 'Hmmm, let's see. The summer of 1971...
That's going back some time. I wouldn't have been here more
than a year myself.'

'Do you remember someone call Roy? He would have been
around your age.'

'Roy?' Jim said the name as if it were a strange plant that
he'd never come across before. 'There were a lot of lads here
every year. Some didn't even last the summer. Not under old
Mr Higgins. He had us working hard for our pay, make no
mistake. Not all of them were cut out for it.'

'But do you remember him? He had dark hair and eyes,'
Birdie pushed. There was something about Jim's ponderous
reply that was rubbing her up the wrong way. Not to mention
that he'd avoided answering the question.

'Dark hair?' Jim mused in the same drawn-out tone that made Birdie want to shake him.

'Are you local? From Dunchurch originally?' Seb interrupted. It seemed to catch him unaware, and he immediately nodded.

'Been there since I was fourteen.'

'Excellent, so there's every chance you *would* have met Roy,' Seb continued in an encouraging voice.

'It does stand to reason. Come on, Jim. Think back.' Lord Montague gave the gardener an encouraging nod. The nudge from his employer seemed to do the trick.

'You know, I think you're right. There was a Roy. Not here for very long. Bit of a fighter, now I think about it. Pretty sure old Higgins gave him the boot after a few months.'

'Do you know where he lived?' Seb probed.

'No. There were a few housing estates close by. Still are. Could have come from one of them.' He looked at Lord Montague, as if asking permission to go back to his work.

'What about the name El Greco?' Birdie pressed, before Lord Montague could say anything. 'That was the nickname he'd been given by some of the other workers. It's not something that's used all the time.'

Jim's hands twitched before he slowly shook his head. 'Nope. Never heard that before. Maybe it's the wrong Roy? I've got to get on. Can't leave this lot alone for more than five minutes without them pulling out something they shouldn't.'

Lord Montague glanced at Birdie, and she reluctantly nodded in agreement. Once Jim was dismissed, he hurried away with more speed than he'd shown during the conversation. Their host gave them an apologetic smile.

'Sorry about that. He's what I would call a slow burner. But he's a marvel with the trees. Probably talks to them more than he does people. What he said is correct. Back then, there would have been a huge crew of gardeners working all year around.

My father cut the staff right back after Uncle Charles passed. I've kept it even leaner than that. Soaring costs, as I'm sure you're only too aware.' He grimaced in Seb's direction.

'Yes, it's not easy managing such a vast estate,' Seb agreed.

'Is there anyone else who might have known Roy?' Birdie asked in a hopeful voice.

'I'll check with the estate manager tomorrow. He'll be able to go through our staff records. Unfortunately, they don't go back as far as the seventies, thanks to a flood in 1982. Would you like to come back to the house for some refreshments?'

'No thank you,' Seb answered for them both. 'We don't want to intrude on your weekend more than we have.'

'In other words, you're happy for me to return to watching that grandson of mine sleeping.'

Birdie grinned. 'You never know, he could have woken up by now. There may even be gurgling involved.'

His eyes twinkled as he smiled. 'Little chap is adorable when he does that. I'll ask my manager to call you if he discovers anything. It's grand to see you, Clifford. Give my regards to your parents and brother.'

'I will do,' Seb said before they made their way through the sweeping garden towards the car. 'Thoughts on Jim?' he asked once they were out of earshot.

'I think he's either got the worst memory in the world, or he's lying through his teeth.' Birdie growled, turning to look back at the gardener. His head was bent, concentrating on whatever it was he was doing. 'If Lord Montague wasn't with us, I would've pressed him a lot harder. Did you see his reaction when I mentioned El Greco?'

'I did.'

'He clearly knows something, and now we're walking away with nothing.'

'Not quite true.' Seb took out his keys and unlocked the car.

'We now have confirmation that Roy and his family lived in the area.'

Birdie's mouth opened, and she stared at him before recalling Jim's words.

There were a few rough housing estates close by. Still are. Could have come from one of them.

Her pulse spiked with the buzz of a breakthrough and she grinned at Seb. 'That's brilliant. I was getting so annoyed at him avoiding the questions until you cut in, forcing him to answer before he could think about it. And let me guess, you already know the names of the estates that were here in 1971.'

'I do,' he agreed easily. 'I undertook some research last night. There were three at the time but only one of them had a Greek community club. Gotham Park Estate. Also, Jim mentioned that Roy was a fighter, which means there's a chance he's also got a criminal record. The same as his father.'

'Which is both a good thing and a bad thing.' Birdie tapped the roof of the car as she continued to think. 'If he's in the system, he's easier for us to track. But it also means he could be dangerous.'

'It does. The other problem is that we need access to the system.'

Birdie's mind was already going down that same path.

While they tried not to ask her old colleagues at Market Harborough Police Station for too many favours, this time it would hopefully be worth it.

'I'll go and see Twiggy first thing in the morning. I haven't caught up with him since my birthday, so it will be nice to say hello. Hopefully, he'll agree to help us find Roy.'

THIRTEEN

Monday, 11 December

'Well, well, look what the weather's brought in.'

Neil 'Twiggy' Branch peered up from the front desk as Birdie stepped into her old workplace, a gust of wind following her. She quickly shut the door and grinned. They'd been partners at Market Harborough Police, and were still great friends, even though she'd resigned to join Seb in the business.

'Been promoted to reception, have you?'

'Very funny. I'm helping out,' he said, rolling his eyes.

'You look good, Twig. No signs of icing sugar or pastry crumbs around your mouth.'

'I'm a lot better at hiding the evidence these days,' he said, though his eyes were twinkling. She knew that after years of his wife, Evie, trying to get him to stay on a diet, he'd finally taken it seriously and cut back on his daily visits to the bakery. He looked better for it. The middle-age spread had gone, though his brown hair was still as unruly as ever. 'And before you ask, I went to the doctor last week and he's pleased with my progress. Or should I say, *lack* of progress.'

'You know me too well.' The tension in her jaw eased.

When Twiggy had first been diagnosed with frontotemporal dementia, it had been a crushing blow to everyone who knew and loved him, so the fact it hadn't got any worse was a relief.

'That's what you get for being stuck with me as a partner. Speaking of partners, how's the viscount?' Once upon a time this comment would've been delivered as a jab, but the two men had finally pushed aside their differences and were now on fairly friendly terms.

'If you mean, Seb, he's good. He's even started wearing jeans sometimes.'

'Wonders will never cease.' Twiggy whistled. 'Anyway, what brings you through our illustrious doors?'

'Can't a girl just come and say hello?' Birdie said. 'How is everyone?'

'Busy fighting crime,' Twiggy promptly replied and then gave her a smile. 'Well, I hope they are. Mrs Maddison has been calling a lot about her cat lately. Oh, but not Sparkle,' he added, referring to DC Gemma Litton. 'I probably haven't told you, but she's been promoted to sergeant and works in Rugby.'

'Wow, that's fantastic.' She made a mental note to call her former colleague later.

'Sure is. We didn't have time for a proper knees-up, because there were a few open cases at the time, and she had to get the little ones settled into a new routine. But we're getting together in the new year for it. You'll have to come. I know she'd love to see you.'

'Never met a party I didn't want to go to,' Birdie assured him, as a young PC she hadn't seen before walked into the room juggling a box of files.

'Hey, Twig. Thanks for minding the desk.'

'No bother.' Twiggy walked around to the front of the

reception desk and ushered Birdie up the stairs and over to his
desk. 'Now, what's this really about?'

'It's the case we're working on right now. We desperately
need to track someone down. There's a good chance he has a
criminal record. Will you help?'

Twiggy frowned and ran a hand through his wayward hair.
'You know how it works here. What would happen if the wrong
person decided to follow up on why I was accessing the
database?'

'I know, Twig. I know. I promise this isn't a run-of-the-mill
case. It's literally a matter of life and death. The man we're
looking for is called Roy and we know that age-wise, he's somewhere in his late sixties. We believe he was living in Dunchurch
in 1971, possibly in Gotham Park Estate, and he might be
Greek because he was sometimes called El Greco.'

Twiggy's lips pressed together and he studied her face
before finally nodding. 'Okay. But you owe me one.'

'Thanks so much, Twig,' she said as Sergeant Jack Weston
walked into the room, his cheeks red from the winter air. He
was holding a large shopping bag in one hand and at the sight of
her, he raised an eyebrow.

'Birdie. Good to see you.'

'You too, Sarge.' She grinned at him. They'd always got on
well, but he was fond of saying that he liked her more now that
he didn't have to put up with her sloppy timekeeping. 'Looks
like you're busy buying Christmas presents. Hope you've got
me something nice.'

'Still as cheeky as ever, I see.' He turned to look at Twiggy.
'Anything happen in my absence?'

'No, Sarge.'

'Right, I'll leave you to it. Don't distract Twiggy for too long,
Birdie.'

'As if,' Birdie said, saluting and grinning in her old boss's
direction.

Sarge rolled his eyes and then left the room, heading in the direction of his office.

Birdie had popped in enough times to say hello to the team that her presence wasn't suspicious. But all the same, they sat in silence, waiting until the sound of Sarge's footsteps had disappeared down the corridor.

'Right. Give me the details again.' Twiggy turned back to the computer and logged into the system. Birdie did so and then resisted the urge to look at the screen, instead forcing herself to wait until he'd finished his tedious two-finger typing. 'Okay, looks like we might have something here.'

'Let's hear it.' She spun back around and leant forward.

'There's a Roy Pappas in here. He's sixty-eight years old and is serving time in a maximum-security prison for armed robbery and assault. It was at a stately home where he was working. Somewhere near Braunston.'

'That's still in the Warwickshire area,' Birdie said, her elation curtailed by the fact he was in a high-security prison and therefore dangerous. Not to mention difficult to access. It really was starting to sum up this case. 'His sentence?'

'Fifteen years, and he's served ten so far. He'll be drawing the pension by the time he gets out. But there's a history of other charges. Take care. He's dangerous. I've sent a photo of him to your phone.'

Her phone dinged a moment later, and Birdie opened up the image. Roy Pappas's face was weather-beaten and a long scar ran down one cheek. The long jawline and the way his eyes were set reminded her of Conrad.

'This could be him. Where is he? Is it Marshdown?' she asked, referring to the high-security prison five miles out of Market Harborough.

Twiggy nodded. 'I take it that means you want to interview him?'

'If this is our guy, then yes. Though now I have a name, we

can do more research to see what else we can find. What are the chances of getting in to see him?'

'Not really my area of expertise, but I might be able to help you at least get a foot through the door. Back when dinosaurs roamed the earth and I was a police cadet, I trained with a guy called John Rogers. He was a good sort, but decided the force wasn't for him. He ended up going into the prison service and is now the governor there. If you do need to speak to Pappas, contact Rogers and use my name.'

'Thanks, Twig.' Birdie felt unexpectedly teary, but she swallowed it down. She was getting way too soft and sentimental in her old age. But all the same, she stood up and gave her friend a hug.

'All right, all right,' he complained. 'No need to go all girly on me. And hey, make sure you and Clifford take care. Whatever this case is, Pappas doesn't look like a guy to be messing with. You hear me?'

'I do,' Birdie promised just as a loud thump came from down the corridor, in the direction of Sarge's office. It was possibly from his phone hitting the wall. She raised an eyebrow at Twiggy and shrugged her coat back on. 'I'd better clear off while I can. Give my love to Evie and the girls. Tell them I'll swing by and see them after Christmas.'

'Will do.' He turned back to his computer and Birdie hurried out of the station into the cool December weather. If Pappas was Conrad's father, then they needed to speak to him as soon as possible.

FOURTEEN

'Okay, thank you.' Seb finished the call to the builder and made a note of the appointment he'd just arranged in his calendar. The bout of bad weather had caused some of the guttering to come loose around the side of the house, and he wanted to get it fixed before it could cause any real damage. He then updated the detailed spreadsheet that he kept for his cousin before dealing with several more administrative tasks involving Rendall Hall.

He was finishing the last of them when Elsa gave a bark of excitement as Birdie pulled into the driveway. A few minutes later, the front door flew open and her hurried steps echoed down the hallway before she burst into the office. Her movements had a frenetic energy and her eyes were gleaming.

'I take it you have good news.' Seb closed the spreadsheet as Elsa got to her feet and nudged Birdie's leg.

'Is it that obvious?' She dropped to her knees and gave the dog a long hug.

'Let's just say, if this were a poker game, you'd owe me a *lot* of money,' he said, though her enthusiasm was contagious. 'How's Twiggy?'

'He's great, and – miracle of all miracles – he's kept off the weight he lost, which must be a first. He sends his regards and all that stuff.' She finished patting Elsa and gave a vague wave of her hands before settling down at the chair by his desk. 'There's a Roy Pappas who is currently serving a fifteen-year sentence at Marshdown, for armed robbery and assault.'

'High security. That's not ideal.' Seb pressed his lips together.

'At least we know he's not going anywhere,' Birdie pointed out as she lifted her phone and tapped away at the screen. 'I've sent you his photo. Let's do some research and see what we can dig up on him. Good news is that Twiggy knows the prison governor, which might work in our favour. I'll start looking for Pappas on social media and in newspaper articles, and you can look into his last conviction. It was at a house near Braunston where, according to Twiggy, he was working at the time.'

'I'm liking this less and less,' Seb admitted as they both settled down to work.

He studied the case and then made a quick call to the owners of the stately home. All they could tell him was that Pappas had only been there a few months before the robbery, and that while he'd been armed at the time, no shots had been fired. But he had knocked the butler unconscious in a fight. The police had since discovered the references he'd used were fake, as had been the name he'd used to get the job.

Seb made a note of the name and searched for it online but came up blank. Did that mean Pappas had used other names in the past? He put through a call to the detective sergeant who had worked on the case and, after a quick conversation, all he'd gleaned was that Pappas was charismatic, but manipulative and extremely volatile if he didn't get his own way.

Seb considered the matter. If Pappas *was* the same Roy

who'd worked on the Montague estate, it would explain how he'd been able to form a bond with Lady Angelica. Especially if she'd felt isolated and was questioning her place in the world. Unfortunately, it also meant that the man they'd be dealing with would likely possess a high level of cunning. He continued researching until Birdie closed her laptop.

'Not much my end. Pappas was only on one social media platform before going into prison and didn't exactly post photos of kittens and sunsets. I discovered that his father was from Athens, and his mother was English. He was born in London. He has a couple of friends on the site, and that's about it. I take it from your face that you didn't fare much better?'

'I couldn't find anything linking him to Lady Angelica. But I've been informed that he can be violent when things don't go his way.'

Birdie's face darkened. 'Suddenly, I'm almost hoping that Pappas *isn't* our guy.'

'The quickest way for us to confirm his identity is to show the photo to Lady Angelica. Then we can decide how much we should tell her about what's happened to him since they were last together.'

'Okay.' Birdie joined him back by his desk as he called their client.

She answered on the third ring. 'Sebastian, do you have news?' Her voice was blunt and to the point.

'We have found someone matching his description. Birdie's sending a photograph through to you now. We're hoping you can tell us if this is the same Roy.'

'Okay, it's just arrived. Hang on, I'm putting down the phone.' There was a fumbling noise and a long silence before Lady Angelica could be heard gasping.

'I think that's a yes...' Birdie whispered.

Seb leant back in his chair as he mulled over the implications. Not only would it be difficult to even speak with Pappas, but if he was as cunning and manipulative as they'd been told, there was a good chance he might use the knowledge about an illegitimate child to his own advantage. Maybe sell a story to the newspaper? Or try to contact Lady Angelica directly?

The silence continued for several moments before Lady Angelica's voice sounded out again.

'I'm fairly certain that's him. He's changed since I last saw him but there's something in his eyes that took me back to that summer...' She broke off and the line went silent for several seconds. 'Sorry. What can you tell me about him? Where is he? Can you visit and see if it's him?'

Seb glanced over at Birdie and they nodded in agreement. This was as close to an identification as they were going to get, so, for now, they had to assume Pappas was definitely Conrad's father. Which meant they'd need to be honest with their client.

'We hope so. But it could be a problem. He's in prison...' There was a sharp intake of breath from down the line. 'Serving a fifteen-year sentence.'

'Prison?' Lady Angelica gasped. 'You know, in all this, I didn't once think about what had happened to Roy. I was so focused on Devon, and on finding the child I'd been forced to give up. If anything, I assumed he would still be working as a gardener somewhere. So much fallout from one stupid night.'

'We're sorry to be the ones to deliver the news.' Seb wasn't surprised it had rattled their client. In a way, it had probably been easier when she'd kept the door to the past closed. But now it was open, she could no longer avoid facing what had happened.

'Don't be. You're doing the job I'm paying for. What happens now? Will you able to visit him?'

'Because it's a high-security prison it might be challenging, but it's not impossible. Leave it with us. If something can be arranged, and we can confirm that he's Conrad's father, we'll discuss a possible meeting between the three of you.'

'I see. Please keep me posted on your progress. Now, if you'll both excuse me, I have a committee meeting to prepare for.'

The call ended and Birdie got to her feet, shaking her head. 'Clearly that's not what she's been expecting. I feel really sorry for her. She said Roy was so different from anyone else she'd met. But at sixteen, we really have no idea.'

'Annabelle had a friend who loved dating men who had criminal records,' Seb said, referring to his ex-girlfriend. 'I could never understand it, but she explained that some women like a bad boy.'

'And some of us might like a bad *girl*,' Birdie reminded him. 'But that aside, think about it. If Lady C had always been living with her rich family, surrounded by equally rich friends at her boarding school, Pappas might have felt like a breath of fresh air. Or, at least, someone so different from anyone she'd ever met that she couldn't see the red flags that might be obvious to her now.'

'It was clearly a shock to hear how different their lives have turned out.'

'Like going to the worst school reunion ever,' Birdie agreed before letting out a long breath. 'But enough of that. We need to meet with Pappas as soon as possible. Let's see if we can get the prison governor on the phone and arrange a visit.'

'I'll ring the prison now and mention Twiggy's name,' Seb said.

'Great. In the meantime, I'll give Conrad a quick call and see how he's going. I won't tell him anything specific yet, but just let him know we're following a lead.'

The governor had a free slot in the afternoon and the arrangements were made for Seb and Birdie to go. He hoped that John Rogers was as helpful as Twiggy had suggested to Birdie. Otherwise, it would be a wasted trip.

FIFTEEN

'The governor will be with you shortly.' The prison guard stepped out of the lift and directed them to a row of uncomfortable-looking chairs that ran along the pale pink wall. Seb had once read that the colour was meant to create a sense of calm, though the sterile scent of disinfectant and the metallic clatter of gates being opened and closed seemed to work in opposition to any soothing effect it might have had.

Once the guard retreated to the caged desk to the right of them, Seb and Birdie sat down. The chair was every bit as uncomfortable as it had appeared, and he twisted slightly to open his suit jacket and smooth down his trousers.

For once, Birdie hadn't complained about his formal attire, and she'd even worn a navy business jacket over a plain white jumper. Next to him she tapped her foot, as if trying to shake her agitation. She took the stairs when she could, but within the prison that hadn't been an option.

'You okay?'

'Yes.' She nodded, though her cheeks were flushed. 'Okay,

not really. But I will be. Let me breathe in some of this Zen-like prison air and think about all the confined spaces. That's sure to help.'

'At least you're making jokes. Which has to be a good sign.'

'It depends on the joke,' she said weakly before giving her arms a good shake. The redness in her face retreated, and she nodded. 'I'm better. This is my first visit here. Usually Twiggy came here on his own. Now I know why.'

So did Seb.

Most of the prisoners in Marshdown were category A, and there was an uncomfortable sense of threat that seemed to seep through the walls. Seb had been to his fair share of prisons in a work capacity and had never enjoyed it. The fact that one of the prisoners here might be the lynchpin to this entire case didn't fill him with confidence. Especially since there were so many external factors that they couldn't control. Not ideal when it came to an investigation.

The lift doors opened again, and this time a lean man in his early fifties stepped out. He had grey eyes and a purposeful walk as he strode towards them. John Rogers.

'Sorry to keep you waiting. Let's go into my office.' He used a swipe card to open the door then ushered them inside. The room had a large whiteboard on one wall and a pinboard on the other, which had on it a collection of Christmas cards, along with several handwritten thankyou notes.

Rogers sat down behind the pale wood desk and gestured to the visitors' seats on the other side. They were slightly more comfortable and once they were settled Rogers fixed them both with a sharp gaze. Seb suspected that he didn't miss too much that went on in his prison.

'What brings you both here today, Mr Clifford and Ms Bird?'

'Please call us Sebastian and Birdie.' Seb leant forwards and gave him a business card. 'We are here to see you as part of a current investigation.'

'Clifford Investigation Services?' The governor studied the card and then put it down on the desk. 'I seem to remember reading an article on you. Weren't you involved with the Liam O'Rourke case down in London?'

'That's correct.' Seb nodded. It was the case that been reported in the national papers and had been responsible for bringing in a regular supply of work. 'We're based in Market Harborough, but our work takes us further afield.'

'Including my prison.' John Rogers raised a curious eyebrow. 'So what is it I can help you both with?'

'We'd like to talk with Roy Pappas. Before I joined the agency, I was a DC at Market Harborough, and Neil Branch was my partner. Twiggy,' Birdie said.

'Twiggy was your partner, eh? You must have had your hands full.' Roger's mouth twitched into a smile, and Birdie returned the grin, eyes bright.

'I'm pretty sure he'd say the same thing about me. Which is probably why we worked so well together. He said to mention his name to you.'

'I bet he did. As long as he didn't tell you about some of the things we got up to at the police training school.'

'No, but now I'm curious,' she said.

He shook his head. 'My lips are sealed. Though let's say it made me realise the police force wasn't for me. I only lasted a couple of years before transferring over to the prison service. What's this case you're working on, and how does Pappas fit into it?'

'Our client has a son who's in need of a kidney transplant and there's no one in the family who's eligible as a donor. They hired us to trace a child she'd given up for adoption, in the hope of them being tested as a possible match. We've found the son, but he'll only agree to it if he can meet both of his birth parents and talk to them together,' Seb said.

'And Pappas is the father?' Rogers let out a long whistle. 'That is quite a can of worms you've opened up.'

He wasn't wrong there. Once again, Seb wished this case hadn't led them in such a dangerous direction. Especially with the time constraints of Devon's illness hanging over them.

'It's not ideal. We haven't been able to glean much information about Pappas, apart from what's in the media. Could you elaborate?'

Rogers sat back in his chair, his eyes thoughtful. 'I won't lie. In the past, Pappas has been very unpredictable and quite a handful. He'd be calm for weeks and then he'd be in the middle of a brawl for what seems like no reason. He's a career criminal and has been in and out of the system since he was a teenager, most of his crimes involving violence. He's divorced and has a couple of adult kids, but none of them visit, and from what I can gather, there's no relationship with them. Does he know about this adopted child?'

'Not as far as we're aware. Our client didn't inform him that she was pregnant and was sent away by her parents. By the time she returned, Pappas was gone. She didn't see him again.' Seb let out a sigh. 'You said he was difficult in the past. Has he changed?'

'He's sixty-eight now and is beginning to slow down. A couple of years ago, he decided to join a new programme to design and build a garden for a national flower show. The garden was awarded third place and Pappas was a key part of the team. It was the first time he'd ever stayed out of trouble for a prolonged period. He's now started mentoring some of the newer inmates in the programme.'

'Does that mean he can have visitors?'

Rogers nodded. 'He hasn't lost privileges in the last twelve months, and his behaviour has markedly improved since we started running the programme. I am satisfied your visit will be useful. However, he will need to agree to it.'

Birdie tapped her foot and grimaced. 'How long will that take?'

'The system is faster than it once was. I can try to arrange something for tomorrow. But it is my strong recommendation that Clifford do the visit alone.'

Birdie's jaw tightened and her fists tightened by her side, but she didn't say anything out loud. Seb glanced at her, impressed by her restraint.

'Why's that? Do you think he would react violently?' Birdie asked.

'I'm not worried about your safety. Pappas is a hard man and I believe his violent outbursts are because he struggles to deal with his emotions. What you need to discuss is going to be awkward, and he might be more open to listening to what you have to say if he doesn't feel threatened or pushed into a corner. It's my opinion that a male might be able to do this better.'

The muscle in her jaw relaxed, and she nodded. 'Okay, if you think that's the best approach. What will you tell him about the visit?'

'It's probably best to keep it vague. He's very shrewd and is always looking for an angle. However, his interest in gardening hasn't waned.'

'Tell him we're interested in the gardening programme the prison runs and we'd like to talk to him about his involvement,' Birdie suggested.

'That would mean lying to him,' Seb said. 'That's hardly ethical.'

'Do you have another idea?' Birdie asked.

'It's not ideal. But if you explain straight away your reason for being there, I'll give my permission,' Rogers said. 'If Pappas agrees to speak to you we can book it in for tomorrow morning at eleven.'

They both shook his hand before being guided out to the exit.

Once they were in the car park, Birdie sucked in a lungful of air and leant against the side of the car. 'To think I was annoyed that I couldn't be there to interview Pappas,' she said. 'But now I've been in those lifts, it's not something I want to repeat in a hurry. Though I am worried about how the interview will go. It sounds like he's not just dangerous, but fickle as well. A real loose cannon. Goodness knows if he'll agree to see you, let alone Conrad.'

'This case is a series of moving parts, and it's our job to make sure it all comes together,' Seb said as a gust of wind blew against their backs and the late-afternoon skies darkened from grey to black. 'It's worth remembering that at one time, Lady Angelica had a connection with him. We have to hope that he felt the same way, and is prepared to help.'

Birdie gave him a sceptical look. 'Have you ever known a career criminal who wants to help merely from the goodness of their heart?'

Seb didn't bother to answer because they both knew she was right. Yet they had to figure out a way to ensure that didn't happen.

SIXTEEN

Tuesday, 12 December

Marshdown Prison, with its gravel-coloured exterior and concrete walls, was a grim example of 1960s brutalist architecture at its worst. In the cool winter light, it looked even less inviting than the previous day. Still, at least Pappas had agreed to the visit.

Seb pulled into the car park as his phone pinged with a flurry of text messages from Birdie.

> 10.31
>
> Spoke to Conrad and he knows you're seeing Pappas.

> 10.36
>
> Don't forget, we still don't have proper confirmation he's the father, so make sure you push him on it.

> 10.37
>
> Pappas has a sister and three nephews. Use that to appeal to his softer side. If he has one.

10.41

Good luck.

He bit back a smile and quickly replied before he headed towards the security gate to go through the sign-in procedure. Despite Birdie's desire to avoid using the lift, she would be hating having to sit out on the interview.

Once he'd handed in his phone and keys and was patted down, a security guard led him down a maze of corridors to one of the nondescript private interview rooms, where prisoners and their lawyers would meet. The rooms were monitored but the conversations were private.

'Wait here. We'll bring Pappas in shortly. He doesn't get many visitors, so let's just hope he's on his best behaviour,' the guard said, though his eyes were filled with scepticism. Probably lucky Birdie wasn't there to see it.

He returned ten minutes later with a prisoner who looked more bull than man, with thick shoulders and a barrel chest, though his face was showing his age. Wrinkles radiated from Pappas's mouth and his cheeks were hollow, which emphasised the scar running down the left-hand side of his face. His dark eyes were alert as they honed in on Seb. The guard guided him to the chair on the other side of the table and removed his handcuffs.

'No funny business, Pappas, and don't forget we're watching.' He nodded to a small camera in the corner of the wall, then turned to Seb. 'Governor said you have thirty minutes, but signal if you want to finish sooner.'

'Thank you, I will.' Seb nodded, waiting in silence for the guard to leave, the door locking shut behind him. 'Roy, thank you for seeing me. My name's Sebastian Clifford.'

Pappas settled into the chair and folded his arms, eyes still narrowed and full of scrutiny. 'You don't look the sort to be making a television show.'

'What makes you say that?' Seb said, not wanting to get off on the wrong foot.

'I've worked for enough rich pricks over the years.' Pappas's voice was a rich baritone, which Seb suspected helped get him through the door with his last employer. 'You have that same air. That you think you're too good for the likes of me. So, you'd better speak quickly.'

Pappas's jaw was tight and his gaze stony. Seb gave him a bland smile in return. He'd seen enough posturing in his time to not be put off by it.

'Yes. You're correct. This isn't about a television show. The truth is that I'm a private investigator. I'm here on behalf of my client.'

'Good luck with that,' Pappas growled and got to his feet. 'Only thing worse than talking to a copper is one of you lot. Tell your client that whatever they want, the answer's no. I should bloody well have you and Rogers up on false pretences.'

'I can't stop you from leaving, but I suggest you hear me out before you do that. It might be to your advantage.' Seb locked eyes with Pappas and waited.

Finally, the man let out an amused grunt and settled back into the chair.

'Well, ain't you a cool cat? Go on then, Mr Fancy PI. What's this all about?'

'My client is Lady Angelica Charing, but you might know her better as Angelica Montague.'

'Never heard of her.'

'Really?' Seb scanned Pappas's impassive face, but the man didn't flinch. 'In 1971, when you worked at Rolton Hall as a gardener, you had an affair with her.'

'Maybe. I was a good-looking lad back in them days. The girls all went wild for it.' Pappas shrugged, though he made no effort to stand again. Clearly, he was enjoying toying with Seb.

'You admit to working at Rolton Hall in 1971?' he probed,

almost hearing Birdie's voice in his head telling him to push. She was right. Although Lady Angelica had been almost certain Pappas was the same Roy she'd had the affair with, it was still circumstantial.

'I worked in a lot of places. Can't expect me to remember them all.'

'Not even with all this time in prison to reflect on things?' Seb asked.

The jab landed and Pappas glared at him, waving his arm, as if to hurry things along. 'Never you mind what I think about in here. What does this chick want?'

'Her youngest son is very sick and she's hired us to find a potential match for a kidney transplant.'

Pappas let out a long snort of laughter. 'And she wants mine? She's welcome to it. But can't say it's in perfect working order, if you know what I mean.'

'She was hoping to ask the child she gave birth to in 1972... *Your* child.' Seb gave him a level stare.

The words hung in the air between them, and for the first time, the tough-guy persona slipped, and he sank further down in the chair. It was the same reaction Lady Angelica had shown after hearing that her former lover was now in prison. As if the new information was forcing them both to go back into the past and interpret it in a different way.

Seb allowed the silence to continue while waiting for him to recover.

'Is this some kind of joke?' Pappas eventually spoke, running a hand through his short, thick hair.

'I take it you *do* remember Angelica Montague now?' Seb cocked an eyebrow at him.

'Yeah, I remember her. At first, she seemed so different from that stuck-up family of hers and actually liked hanging around me. Then she buggered off and the next thing I know, I've been given the boot. But she never once mentioned anything about having a brat on the way.'

'She didn't discover her pregnancy until she was back at school, and once her parents found out, they immediately sent her away to have the baby, without anyone knowing.'

'I bet they did.' A grim expression settled back on his face. 'No way would I have been good enough for their precious daughter. What did you say? She's now Lady something?'

'That's correct.' Seb kept his voice matter-of-fact. Disclosing this information to Pappas could be dangerous. But Lady Angelica had been clear. They were to do whatever it took if Devon stood any chance of surviving. 'We have found the son she gave up for adoption. However, he won't consider being tested as a possible match until he's spoken to both of his birth parents. That's why I'm here. To ask if you'll be prepared to meet your son.'

'Not gonna happen.' Pappas once again folded his arms in front of his barrel chest. 'I've already had to listen to two whiny brats tell me how I ruined their life. I'm not about to sign up for that again. Besides, how do I even know any of this is true? You could be making it all up.'

'Why would we do that?'

Pappas shrugged. 'You tell me. To kick a man when he's down?'

'We have proof of the adoption and a quick DNA test will confirm you're his father, if you need convincing.' Seb bit back his growing irritation.

Pappas had a chip on his shoulder the size of a mountain. It had clearly grown over the years, leaving him acting like a hard-done-by victim. Maybe he was. Maybe the way he'd grown up had shaped him that way. But he had been the person to make the choices he had.

In a way, it made Seb's job easier. If Pappas was ruled by

self-interest and poor impulse control, then there was bound to be a price. All Seb had to do was find out what it was.

'I have no interest in being jabbed with a needle,' Pappas declared loftily.

Seb didn't bother to explain it didn't require that. Instead, he folded his own arms and stared directly at the man.

'Let's move this discussion forward. What would it take for you to meet your son?'

'Tired of dancing already, Clifford?' Pappas raised an eyebrow, and then shrugged. 'Fine. I might consider it... if there was something in it for me.'

Finally.

Seb continued to hold Pappas's gaze. 'We'll discuss that with our client. How much do you want?'

'Oh, this isn't about money.' Pappas grinned, clearly enjoying playing with Seb. 'I want to get out of this shithole before I'm too old to enjoy my retirement. I'm thinking a nice beach in Costa Del Anywhere-But-Here would suit me nicely, thank you very much. But that means getting my sentence reduced.'

What?

It took all Seb's willpower not to react to the outrageous request. He fixed the man with a cold glare.

'That's not within my power.'

'That's where you're wrong.' Pappas leant forwards so that his elbows were on the table, his eyes hard. 'You see, I know something about a crime. An unsolved death that happened fifty years ago. If I tell the coppers about it, that'll go in my favour and get the parole board to let me out of this dump.'

He leant back, almost as if he'd been playing poker and had just revealed what he believed was a winning hand. Seb let out a breath. This case was like an onion, with layer after layer gradually unpeeling.

'It might indeed help, but that's not something I can do. It would be up to the police. Tell me what you know. Who died and where did it happen?'

'That's where things start to get fun. It happened at Rolton Hall. You're right. I did work there in the gardens, and that's where I met Angie. She was fit as a filly and just as wild. We had a thing that summer. Then saw each other again when she came back from school at Christmas. One night, she sneaked out to spend time with me. She wanted to go for a midnight drive. But I didn't have a car, so she slipped into the house and nabbed the keys for one of the work vehicles.'

Really? That was new information. Why hadn't Lady Angelica mentioned any of this?

'What happened then?'

'Turns out, she couldn't drive. So she convinced me to take the wheel. We went along one of the old dirt roads on the estate and then there was a huge bleeding thump. I stopped straight away, and we climbed out to see what we'd hit. It was one of the farmworkers. Old Fred. Back then I knew a thing or two about first aid, so I checked his pulse, but it wasn't there. Poor old bastard was dead. It was an accident. I didn't even see him, though judging by the broken whisky bottle, he'd had even more to drink than we had. I'm guessing he didn't see us either. Just stepped right out in front of the car.'

Seb frowned. This wasn't evidence. It was a confession. If Pappas was driving, then he was the one who killed the man and Lady Angelica was an accomplice. He couldn't see how it would end well.

It also meant that their client had concealed it from them.

Lady Angelica been very vague about what had happened to Pappas once she'd been sent away. Correction. She'd lied about it. She'd told them she hadn't seen him.

But clearly, this wasn't true. Because if Pappas was right, then it meant she had seen him at Christmas before being sent away to Norfolk.

Why had she hidden it from them? He could only think of one reason.

Pappas was telling the truth.

'What happened? Did you call the police?'

'I wanted to, but it wasn't like nowadays. There were no mobile phones or anything like that. My parents didn't have a pot to piss in and we didn't have a phone. I said we had to go up to her place to call them. She was bawling and sobbing, and by the time we got to the house, she was making so much noise that her parents woke up, and dear old Dad stepped in.'

Now things were starting to make more sense. The Montagues had sent their daughter away to avoid a scandal. Not only about the baby, but about something much worse.

'Are you saying that Charles Montague wouldn't let you call the police?'

'Yep. And that's not all. His estate manager drove me home, and the next day turned up with a wad of cash. He handed it to my old man and told me not to come back to work.'

'How much did they give you?'

'No idea.' Pappas rubbed the back of his neck and rolled his shoulders, as if trying to get rid of the strain of carrying it all these years. 'I didn't see a penny of it. The old man told me to bugger off to his sister's in London and to lie low for a few months. He warned me not to say a word about what happened. If anyone asked, I had to say I'd been fired.'

'What happened to the body?' Seb asked, his mind working out the timeline. It had clearly happened around the same time as the pregnancy, which would also explain why Pappas hadn't known that Lady Angelica had been sent away to Norfolk.

'I don't know. Because I never went back there. No way would I have crossed my old man. He was a mean old dog, he was. So I went and crashed with his sister in London and did some odd jobs. By the time I got back, Angie was gone. I figured she was at that posh school of hers.'

'To confirm, you don't know if anyone reported Fred missing, or if the police were called?'

'That's right. But he was an old drunk. He'd often disappear for months and then turn up to work like nothing had happened. Can't imagine anyone thinking anything was wrong.'

'You do realise that without a body, this whole thing is pure conjecture.'

'Why would I make it up? Look, I might not know where the body is, but I can damn well guess. It'll be buried somewhere on the estate.'

'Why do you think that? Wouldn't that be a risk?'

Pappas let out a bemused chuckle. 'That's bloody obvious. And you should know, seeing as you're one of them. Montague thought he was protected from life because he was born into money. Acted like there were two sets of rules. One for the likes of me, and one for the likes of him. The grounds are huge. Plenty of hidden little corners to bury a body, with no one being any the wiser. That body will be there somewhere. I know it.'

Seb was quiet as he studied Pappas's face. His eyes were clear and his long jaw was firmly shut. He was like a boulder. An immovable object that wasn't going to be shifted by anything less than getting his own way.

'If we investigate this and take what we find to the police, will you agree to meet your son?' Seb asked as the guard opened the door and tapped at his watch.

'Time's up.'

Pappas got to his feet and stared directly at Seb. 'Yeah, I'll meet him. But not until you show me proof that you've looked into it and taken it to the coppers. We clear?'

'Crystal.' Seb stood up.

He was taller than Pappas and, for the first time, the prisoner blanched, before turning to the guard and walking towards the door.

Once he was gone, Seb rubbed his chin as he prepared to

leave the prison. There wasn't much to go on, especially without a body, or even a full name. They'd have to do more digging to see if there was even enough of a case to bring to the police, let alone convince them to take it further. And the ripple effects could be even worse for Lady Angelica.

Once he'd passed through security and retrieved his phone and keys, he marched back to his car. The case was becoming murkier by the minute. He brought up Birdie's number and called, knowing how anxious she'd be to hear how the interview had gone. But she didn't pick up.

Frowning, he tried again, but after several rings, it went through to her voicemail. Had she taken Elsa out for a walk and left her phone on the desk?

He didn't bother to leave a message because he'd be back in the office in twenty minutes and could give her a proper update then.

* * *

'Come on, come on, come on.' Birdie glared at her phone, willing it to ring. While she'd accepted John Rogers's decision for Seb to interview Pappas alone, it still felt like getting benched by her cricket team. It wasn't that she didn't trust Seb, because of course she did. He was calm but determined when interviewing, and never missed anything.

But... what if he *did* miss something this time? What if he needed her to help get Pappas into a corner? What if—

Stop it.

She was wasting time and there was plenty of other work to do. She reluctantly opened her laptop screen and turned up the soundtrack to *Six*, currently her favourite musical. When Seb wasn't in the office, she didn't bother with headphones. The music helped her focus.

She tapped her foot as she got back to work. She'd tracked

down where Pappas and his family had lived in Gotham Park
Estate. They'd moved there in 1968, but in 1972 had moved
further north to Yorkshire, which fitted in with their timeline
nicely. Of course, if Pappas confirmed he was the father, then
the lead wouldn't matter.

Why hadn't Seb called yet?

She picked up her phone and glared at it some more.
Weirdly enough, it still didn't ring. And there was no point
calling him since if he was in the prison, then he would have
surrendered his phone before the interview.

Her limbs itched with frustration and she stood up.

'Come on, Elsa. Let's go for a bonus walk. And don't worry,
you'll still have your regular one after lunch. This is to stop me
from going mad.'

Elsa, who was curled up on a rug by Seb's desk, lifted her
head and opened one brown eye with mild interest. Suddenly,
she barked, wagged her tail, then darted out of the office and
down the hallway, her nails clattering against the old wooden
floorboards.

Birdie blinked and stared at the empty rug.

She followed in Elsa's wake to the front door; the dog had
her nose pressed up against the wood.

'Okay, what's this all about?' She reached for her coat,
which was hanging on one of the hooks by the door, as the
sound of a car door shutting caught her attention.

Seb? That would account for Elsa taking off so quickly.
Birdie hadn't even heard the car arrive. Then again, her music
had been loud. But why didn't he call to say he was on the way
back? The phone had been right next to her, and even over the
music, she would have heard it.

'Well, aren't you the clever girl, realising that Seb had
returned?' Birdie told her. The front doorbell rang. 'Oh. Maybe
it's not him.' Even Seb with all his manners wouldn't ring his
own doorbell. 'Stand back so I can answer the door.'

Elsa did as she was told and Birdie twisted the handle and swung it open to reveal a teenage girl standing on the doormat. She was tall – like almost six foot tall – with a willowy figure, thick, dark hair that hung over her shoulders, and large brown eyes.

'Hello... Can I help you?'

'Oh.' The girl's eyes widened. 'Who are you?'

'I'm Birdie.' She folded her arms as Elsa poked her nose out from around the side of her leg, nose twitching with curiosity. She was definitely only a teenager. Maybe sixteen or seventeen. At her feet, a large overnight bag was bulging in all directions, and a rucksack hung off one shoulder, with a neck cushion looped around it, as if she'd been travelling. Was she a friend of Sarah's sons?

'Are you here to see Benedict or Caspian? Because they won't be here until Christmas Eve,' Birdie asked.

'That's good, because I don't know them.' The girl danced from foot to foot, and glanced over Birdie's shoulder, as if trying to peer further into the house. 'I'm here to see Sebastian Clifford. Is he around?'

'No, he's out.' Was she a client? She seemed young, but then a lot of their current clients knew about them through word of mouth and came from money. Maybe she was some teenage heiress with a pressing problem and lots of cash? 'What's this about? Is it something I can help you with?'

'Not really. But I'd love a cup of tea if you're offering. If you don't mind, I'd like to wait until Sebastian comes home.' The girl scooped up the overnight bag and gave her a lopsided smile. 'You see, he's my dad.'

SEVENTEEN

Birdie's jaws dropped open, but no words came out.

She could only remember three other times that she'd been speechless. Once was when she'd first met Kim, her birth mother; another was when she'd been accepted into the police force; and the third was... actually, it didn't even matter. What mattered was that this teenager....this *very* tall teenager had called Seb her father.

As in they were related.

But why hadn't Seb told her?

God, did he even know?

More to the point, what was she doing here? And who was her mum?

Birdie's mind whirled with so many questions, none of which she could say out loud. Instead, she continued to stare at the girl. The dark eyes were definitely like Seb's, and the wide mouth was almost identical to his mother's, Charlotte's.

The girl didn't seem at all put out by Birdie's reaction and just wrinkled her nose.

'I know. Weird, right? That's kind of how I felt when I first found out – which wasn't long ago. But then, after the shock wore off, I figured that I'd better come and meet him. Oh, by the way, I'm Keira.'

'I-I'm Birdie,' she said automatically, before groaning. 'Which you already know. Sorry, I'm trying to get my head around this. You'd better come inside. It's freezing out there.'

'Tell me about it. The taxi driver didn't even have the heating on,' Keira explained as Birdie stepped back and opened the door properly. 'Oh my God. You have a dog. Isn't she a darling? Or is it a he? Never mind. You're beautiful either way.' Keira stepped inside and held out her hand for Elsa to sniff.

'This is Elsa, and she's a girl.' Birdie closed the door behind them and rubbed her eyes as Elsa cautiously sniffed Keira's hand. 'She's Seb's dog and is a total angel. I love her so much.'

At that, Keira looked at her and let out a long breath. 'My dad has a dog and you both love her? I just *knew* that coming up here was the right thing to do. Of course, I was a little worried he might be a crazy person. I mean you do all the research, but until you meet someone, you never can tell.'

'That's true,' Birdie agreed, getting used to Keira's oversharing. 'I think we'd better go into the kitchen and have a cup of tea. We can split a Danish pastry if you want. There's only one left, but they're to die for.'

'That would be great. I'm famished,' Keira said, her eyes wide as she seemed to take in the large hallway with the antique marble hall stand and the gold-framed paintings that dotted the walls. 'Wow, this place is something else.'

'It is pretty impressive,' Birdie agreed as they reached the kitchen. 'Why don't you sit at the table and I'll put on the kettle. Where have you come from?'

'London. But I accidentally got on the slow train and it stopped so many times, I swear it would have been faster to walk.' Keira shrugged off her large puffa jacket and sat down on one of the chairs. Elsa curled up close by the side of her feet.

It didn't take Birdie long to cut the Danish in half and pour two cups of tea. Then she sat down and nodded her head at Keira. 'Okay, why don't you tell me a bit more about yourself.'

Keira picked up the sticky pastry, let out a happy sigh, and took a bite. 'This is so good. Thanks. Okay. I'm seventeen and my mum is... *was*... Melanie Austin. She... she... died six months ago.' Tears filled Keira's eyes and she closed them, dark lashes sweeping across the delicate skin under her eyes.

'Oh, Keira. I'm so sorry to hear that.' A lump formed in Birdie's throat as she tried to imagine what it must have been like to lose a parent at such a young age. 'Was it just the two of you?'

'Yup. Mum used to call us the "Awesome Austin Girls", and said as long as we had each other, things were good.' Finally, she opened her eyes and gave Birdie a rueful smile. 'Sorry. I swear, most of the time I can hold it together, but every now and again, it sneaks up on me. We knew about the cancer for ages, so I had time to get used to the idea. But it wasn't until just before she died that she told me who my father was.'

Melanie Austin? Birdie tried to recall if Seb had ever mentioned her. But she didn't think so. She'd only met one of his exes and that was Annabelle, who'd come to them asking for help.

'How long ago did your mum and Seb date?'

Keira gave Birdie an amused smile. 'Date? No, it was nothing like that. They both went to Durham University and had just finished finals. There was some big party, and they hooked up for the night. The next day, my mum went home to London, and nine months later, yours truly was born.' Keira took another bite of the pastry and gave a blissful sigh.

'Which is why Seb doesn't know about you...' Birdie concluded, and Keira looked at her with interest.

'How do you know that? Clearly he hadn't told you, but maybe my mum told him at the time and she forgot to tell me? She was pretty sick and kept drifting in and out.'

Birdie gave a firm shake of her head. 'Trust me, he doesn't know. Because if he did, you would've already met him. And he would've told me about it,' she added, thinking of the numerous conversations they'd had about her own adoption and struggles to find her birth mother. At this, Keira smiled.

'So you don't think he'll be freaked out that I've turned up like this?'

'Oh, don't get me wrong. He'll be totally freaked out. But he won't be mad. If that's what you're worried about.'

'It did cross my mind, which is why I didn't want to contact him first. I figured that if I turned up in person, he'd have to at least speak to me. That probably sounds stupid.'

'Not to me it doesn't,' Birdie said. 'I'm sorry he's not here.'

'Yeah. Can we call him or something?' Keira asked in a hopeful voice.

'I wish we could. But he's in prison,' Birdie said, then winced. 'Sorry. That came out wrong. He's interviewing a potential lead in a case we're working on. The lead's in prison, which means Seb won't have his phone with him.'

'Ah. For Clifford Investigation Service. I read about it after Mum told me his name. Seemed a bit weird at first. I mean his father's a viscount, but for some reason my dad joined the Met and worked in the fraud squad. Then, when I researched all the cases he was involved in, it made more sense,' Keira said before listing out, in chronological order, what seemed like every single case Seb had ever touched in his fourteen years on the force.

When it came to research, Keira obviously didn't do things half-heartedly.

'That's some memory you have there.'

'Don't be so impressed.' Keira waved a hand at her. 'It's not something I do on purpose. I have like this super memory. The technical term is highly superior autobiographical memory. Have you heard of it?'

'As it happens, I have.' Birdie's lips twitched. 'From what I've been told, some people find it a double-edged sword.'

'Preach.' Keira clicked her fingers in agreement. 'Last year, one of my teachers accused me of cheating because in the exam I wrote down everything word for word that she'd taught us. Usually I wouldn't bother, but it was the most boring subject. All about human geography. In the end, my mum had to go up to the school and explain to her.'

'What a pain. I hated geography as well,' Birdie said as Elsa suddenly jumped to her feet at the low rumble of Seb's BMW on the drive outside.

Keira sat up bolt straight in her chair, eyes wide. 'Is that him?'

'Yeah.' Birdie got to her feet, wondering too late if she should have sent Seb a text to give him a heads-up. But she'd left her phone on her desk, and besides, this wasn't really about her. This was something that he would need to talk with Keira about. 'Time to introduce you to your father.'

EIGHTEEN

Tuesday, 12 December

Seb tapped his fingers on the steering wheel as he pulled into Rendall Hall. It was almost lunchtime, and considering the new developments on the case, he was going to suggest he and Birdie leave the office and go to the pub. It was amazing how many breakthroughs happened simply by changing their scenery.

The front door burst open and Elsa bounced out, racing towards him. His mood lifted as he swung his legs out from under the steering wheel and greeted her.

'Hello, there. Let me guess, you've conned Birdie into taking you for another walk? You really do have her wrapped around your paw. No... Move away so that I can climb out, and then we'll negotiate.'

He extracted himself from the car and closed the door before looking over at Birdie, who was standing by the front of the house. Her expression was half curious, half apologetic. His gaze shifted to the person next to her.

She had to be around seventeen, with dark hair and huge

eyes, and the way she towered over Birdie made him guess she was at least six foot tall.

He frowned. Was she one of Birdie's friends? She had a gang of both girls and guys that she went out with, but this girl was at least ten years younger than Birdie. Perhaps she was a new member of the cricket team.

As he got closer, there was something about the tilt of her head and an effervescent energy that exuded from her that reminded him of—

Melanie Austin.

Seb's brow puckered together. Now that was a name he hadn't thought of in a long time. It had been even longer since he'd seen her, which had been on the last day of finals, at a party. *Eighteen years ago.* He blinked, once again cursing the memory that never let him forget anything.

He glanced again at the young girl.

Part of her looked very much like Melanie, but her height had come from elsewhere and her mouth was straight... like...

No.

Surely not.

He came to a halt and locked eyes with his business partner, who had taken another step towards him.

'Birdie, what's going on?'

'I think you'd better come inside, Seb. There are some things you need to know.'

At the same time, the tall girl grinned and ran towards him. 'She's talking about me. I'm Keira. And I can see it in your face already. You know who I am, don't you?'

Seb swallowed as he stared at the girl in front of him. The mouth was exactly like... his mother's side of the family.

'All the same, I think you'd better tell me. To be clear,' he managed to say.

She gave him a lopsided grin and patted his arm, as if

making sure he was real. 'Sure, Dad. I'm your daughter. It's so cool to finally meet you.'

Dad.

She'd called him *Dad*.

The word sounded foreign but familiar at the same time. He collected himself. The time for self-reflection wasn't now. Birdie was right. They really needed to go inside and discuss this.

'Umm... Yes... Right...' He couldn't take his eyes off the girl.

'I think what Seb's trying to say is that it's good to meet you, too,' Birdie said, coming to his rescue.

'Yes, that's right. It's very nice to meet you, Keira. Let's have some lunch and you can tell me about yourself.'

'I've never seen him speechless before. Excellent job, Keira,' Birdie added.

'Er... I didn't mean to, it's—'

'I'm joking,' Birdie said, with a wave of her hand.

Never before had Seb been so grateful for Birdie's sense of humour and how she could ease the tension.

'Cool,' Keira said, grinning.

Seb's heart lurched. The grin. It was totally Melanie. He sucked in a breath. He had to hold it together.

They went inside and Birdie heated the homemade soup her mother had given them and Seb sliced some fresh bread, all the time glancing over at Keira, who was playing with Elsa.

'Lunch is ready,' Birdie said.

They retreated to the long farmhouse table at the far end of the kitchen. While they ate, Keira filled him in on aspects of her life, including Melanie's death six months previously from cancer, and the fact that she hadn't known his name until then.

'So, Mum really never told you about me?' Keira double-checked once Birdie stood up and cleared away the plates.

Seb shook his head. 'No. Our paths didn't cross after that last night at college, and the only thing I ever heard about her was she'd become an art teacher. There had never been any mention of a child— Of you,' he corrected.

'Probably because my nan always treated my mum like she'd done this terrible thing by having a child out of wedlock. I think that's why she never talked about it.' Keira toyed with the napkin in her hands, before looking up, her expression thoughtful. 'You do remember her, right? You're not being polite? I did read that your dad is a viscount. You could just be very well mannered.'

Seb let out a reluctant smile. 'No wonder you and Birdie hit it off so well. While I admit to being polite, I do remember Melanie. She studied art history, but only did it because her mother thought that working in an art gallery would be a good way to meet men. She really wanted to be a painter and loved Frida Kahlo. Let's see, what else? She was born two days before Christmas, which means it would have been her thirty-eighth birthday in two weeks. She also loved listening to Radio Two and refused to put on Radio One, calling it too young and silly for her.'

Suddenly, Keira let out a sharp gasp. She stared at him, her mouth slightly open.

Seb stiffened. Had he gone into too much detail? How stupid of him. Her grief would still be so raw from her mother's death, and he would no doubt be stirring it up. He shook his head. 'I'm sorry. I shouldn't have said so much. I have this memory which doesn't give me much choice, and—'

'No, no, no.' Keira waved her hand at him. 'I wasn't upset, I was excited. All that stuff you remembered in so much detail, even though it's been eighteen years since you saw her. It just hit me that you might have HSAM, too. That I got it from *you*?'

Seb blinked, and Birdie, who'd finished loading up the dishwasher, grinned at them both. Clearly she'd figured it out already and had kept it to herself, not wanting to overstep the mark.

'Look, I'm going to take Elsa out for a quick walk and let you two keep talking,' Birdie said.

Without waiting for an answer, she hurried away, with Elsa following happily behind her.

Seb ran a hand along his jaw. Keira was still seated but had one leg tucked up and was leaning forwards, so that her dark hair fell across her face. Suddenly, despite how tall she was, he could imagine what she'd been like as a child. That in many ways, she was still a child.

'How are you feeling? This must be a lot to take in,' he asked.

'It's pretty surreal, for sure. In a good way, though. I wasn't sure what to expect, or if I'd even feel like I was related to you. But I do. It's like finding part of a jigsaw puzzle that's been missing for a long time.' She gave him a nervous smile. 'Are you mad about all this? You know, me just turning up here.'

'Of course I'm not,' he told her firmly. 'Surprised. But not mad.' And he meant it. Despite the shock of suddenly discovering he was a father, it didn't feel wrong, or bad. It felt *right*. 'As for Melanie not telling me. While I would have loved to have known from the beginning, so that I could have supported you... and her... I do understand. Your mother was fiercely independent and I know she was only doing what she believed was right.'

Keira swallowed, her eyes glistening with unshed tears. 'That's a really nice thing to say. Birdie told me you'd be like this.'

'Did she indeed? Well, Birdie's often right. But we'll keep that to ourselves or I'll never hear the end of it.' He grinned. 'Now, we need to talk about you. From what Melanie told me about her parents, I imagine they wouldn't be too happy that you've skipped school unexpectedly to visit me.'

At this, Keira dropped her head and Seb's stomach tightened.

'I didn't exactly tell them what I was doing. They're really strict and live out in Aylesbury. They didn't get what it was like for me and Mum living in North London for the last ten years. I grew up riding the Tube and getting around on my own. It's no big deal. I can take care of myself.'

'Except they're your grandparents and must be worried about you. Or, they will be when you don't come home from wherever it is you told them you were going.'

She swallowed and glanced over at the crammed overnight bag and rucksack that were leaning against the wall. 'Are you sending me back there?'

He shook his head. 'I meant that if you're here, you must call them and let them know.'

'Now?'

'Now,' he agreed. 'I would like to speak to them as well.'

'Seriously? They're pretty intense, and when they read the Riot Act, they'll start at *A* and not stop until they get to *Z*.'

Seb bit back an amused smile. 'It's okay. I think I can handle it.'

Keira studied him, her mouth in an uncertain line, before she reluctantly retrieved a phone from the back pocket of her jeans. 'Okay, I'll call them. But don't say I didn't warn you.'

'I consider myself fully warned,' he assured her as she brought up their number and made the call. Her own conversation was brief and by the time she handed over the phone, her face was drained of colour.

'Hello, it's Sebastian Clifford. I know this is a worrying situation for you both. I want to reassure you that Keira is safe.'

'I'm Jim and my wife is Diana,' the man at the end of the phone said. 'We know nothing about you.'

'I don't understand how you could not have known about Keira all this time?' Diana said, getting straight to the point, her voice stern.

Seb sighed. 'Melanie didn't tell me about the pregnancy. We were young university students enjoying ourselves at the time. It was a brief relationship that didn't last. If I had known, things would have been different. I want to make up for lost time with Keira.'

'We know nothing about you, other than Keira said you're a private investigator. What's your background?' Diana asked.

'After university I went into the police force and recently left to open my own investigation service. I'm currently living at my cousin's house in East Farndon, while she's overseas. I'm operating my business from here.'

'And your parents?' Jim asked.

'My father's Viscount Worthington,' Seb said, hoping he was doing the right thing by mentioning it. Often people were intimidated by his father's title. But it wasn't as if they weren't going to discover his background eventually.

'I see,' Jim said.

Silence hung in the air for a few seconds.

'It's still not appropriate for a young girl to be living with someone she hardly knows, even with your background. You should send her back to us,' Diana said, her voice breaking.

'Diana, I do appreciate your concern. But technically at aged seventeen Keira can live where she chooses.'

'Are you married?' Jim demanded.

Seb frowned. 'No, I'm not. I live here on my own.'

'What if some criminal comes looking for you while Keira's there?' Diana suddenly asked.

'My work can be unpredictable at times. But Keira's safety would be my top priority. My home and office are secure. I have a dog.'

'I still don't like it. A teenage girl living with a single man – people will talk,' Jim said, sounding worried.

'I'd like to drive down to meet you face to face, so we can get to know each other,' Seb said, although he wasn't entirely sure how to arrange it. Especially when they were in the middle of a pressing case.

'That's a good idea,' Jim agreed. 'But until that time we'd rather Keira wasn't alone with you in the house.'

'I'll sort something out,' he promised.

He ended the call and shook his head. Glad to have got the conversation over.

'What did they say?' Keira asked.

'They don't want you staying with me here until we've met.'

'Oh no.' Her face fell. 'That's stupid. Well, I'm not going back there. I'll—'

'Stop,' Seb said, holding up his hand to silence her. 'No one is making you leave. We'll work something out.'

'Thank you.' She flung her arms around his neck and gave him a hug.

Seb froze. 'Okay,' he said, his voice sounding strange.

Keira dropped her arms to her sides. 'You're not a hugger?'

'Afraid not.'

'Not even with Mum? Because she was the best hugger in the world.' Tears formed in the young girl's eyes and she blinked them away.

'I'll learn,' he promised, his heart going out to her. She'd been through so much at such a young age.

Keira sniffed. 'Sorry. I really miss her.'

'I understand. Can I get you anything?'

'No, thanks. I want to phone my friend, is that okay?'

'Of course, you don't need to ask. Why don't you go to the snug. It's out of the kitchen and down the hall. You can't miss it. The door will be open.'

'Thanks, Dad,' Keira said, heading out of the kitchen.

Seb stared at her retreating back.

Would he ever get used to being called *Dad*?

* * *

Ten minutes later he was still trying to decide on a solution regarding where Keira was going to stay when the front door opened and Elsa reappeared. She gave him a friendly glance and then curled up in her bed by the radiator.

'I think I've worn her out,' Birdie announced, peering around the kitchen. 'Where's Keira? Don't tell me something's happened.'

'She's in the snug, calling one of her friends. I thought she might want some privacy,' he explained, before filling Birdie in on the conversation with Keira's grandparents and their request for her not to stay with him in the house.

'Of course. I should have thought of that sooner,' Birdie said in a brisk voice. 'She can stay with me tonight and we'll work something out for tomorrow. And – grandparents aside – it's probably a good idea for you both to have some space to decompress. How are you feeling? Is it weird?'

It was a good question. If someone had asked him yesterday how, theoretically, he would take this kind of news, he'd have probably answered differently. But now...?

'No. Despite how unexpected it is, it doesn't feel odd. It feels almost right in a way. I'm looking forward to getting to know her.'

Birdie grinned. 'Welcome to the mad world of non-traditional families. She's like you in lots of ways, which is a little unnerving. Especially now that I will be around *two* people who won't forget a single thing I say.'

'We'll try to use our power sparingly,' Seb assured her as Keira reappeared in the room. Her eyes were bright, but her face was pale with fatigue. She looked tired.

'Birdie and I have been talking,' Seb said, 'and she's offered for you to stay with her and her family tonight. How do you feel about that?'

'I suppose my grandparents were worried you might have wild bachelor parties here?' Keira said, rolling her eyes. She gave Birdie an uncertain look. 'Is that okay? I don't want to be a pain.'

'You'll have to try a lot harder to be a pain,' Birdie replied, giving her an easy smile. 'Though I do warn you, I have two brothers who are animals when it comes to the bathroom.'

Keira's expression brightened. 'I'm an only child but my mum's best friends, Eric and Fiona, have three boys and we all grew up together. It's like having brothers – right down to the farting and burping. But thanks... if you're sure?'

'I am,' Birdie assured her. 'Do you want to give me and Seb ten minutes to discuss the case we're working on, and then we'll go back to mine? Why don't you go back to the snug for a bit?'

'Cool.' Keira scampered away, closely followed by Elsa.

Once she was gone, Birdie turned back to Seb.

'Okay. Tell me what happened with Pappas. Where are we up to?'

'You're not going to like it.' Seb forced his mind into work mode.

It seemed like a lifetime ago that he'd been at the prison. Once he'd given Birdie an update and when he was finished, she swore softly.

'Clearly he didn't take the news about his own secret child quite as well as you did.' She picked up the notebook that was never far from her side and tapped her pen against her chin. 'We need to ask the police to look into something that happened over fifty years ago before Pappas will even agree to meet Conrad? Bloody hell. What else does he want? A back massage? Peeled grapes?'

'It's not ideal. Tomorrow we'll visit Lady Angelica.'

'Agreed. I want to see Lady C's reaction when we ask her what happened that night. Especially when she realises we know she lied to us about it.' Birdie's eyes flashed with annoyance.

'Considering Devon's life is on the line, I suspect she has a very good reason,' Seb gently reminded her.

Birdie sighed and glanced at the large clock on the wall. 'It had better be more than just saving her own skin. Anyway, I'd better text my mum and let her know what's happening, then I'll take Keira back to the house. What are you doing tonight? Work on the case?'

Seb shook his head. 'No. I need to think through a couple of things. Also, Keira mentioned Melanie's friends, Fiona and Eric. They were both at uni with us. I'd better give them a call and let them know Keira's here. They might be able to tell me more about Melanie's life, and why she decided to keep me in the dark.'

'And by implication, so did they.'

'Yes and no. We didn't keep in contact after university. I'll get the details from Keira.'

Birdie's brows knitted together. 'Are you upset that Melanie didn't tell you?'

'Keira asked me the same question. How can I be? Melanie would've thought she was doing the right thing, so I can't hold it against her. For my own sake, I'd like to find out more.'

'Preaching to the choir,' Birdie assured him. 'I'm always here if you need to talk.'

'Thanks. I appreciate you having my back.'

'We're partners. That's what we do. Oh... if I do take Keira to the pub tonight, you're paying.'

He laughed and extracted some notes from his wallet.

They headed for the snug, where Keira was sitting on one of the chairs, staring out of the window to the garden beyond. At the sight of him, she grinned. Seb returned the smile. It really had been quite the day.

* * *

'I'll have a chardonnay, thanks,' Keira said as they reached the bar of the Old Bell that evening. The original plan had been to stay in the house, but her parents had some friends turn up, and both of her brothers had been at home, staring – or should she say *drooling* – over Keira. So, the pub had seemed like a good idea.

'Nice try,' Birdie retorted. 'Come back and see me next year after your birthday. In the meantime, juice or soft drink?'

'Just checking to see how strict you are.' Keira gave a wide smile and released a dimple. 'Ginger beer, if they have it. Besides, I'm wiped out, so it's for the best.'

'Glad we're in agreement.' Birdie pointed to a table. 'Why don't you nab that one while it's free, and I'll bring them over. Crisps?'

'Always,' Keira said, nodding, as she threaded her way through the half-full pub.

Birdie joined her a couple of minutes later and took a long gulp of her cider, before placing her glass on the table. 'Sorry if my family were a bit much.'

'Are you kidding me? I love them already. That's why I decided to come here. It's been six months since Mum died and I'll go mad if I stay with my grandparents much longer. They've been on my back for dropping out of my A levels.' Keira poured the bottle of ginger beer into her glass and took a sip.

Birdie widened her eyes. She couldn't blame them for not wanting their granddaughter to drop out of school. Then again, there were extenuating circumstances. And considering the way she'd been around Birdie's own family, it was obvious she wanted to be somewhere that she felt a part of.

'Why did you drop out? Did you fall behind with your work?'

Keira nodded. 'Summer was rough – what with the funeral and then having to move in with my nan and grandad, who are super strict. I thought it would get better when school started, but they made me go to a local comprehensive, which was horrible. Everyone was so bitchy... but then my old friends kept talking about going to parties and getting drunk, which seemed stupid. It felt like I didn't belong anywhere.' She toyed with her glass before suddenly blurting out: 'Do you think Seb will let me live with him?'

'What makes you think that he'll be less strict? He comes from a super posh family and grew up with royalty. That's some serious shit.'

'I know. I checked out everything I could about him and his family. I also know he's a rebel. I figured he wouldn't be quite so strict, because he knows what it's like. Also' – she wrinkled her nose – 'before she died, Mum said sorry to have kept it from me for so long, and that Seb was the nicest man she'd ever been with. Unlike most of her other boyfriends, who shall remain nameless on account of them all being horrible pigs.'

'Sounds like she was giving you permission to connect with him.'

Keira nodded. 'I think so. But you won't say anything to him, will you? I figure it would be better if I asked him directly.'

Birdie nodded in approval. 'Of course I won't. This is between you and your dad. But you're right to trust him. He's a good guy.' She fished out one of the ten-pound notes Seb had given her. 'And I'm sure he'd want to buy us another drink and some more crisps. If you're game, we could have a game of pool with some of my friends from the cricket team. A few of them are in the corner over there, and they're pretty cool.'

'Yes, please. That sounds awesome.' Keira beamed. 'I think I'm going to like it here.'

NINETEEN

Seb peered out of the window. The sky was dull grey and a glittering frost clung to the lawn and naked trees as winter took hold. The growl of a car engine announced Birdie's arrival as she unceremoniously sped along the driveway and came to a halt next to his own car. He watched her climb out, while Keira awkwardly uncurled her legs from the passenger seat. Another thing they had in common. Small cars were a challenge. He shook his head, still marvelling at the turn of events.

He'd had a long conversation with Fiona and Eric the previous night. Melanie had never admitted Keira was his daughter but they'd always suspected. Far from being concerned that Keira had turned up on his doorstep, they'd been relieved.

Melanie's parents were old-fashioned and were not only dealing with several health conditions but had struggled with the death of their only daughter. Fiona and Eric had offered to let Keira live with them, so as not to interrupt her schooling and make sure she could get the support she needed. The grandparents had refused to even consider it.

Keira had been devastated, but they hadn't wanted to push the matter, since they didn't want to worsen Keira's relationship with her grandparents. Although he suspected they'd failed in that aim.

He closed his eyes, knowing that it would take a good deal of work to navigate the situation, without hurting their feelings further. Not to mention, trying to come to terms with it himself.

'Cold enough for you? I hope the kettle is on.' Birdie bustled in, a halo of chilly air surrounding her.

Since it was the same thing she asked most mornings, he nodded and set about making coffee. He placed the steaming mugs in front of them and smiled as Keira told him all about Birdie's family and going to the pub and how many people she'd met, and how great it was.

'So much better than being stuck at Nan's house watching soap operas and having to sit on the couch all night. It was the best fun I've had in ages. Apart from sleeping on a blow-up bed, which was a challenge.'

'Sorry about that,' Birdie said, with a rueful smile. 'But that aside, if you think Tuesday night at the Old Bell was good, wait until you see Friday lunchtime at the local chippie,' she teased.

Keira grinned. Seb was pleased that they already seemed to have developed a friendship. Would he be able to have such a relaxed relationship with his daughter? He certainly hoped so.

He glanced at the clock on the wall. They had a busy day, and he wanted to make sure they didn't miss Lady Angelica. He stood up and gave Keira an apologetic smile.

'I'm sorry we have to go out this morning.'

'It's okay. Birdie told me last night that you're working on a complicated case with a tight timeframe.'

'I did say Keira could hang out at my house with Mum. She's babysitting Lacey.'

'I'd rather be here, though. Birdie said that was okay.'

'Are you sure you won't be bored? I've no idea when we'll be returning.' Seb studied her face, hating the idea of leaving her alone so soon after she'd arrived.

Keira shook her head, eyes wide. 'No way. There are tons of books here and I love reading. Plus, Birdie said you didn't have a website. If you want, I can set one up for you. I'm not into art the way Mum was, but I've done loads of graphic-design stuff and always did her sites for her. It'll be fun.'

'You have a strange idea of fun. But I don't mind if Seb doesn't,' Birdie said, getting to her feet. 'We did buy a domain name, but that's as far as we've got.'

'Cool. I'll do some research and sketch out a few ideas to see what you think.'

Seb nodded. 'Okay, but you have my number if you need anything.'

'Got it. Now go, so that me and Elsa can get some work done.' She made a shooing motion with her hands, and Seb bit back a smile. They still had much to discuss, but the fact she already felt comfortable around him was a good sign.

The drive to Fleckney was filled with conversation about Keira until they turned down the long driveway and it turned back to the case.

Birdie's brow was pensive. 'A fifty-year-old murder is always going to be a long shot. Not helped by us not even knowing who the victim was, apart from being called Old Fred.'

Seb agreed. It wasn't ideal, and usually they'd have done more digging before talking to Lady Angelica, but they didn't have the time. Hopefully, their client would be more forthcoming this time. He parked in the same space as yesterday and they hurried around the path leading to the entrance.

Gibbs met them at the door, though his face was grim.

'You don't have an appointment,' he stated in a flat voice.

Seb was unperturbed. 'That is correct. But we urgently need to speak to Lady Angelica. Is she at home?'

'She had a very late night. I will—'

'It's fine, Gibbs. Could you please bring a pot of coffee to my office?' Lady Angelica appeared in the hallway. She was fully dressed, but her eyes were dull and tired. It appeared that she hadn't had much sleep. If any.

Next to him, Birdie sucked in her breath as the unspoken word danced between them.

Devon?

'Of course.' Gibbs retreated, and they followed their client into her study.

'Sorry about my appearance. Devon had a tough night, resulting in him being admitted into hospital. He's stable now, but—' She broke off and composed herself. 'Well, let's not go into that. What's happened? Do you have an update for me? I do hope it's good news.'

'I was at Marshdown yesterday and spoke to Pappas.'

'Did he agree to meet our son?'

'Tentatively. Providing we met his conditions.' Seb gave her an update over coffee brought in by Gibbs, not leaving anything out. 'He wants us to instruct the police to investigate Fred's death.'

'I don't know what you're talking about? I don't know anyone called Fred who died.' Lady Angelica's brows lifted up, her expression perplexed.

Birdie's mouth tightened. 'Are you saying that Pappas is lying? You told us that you didn't see him when you went back to your family estate at Christmas. But according to him you met up and spent an evening getting drunk, before stealing a car.'

Lady Angelica swallowed and closed her eyes. It was clear this was something she would have preferred not to discuss.

'I know. It was wrong of me not to have told you everything, but I was hoping at least some of my shameful past wouldn't come to light.'

'We can't help you if you don't tell us what we need to know. If we are to persuade the police to look into it, we need all the facts. Don't leave anything out.' Birdie's voice was firm and it had the desired effect of breaking through whatever memories their client was lost in.

'Okay. By the time I was home, I knew I wouldn't be able to hide the pregnancy for long and that my parents needed to be told. But... I wanted to see Roy one last time. It was a stupid idea. I think... I wanted to pretend that everything was going to be okay. We had a lot to drink. It was different then. No one knew how risky drinking was for a pregnant woman. We went for a joy ride along some of the dirt roads on the property. It was fun... until we hit something. Except, when we got out of the car, we discovered it wasn't a something but a *someone*. A man. I swear we hadn't seen him. Roy was driving, and he checked the man for a pulse before saying we needed to call an ambulance. But when we got back to the house, I was so upset that my parents sent me straight to my room.'

'What happened the next day? Did you ask what had happened to him?' Seb probed.

'Of course I did. My mother said the man was fine and had been discharged from hospital. She fully intended to ground me and ban me from seeing Roy, which is when I broke down and told her about the baby. You know the rest. I guess it explains why they made sure I left the house the same day.'

Her voice was steady and she didn't avoid eye contact. Seb nodded. This time she was telling them the truth.

'Tell us more about the man that Pappas hit. Was he old or young? What was he wearing? Did it seem like he'd been drinking?' Seb asked.

She shook her head. 'I really have no idea. It was dark and I was drunk. When we got out of the car, it was Roy who rushed over to him. He'd done a first aid course and seemed to know what he was doing. I'm ashamed to say that I was quite hysterical.'

'When you got back to the house, did you hear them call for the ambulance, or see it arrive?'

She shook her head. 'No. I felt so sick from drinking that after vomiting in my toilet, I lay down on my bed and went straight to sleep. I accepted what my parents told me the next day. It didn't enter my head to question it.'

'Pappas said the victim lived on the estate and was called Fred. Do you recall ever hearing that name or meeting him?' Seb asked.

Lady Angelica shook her head, her eyes foggy with fatigue. 'We had a large staff. I knew some, but not many. I was at boarding school most of the time, remember, and only noticed Roy because he was closer to my age and was handsome. Although, now I think about it, when I got the keys for the car, I did see a couple of people who worked on the estate. The daughter of our housekeeper, and a young man who I believe might have worked in the garden. But I can't tell you their names or, indeed, if they actually saw me.'

Birdie leant forwards her eyes wide. 'Was the gardener's name Jim by any chance?'

'Sorry, Birdie, I don't know. Why?'

'When we visited your cousin, we spoke to Jim, the head gardener, who has been there for over fifty years. We were hoping to learn more about Roy, but he wasn't very forthcoming.'

'I wish I could remember more, but it's all such a blur. It's sometimes hard to remember what's real and what's not. What happens now? Will you take the case to the police?'

'Not until we have more information,' Seb said. 'Also, before we do, it's important to discuss the implications of it becoming a police case. Pappas wanted the case investigated to improve his chance of parole, but there's a good chance he might have an ulterior motive. It's entirely possible that he wants to seek revenge on you or your family.'

Lady Angelica gave a long sigh. 'I always knew that going down this road could cause problems. But all I care about is trying to save my son's life. What happens if you can't convince the police to look into the case? Is there another way to persuade Roy to see our son? Should I go speak to him directly?'

Seb's mind flashed back to the man he'd met in prison. There was a darkness in his eyes and a ruthlessness to him. Maybe it hadn't always been there, but years of bad decisions and anger at how his life had turned out had deepened the grooves until it was a constant companion. Either way, he didn't think anything would change if he saw Lady Angelica again.

'I don't recommend it. Whoever he was back then, he's not that person now.'

'Seb's right. For now, our priority is finding out about this Fred, and if anyone else knew about the accident.' Birdie got to her feet and Seb followed.

'Please do whatever it takes. Devon's life depends on it.'

'We're working as quickly as we can. As soon as there's an update, we'll be in touch,' Birdie promised as they walked out of the room to where Gibbs was waiting with their coats. But it wasn't until they were back in the car that she turned to him. 'Do you think she's telling us the truth this time?'

'Yes. Now that Devon's dangerously ill, she's told us as much as she knows. It's up to us to find out what really happened that night. Apart from Pappas, Jim's our best chance. He's the only other person we know who was working at the estate then.'

Birdie reached for her phone. 'You drive and I'll call Lord Montague to make sure Jim's available and that it's okay for us to interview him. And this time, we need to make sure that he tells us the truth.'

TWENTY

Birdie rolled her neck and closed the car door. With the amount of travelling they'd done in the last week, the travel expenses for this case were going to be through the roof. But they couldn't risk speaking to Jim on the phone. They needed to see his reactions to discern whether he was answering their questions truthfully.

'Lord Montague said we could go straight to the south garden and talk to him directly.' She craned her head towards a large greenhouse. 'I've got no idea where that is. Any clue?'

Seb pointed to a clump of camellias at the end of a well-mown lawn. 'The house is north-facing, so south is in this direction. I suggest we change into our wellies. I brought a couple of pairs with us.'

She raised an eyebrow. 'Aren't you a good Boy Scout?'

'Not sure about that.' Seb produced the wellington boots and they pulled them on before heading over to the shrubs.

Jim was raking when they reached him, but stopped, not quite able to hide his frown.

Interesting.

'Good morning, Jim,' Birdie said, smiling. 'Lord Montague said we could talk to you further about an event that happened when Roy Pappas worked here.'

He shrugged and started raking again. 'I've already told you, I hardly knew him.'

'So, how do you know who we're talking about then? When we saw you last, you didn't seem to know Roy's last name.'

Jim swallowed, his Adam's apple bobbing up and down. If Birdie wasn't mistaken, he swore under his breath.

'Oh. I was assuming that's who you meant.'

'Really?' Birdie glared at him.

'Why don't we start again, shall we?' Seb said, his arms folded. 'The Christmas of 1971, Roy Pappas worked here and said that while he was driving a vehicle on the estate, he accidently hit someone.'

'I don't know what you're talking about.' Jim's grip tightened on the rake.

Birdie narrowed her eyes. 'We don't believe you. From the moment Pappas's name was mentioned, you've been evasive. Now we know about the accident, we believe that's the reason. And before you deny it, you were seen that night.'

'By who?' Then he groaned again, realising he'd made it even worse.

It had been a gamble to suggest he was the person Lady Angelica had passed that night, but it seemed to have paid off.

'Start talking,' Birdie demanded.

'Okay, okay. I'd been seeing one of the girls who worked up at the big house. Nancy, her name was. We met up most nights. I guess someone could have seen us...' He paused.

'Continue,' Seb growled.

'We'd been messing around in the summer house. The place was locked up in winter but it was easy to get into back then –

before they started restoring it. We were leaving when there was all this noise. Nancy freaked out and scarpered, but I couldn't risk being caught in the grounds after hours, so I stayed hidden.'

'What was the noise? What did you see?' Birdie pushed.

'There were four men, including Lord Montague, and one of them was pushing a wheelbarrow.'

Next to her, Seb sucked in his breath. 'Are you sure Lord Montague was there?'

'Oh, yeah. He walked like he had something up—' He broke off. 'Well, anyway. It was definitely him. The moon was pretty bright that night. It's why Nancy and I had gone there because it was easy to find the path without a torch.'

'What happened? Did you see what they did?' Birdie asked.

'Um...' Jim said, hesitating.

'We need to know,' Birdie pushed.

'Okay. Yes. I didn't know what to think and so I followed them as far as I could, keeping out of sight. They went to the summer house, and I remember thinking it was bloody lucky me and Nancy weren't still in there. But it turned out that they didn't go inside. Instead, they went round the back and started digging.'

'Do you know what was in the wheelbarrow?'

'I didn't stay long enough to check. But whatever it was, it was big.'

'Could it have been a body?'

Jim gave a loud sigh. 'Yes. It could have been, I suppose, but I didn't think about it then.'

'Pappas mentioned an old gardener called Fred. Said he had a drinking problem.'

Jim's nostrils flared. 'He had a problem all right. And a death wish. The old boy would be off his face while driving the tractor. The amount of times we had to haul him out of a ditch

was past counting. But there was no talk of anything bad
happening to him. He'd often go on huge benders and disappear
for months at a time.'

It was the same thing Pappas had told them.

Did this mean he was right? That Fred had been killed, and
that his body had been buried?

'Did no one question the fact that Fred didn't return after
several months this time?' Seb's jaw was tight.

'Not that I remember. Is that it, because I need to get back
to work?'

'No it's not *it*,' Birdie said. 'Please show us exactly where
they were digging.'

'You've got to be joking. It was a long time ago,' he
complained, but after realising that neither of them were
moving, he let out an irritated sigh. 'Fine.'

He motioned for them to follow him down a long path. It
came out beside a red-brick building that was two storeys high
and had what looked like a turret.

Birdie turned to Seb in confusion. '*That's* a summer house?
It looks like something from a fun park. The windows are tiny.'

Seb let out a reluctant chuckle. 'Ever heard of a folly? It's a
building that often serves no real purpose other than to look
ornate and over the top. I'm guessing that a previous Lord
Montague decided he needed his own folly. It appears to me
that it was built prior to the design of the garden.'

'You'd be right about that,' Jim said as they reached the
ornate building and skirted around to the left-hand side of it.
'These days it gets used for holiday rentals, would you believe.'

'Is anyone in there now?'

'No. The heating isn't working, so they've cancelled the
bookings.' He came to a halt at a large holly bush. The glossy
green leaves spread out in all directions, displaying the plump
red berries. There were several much smaller bushes on either

side of it. He swore under his breath. 'I told the lads to cut this
back last week. They're going to have hell to pay when I see
them.'

'Why didn't you check the work at the time?' Birdie studied
his face, and Jim looked away, cheeks reddening.

'No reason. Just busy. Anyway, I think it was here.'

'We're going to be talking to the police about the matter,
which means there's a good chance they'll want to question you.
I suggest you tell them the truth.' Seb walked closer to the bush
and dropped down to his knees, inspecting the area around it.
Jim swallowed but dipped his head in agreement.

'There's no point in trying to hide it, now that you know. I
kept quiet at the time because you know the old saying, don't
bite the hand that feeds you. Lord Montague paid my wages
and I would've been out on my ear if I'd ever said anything.'

'So you did suspect it was a body? You said you didn't.'

'Look, I didn't want to get involved.'

'Lord Montague is dead and has been for many years,'
Birdie retorted, irritation prickling her skin. 'If someone was
killed, then they deserve more than being left in a hole behind
some kind of folly.'

'Fine. You've made your point.' He scowled and went to
leave, but Seb stepped in his way.

'One more thing. Was Roy Pappas with Lord Montague
and the other men?'

'Yes, he was. Who do you think did the digging? Now, I
really need to get back to work.' With that, he turned and disappeared around the side of the summer house, as if wanting to
put as much distance between them and himself as possible.

'It seems like he avoids this part of the garden like the
plague because he's convinced there's a body down there.'
Birdie stared at his retreating back.

'I agree, and if he's correct about Pappas being part of the burial party, then our *friend* in prison didn't tell me the whole truth.'

'You think?' Birdie muttered as she retrieved her phone and took several photographs of the holly bush and the back of the building.

'I suspect he thought we wouldn't look into it if he said he was involved.'

'Yeah, well, that's where he's wrong,' Birdie said. 'When we get back, I want to research old newspaper articles to see if I can find anything about a missing person, or who Fred was.'

'There's a good chance his disappearance wouldn't have made the news. Even if Lady Angelica did believe the person they'd hit hadn't been killed, if there was a large manhunt for the missing man, surely she would have heard about it.'

'Unfortunately, we can't dig the body up and see for ourselves.'

'Not if we want to involve the police. Tampering with a possible crime scene would work against us. We'll put together everything we have and leave it to the proper authorities.'

'We'd better head home before the weather turns bad again.' Birdie looked up at the darkening sky and shivered. It was only three in the afternoon but it felt like any moment it would be black. She was starting to see why Jim had such an aversion to the place. It was giving her the creeps as well.

'Good idea. I want to phone Keira's grandparents to try and persuade them that it's better for her to stay with me. Being so tall, sleeping on a blow-up mattress will play havoc with her back.'

'That's a great idea. Have you mentioned this to Keira?' Birdie said, nodding her approval.

'No. I don't want to get her hopes up in case they don't agree.'

'Has she told you yet about giving up school?'

Seb frowned. 'No. We haven't had that discussion. But we most definitely will.'

'Look at you stepping up. I'm super impressed at how well you're doing all this *dad* stuff.'

'Thank you. Now, let's get going.'

TWENTY-ONE

Wednesday, 13 December

Seb placed his phone on the side and returned his attention to the hob, where the pasta sauce was bubbling away. Birdie and Keira were in the sitting room, curled up on the sofas having a heated conversation about how far they'd go to get tickets to next year's Glastonbury. Both of them had extreme views on it.

He took out three bowls from the cupboard and searched around for a platter for the garlic bread. His conversation with Keira's grandparents had gone well. They realised that sleeping at Birdie's family home wasn't ideal and hoped that she'd see sense and return to living with them. In the meantime, they'd agreed that she could stay with him at Rendall Hall.

He'd been considering how practical it would be for Keira to move in with him permanently. But he hadn't broached the subject with the elderly couple on the call, who he realised were finding it difficult to look after Keira, and grieve for their daughter, while still caring for themselves and their own health issues.

It had to be Keira's decision... Although he wasn't going to bring it up, in case she felt pushed into a corner.

Once the bowls were on the table, he called them through.

'Smells amazing, I'm starving,' Birdie announced as she tucked a giant serviette into her shirt and sat down. She glanced at Keira, who was staring in her direction. 'I'm wearing a white T-shirt, and if you think I won't spill anything on it, then you have a lot to learn about me.'

After Seb had let Keira know that she could spend the night at the Hall, they'd made small talk for the rest of the meal, and once Birdie had left for the evening, they returned to the sitting room, where Elsa was waiting for them.

'That was the best food I've eaten in ages.' Keira collapsed onto the sofa in a dramatic heap. 'Nan's on some stupid diet that involves mushed-up vegetables, no salt and nothing that begins with the letter C.'

Seb raised an eyebrow. 'The letter C? I assume it's based on scientific research.'

Keira giggled. 'Okay, so maybe I made the last part up. But it's truly horrible food. Which is what I wanted to talk to you about... I was thinking that maybe... Maybe, um... Maybe I could live here with you all the time.'

Seb caught his breath, pleased that she'd been the one to ask him.

'Are you sure you won't be bored? It's nothing like North London.' He scanned her face for signs of uncertainty.

'It might be small, but I like it already. Birdie introduced me to some of the girls in her cricket team, and you should have seen how excited they were to meet me. They reckon I'll make a good bowler because of my height and want me to try out for the team next year. And,' she added, stopping to draw breath, 'I reckon there's loads I can do to help you and Birdie with the business. Not just with the website, but doing admin and answering phones. That way you wouldn't need to take all the calls yourself. And I love researching.' As she spoke, her brown eyes, so like her mother's, glittered with excitement, though her hands were laced together in a nervous tangle. 'Please.'

'I'd love for you to live here, and for us get to know each other better. But—' he quickly added before she could finish jumping up from her seat. She dropped back down on the sofa and stared directly at him, worry flickering in her eyes. 'It's not going to happen unless you agree to attend school and finish your A levels. Birdie mentioned that you'd left.'

'Phew. Is that all? I thought you were going to say something terrible. I mean, school's easy enough.' She tapped her head as if to remind him that they shared the same memory. 'I'd always planned to finish once I'd figured out where I was going to live.'

'Good to know,' Seb said, trying to hide his amusement. Keira had so much energy and enthusiasm that he hadn't realised how quiet his life had become. Not during the day when he was with Birdie, but when he wasn't working. 'Have you given any thought as to your next steps after A levels? University, for instance.' He didn't want to push his daughter into higher education, but if she didn't go, her future choices would be limited.

'Actually, I have. For ages I couldn't decide what to do and everything the career advisor suggested sounded so boring. When Mum told me about you, I did some research. You studied criminology, which I hadn't considered before and it looked cool, so I checked out which courses were available. My HSAM will help, but there's more to it than that. It involves thinking and solving problems. Is that why you picked it?'

'At the time it wasn't. But once the course was underway, I quickly realised how much I enjoyed being challenged. When I joined the police force, it proved very beneficial.'

'If I help you and Birdie on some of your cases, I'll get a better idea if I'm going to like it or not. What do you think?'

'Possibly. Although you won't be allowed access to all our

cases. Some are confidential.'

'Like the one you're doing now?'

'Correct.'

'Don't worry, I won't snoop where I'm not allowed.' She made a zipping motion across her mouth, and then immediately broke it by laughing. 'Unless I sign an NDA.'

'You know about non-disclosure agreements?' Seb asked, unable to hide his surprise.'

'Of course I do. And I'm happy to sign one for any of your cases.'

'Okay. I'll bear that in mind.'

'Thanks. And also thanks for everything. I'm so happy.'

'Likewise,' he said, returning her smile. 'However, there is one other thing,' he added, rubbing his chin. 'I'd like you to meet my parents, brother and his family.'

Keira gulped, the laughter leaving her face. 'Oh. The thing is I've never met a viscount before. What if they don't like me? Or think that I'm not good enough to be part of the family?'

'That's nonsense. I promise that once you get to know them, you'll find that they're no different from anyone else. They will be thrilled to know they have a granddaughter. My brother Hubert has two boys. A girl would be a most welcome addition.'

Keira didn't look convinced despite nodding. 'Okay. But promise not to leave me in the room alone with them.'

He nodded. 'I promise. I'm going to phone and give them the news. Would you like to speak to them?'

She shook her head. 'No thanks. Do you mind if I have an early night? Tell them I really want to meet them... which is almost true.'

Seb wished her a good night before picking up his phone. He didn't blame Keira for being nervous. Birdie had been very much on edge the first time he'd taken her to his parents' house in Ovington Square.

Once they got used to the fact that Keira was now part of

his life, he knew they'd be delighted. Even more so when they met her.

'Sebastian, how lovely to hear from you.' His mother answered on the second ring. 'I was in Harrods earlier doing some Christmas shopping and thinking of you. You must have known.'

'I must have,' he agreed. 'How are you and Father?'

'Both in good sorts, thank you. Although your father's doctor has instructed him not to overdo it during the silly season. That means no brandy sauce or sherry in the trifle this year. Have you phoned to let me know you've changed your mind about being with us on Christmas Day?'

'Sorry, Mother, it's not possible. The twins will be here and, with Sarah away, I don't want them to be alone,' he explained, not for the first time. His mother let out a reluctant sigh, which he ignored. 'But there's another reason I'm calling. Is Father there? I'd like to speak to you both together.'

'Yes, he's on the sofa reading. Phillip?... Put down the book. Sebastian would like to speak to us. I'm putting him on speaker.'

'Hello, Father. How are you?'

'Much better when I can return to my book, I'd reached a very compelling part. What's this about?'

Seb took a deep breath. 'Yesterday, a rather surprising thing happened. I discovered that a woman I knew while at university had a daughter nine months after we graduated and that I am the father.' It was to the point, but in his experience that was best when discussing anything of importance with his parents.

There was silence at the other end of the phone, and Seb could almost imagine his mother and father staring at each other.

'Good Lord,' his father finally uttered. 'Are you serious?'

'Of course he's serious.' His mother made a clucking noise. 'Why ever would he call us saying something like that if it wasn't true, Phillip?'

'Right, right. Tell us more.' His father's shocked tone was replaced with curiosity. 'If it happened after university, the girl must now be seventeen?'

'That's correct,' Seb agreed, before explaining about Melanie's tragic death and that neither he nor Keira had known about each other until recently. 'I want you to meet her as soon as possible.'

'It's not an ideal situation, my boy. Suddenly a child appears out of nowhere. What will people think?'

'I'm not concerned about that, Father. It doesn't matter. We're not living in the Dark Ages.'

'I agree,' his mother said, her voice watery, as if she was about to cry. Which was most unlike her. 'We'd very much like to meet Keira. Wouldn't we, Phillip,' she added, her voice stern.

'Of course,' Seb's father said, gruffly.

'Excellent. Would tomorrow suit, Sebastian?' his mother asked.

'Unfortunately, we're in the middle of an urgent case. Once it's over, I'll call and arrange a time for us to visit. Thank you both for taking the news so well. You're going to like Keira very much.'

'Of course we will,' his father retorted gruffly. 'Now, if that's all, I need to get back to my book.'

Sebastian smiled and ended the call.

That couldn't have gone any better. He'd let Keira know in the morning.

He poured himself a drink and walked back into the office. Birdie had updated the large whiteboard they used, and he stood in front of it, going through all the information they'd gathered. There was still a question mark next to Fred's name but even without confirmation that he'd disappeared permanently, hopefully they had enough to convince the police to delve deeper.

TWENTY-TWO

Thursday, 14 December

'You're early.' Seb looked across from the coffee machine to where Birdie was standing in the doorway of the kitchen. The cool air surrounded her and her eyes were blinking, as if trying to wake herself up.

'You don't have to look quite so surprised. You'd better make that coffee double strength.' She shrugged off her heavy coat and hung it over the back of one of the chairs.

'Consider it done. I wasn't expecting you for at least another hour.' Seb reached for another mug.

'You and me both. But Dad had to go into work early and made such a racket that I couldn't get back to sleep. Plus, there's still so much up in the air, and so little time. I just wanted to get back to work. By the way, where's Keira? Let me guess, sleeping in?'

'No, it appears she's an early bird.' He nodded at the remains of his daughter's breakfast that was beside the sink. 'She's coming back to tidy up, but wanted to work on our website first. I'm not sure if that means she's leaving it for me.'

'As someone with two younger brothers who can be complete slobs when they choose, you definitely need to leave it for her. Start as you mean to continue,' Birdie advised as he poured her coffee, added a splash of milk, and handed it over.

'I'll take your word for it then.'

He had a feeling that there was going to be a steep learning curve when it came to having a teenager in the house.

'So what are we going to do about Pappas?' Birdie wrapped both her hands around the mug. 'He denied being there when the body was buried, but Jim says he was. Which means if this case is investigated, he might be in more trouble, not less. It could be a problem if he reneges on his deal to meet Conrad.'

Seb nodded in agreement. 'Pappas must have known the potential risk of taking the case to the police, bearing in mind that he was driving when Fred was hit. Although I suspect he thought that, with Lord Montague dead, no one could prove he was involved in the burial.'

Birdie blew on her drink and took a sip. 'Which means he doesn't know Jim was around that night and saw him. Now it makes more sense. Pappas is stuck in prison knowing he still has five years to serve, and he's not getting any younger. Then you come along and want something, so he figures he has nothing to lose by telling you. Because, hey, he's already inside. So, he agrees to see Conrad as long as the police are involved.'

'Even though whatever transpires, it might not help his case,' Seb added.

'I guess he's desperate enough to be clutching at straws,' Birdie said, taking another sip of her coffee.

'True. And remember, it's not our job to convince the police to reduce his sentence. The agreement was to convince them to look into it. Unfortunately, we can't ask Twiggy. We'll have to visit the Rugby force. Unless Twiggy would agree to take it to them on our behalf?' Seb said, conscious of the time delay that might cause.

'Actually, that won't be necessary.' Birdie placed the mug on the table, her eyes gleaming. 'Sparkle's based there. Do you remember her? Gemma Litton. Twiggy told me the other day that she'd passed her sergeant's exams and is a DS at Rugby. At the very least, she'll listen to what we have to say. I'll call her now and see if she'll see us today.'

The conversation didn't take long and Sparkle, who was catching up on paperwork at the station, said they could come in straight away. Seb and Birdie then went through to the office, where Keira was working. Once Seb had explained where they were going, Keira told them she'd arranged to go out for lunch with one of the younger members of Birdie's cricket club.

'So, you don't need to worry about me and I'll make sure to take Elsa for at least two—' Elsa interrupted the sentence with a bark, and Keira laughed. 'Okay, *three* walks.'

'Remember to clean up after your breakfast,' said Birdie, raising an eyebrow.

Keira wrinkled her nose. 'Absolutely. I'll do it now.'

* * *

Forty minutes later, they were waiting in the foyer of the police station, where a harassed-looking desk sergeant was dealing with a steady flow of people. The drive over had been uneventful, and Seb had filled Birdie in on his conversation with Keira and the possibility of her living with him on a full-time basis. Judging by Birdie's reaction, she approved, although she had teased him that when Sarah did eventually come back, he might need to buy something more permanent now he was a family man.

He suspected she was right, and it was something he'd consider in the new year. But for now, the case demanded his full attention.

Sparkle chose that moment to step into the foyer.

'Well, aren't you a sight for sore eyes?' Sparkle said to Birdie, before giving Seb a wide smile. 'Nice to see you again, Clifford. Let's get out of this madhouse and go upstairs.'

'Gladly. Plus, we have treats.' Birdie held up the box of jam doughnuts that they'd picked up on the way.

'Oh dear, that can only mean one thing. You're trying to butter me up. Not that I'm complaining.' Sparkle ushered them into one of the empty interview rooms before disappearing, then returning several minutes later with three mugs of coffee and some plates. Once the officer had taken a bite of the doughnut and wiped away the sugar from her mouth, she raised an eyebrow. 'So, you'd better spill. What's this all about, Birdie? You were most mysterious on the phone.'

'We have a possible cold case for you. Though it's a tricky one. We're in the process of an investigation and interviewed a man called Roy Pappas. He's ten years into his sentence at Marshdown and claims to know where a body is buried. He says in that in 1971, he accidentally hit and killed a man while driving with his girlfriend – who was the daughter of Lord Montague, over at Rolton Hall. He says Lord Montague, who was his employer at the time, covered it up, and paid him off, worried it would create a scandal.'

Sparkle was quiet as Birdie went through the details, including the demand by Pappas for the police to have input in the possible reduction of his sentence. By the time Birdie had finished, the officer was frowning.

'Pappas seems like a piece of work. Especially if he's known about this all these years and only mentioned it now because of self-interest. It's going to make it harder to convince my governor to investigate, without knowing if this Fred did actually go missing.'

'We couldn't locate him,' Seb admitted. 'But if Fred did have a drinking problem, there's a good chance he'll have had a police record. It might be a good place to start.'

Sparkle tapped her finger against her lips, then nodded. 'Agreed. Let me have a quick word with my boss now. If I get the okay, one of my team can go through the records to see what they can find, and we'll pay a visit to Rolton Hall so you can show me the site. But I can't promise anything yet.'

'Thanks, Sparkle.' Birdie finished off the rest of her doughnut as her former colleague left the room. Then she turned to Seb. 'Do you think they'll agree?'

'It's promising. If DS Litton's team can find out who Fred was and confirm that he disappeared at some stage, it will give credibility to our claim.' He stretched his legs, trying to get comfortable in the hard chair, when his mobile buzzed with a text message from Lady Angelica.

> Any news? Devon's home from the hospital, but the doctor's very worried.

He showed it to Birdie, who swore softly under her breath while he sent Angelica a quick update. By the time he'd finished, Sparkle had reappeared, a faint smile playing around her mouth.

'The guv has okayed it. I've got my team looking through the records now, and they'll call if she has anything. Which means we'd better take a road trip. We'll meet you there. I haven't been to the Rolton Hall before, but have driven past it a few times.'

Seb got to his feet. 'Excellent. We'll see you there.'

'You'll need your wellies,' Birdie said. 'The place is like a mud bath.'

'That's why this job never gets boring,' Sparkle said, shaking her head. 'I'll see you both soon.'

'That was promising,' Birdie said as they reached the car. 'I'll call Lord Montague and give him an update while we're on the way.'

* * *

When Birdie and Seb pulled up outside Rolton Hall, Jim was standing in the visitors' car park, wearing a thick wool coat and scarf wrapped around his neck. He appeared freezing. Hardly surprising. The harsh winter wind was whipping through the estate. Lord Montague had been shocked by Birdie's disclosure regarding there potentially being a body buried in the grounds of his home, but had offered his full support to the investigation.

Sparkle and another officer pulled up a few minutes later, and once introductions were made, Jim led them towards the summer house.

Their muddy footprints from the previous day were still visible as they carefully navigated their way along the path until they arrived at the small clearing in the woods where the summer house was nestled.

At the sight of it, Sparkle had the almost identical reaction to Birdie's. 'What is that thing?' Her wide eyes took in the ornate details of the building.

'Apparently it's a folly,' Birdie said dryly. 'Rich people built them hundreds of years ago for no apparent reason.' She turned to Jim. 'Can you lead us around to the back where you saw them dig the hole?'

'Why didn't you go to the police at the time?' Sparkle asked the elderly gardener, the amusement gone from her voice. 'If you suspected a crime had been committed, it was your duty to report it.'

The man's cheeks reddened. 'I was just a kid and had no idea what was going on. It was different back then. Coppers didn't want to get involved with anything going on here at the hall. And I had no idea anything had happened to Old Fred. I didn't make any connection.'

Sparkle's mouth tightened but she didn't push it further. Instead, she followed him around the muddy trail. It all appeared the same as it had yesterday. Nothing had been disturbed recently.

Sparkle took several photographs from different angles, and then walked over to another, smaller patch of holly. She took more photos and called Jim over.

'Have these holly bushes all been here for the same amount of time?'

He swallowed and reluctantly nodded his head. 'Yeah, give or take.'

'You see how this one's much bigger than the others.' Sparkle glanced at Seb and Birdie, indicating to the smaller bushes on either side. 'I was at a workshop recently talking about clandestine graves and how sometimes they can lead to excessive plant growth.'

Seb's brows pulled together. 'I am aware of that, but studies only pointed to shorter timeframes. This particular site goes back over fifty years.'

'Maybe the body gave the plant the head start it needed? But it's certainly enough for me to convince the guv to let us dig. If you'll excuse me, I'll give him a call.' Sparkle walked back along the path until she was no longer in earshot.

While they waited, Jim moved from leg to leg, clearly nervous.

'Is that why you make sure someone always cuts the holly bush back?' Birdie demanded.

'Just doing my job,' he replied, though he couldn't stop moving his legs. 'You really think they're going to dig it up?'

'I believe we're about to find out,' Seb said as Sparkle reappeared.

Her phone was no longer in her hand and she'd taken the large backpack from her shoulder and was unzipping it.

'Well? What did he say?' Birdie demanded.

'We've got the green light.'

'Yes.' Birdie punched her arm into the air and Seb let out a breath.

It hadn't been their intention to obtain justice for the unknown Fred, but he and Birdie would have hated to have left without getting to the truth. It meant he could revisit Pappas and arrange for him to meet with Conrad.

'I need to cordon this off. I've sent DC Harris back to the car— oh, here he is now. Jim, once the area is contained, I want you to give the officer here a full statement.'

'How long will that take?' he growled.

Sparkle fixed him with a stony glare. 'Less time than if you accompany us to the station. But it's your choice.'

'Fine,' he muttered. He walked over to the far side of the holly bush and folded his arms.

'I'd better find Lord Montague, and let him know what's going to happen,' Sparkle said.

'You'll find him more than happy to cooperate,' Seb assured her as they all headed back towards the main building. 'It was his uncle who had the title and was possibly involved in the cover-up. After the uncle died, Darcy's father inherited the title and the estate. It has since passed to Darcy and I believe he's more interested in justice than trying to hide family skeletons.'

'Good. Because it appears like a skeleton is what we're going to find,' Sparkle said in a dry voice. 'I'll arrange for a forensic anthropologist to supervise the dig, and then we'll see exactly what's buried there.'

'Would you mind if Seb and I tag along?' Birdie asked. 'As observers. It's not really part of our case, but we'd both like to see what happens,' she quickly added.

Sparkle nodded. 'It's the least I can do. Thanks for bringing this to me. I've been itching for the guv to start giving me bigger cases. I owe you both.'

'Right, I think we need to talk to Conrad face to face and

make sure he hasn't changed his mind,' Birdie said, once they'd parted ways with Sparkle.

'I'll contact Marshdown and ask John Rogers to let Pappas know that the case is officially open, and we'll be arranging the visit.' Seb took out his phone and made the call.

Once he'd spoken to Rogers, he started the engine and drove back down the long drive that connected Rolton Hall to the road.

'Finally, we're getting somewhere,' Birdie said, rubbing her brow. 'This case has become more like a juggling act than anything else and I want it all wrapped up before any of the balls drop to the floor.'

Seb let out a long breath. His sentiments exactly.

TWENTY-THREE

It was almost eleven o'clock when they reached Conrad Olsen's house. The coffee they'd grabbed on the way had definitely helped Birdie forget the unearthly time she'd woken up, aided by the adrenaline surge of the police agreeing to follow through with the investigation of Old Fred's death.

As she'd watched Sparkle put the wheels in motion, Birdie had momentarily missed her old job in the force, but it had quickly passed. No way could Birdie give up the new freedom she had working as a private investigator. Yes, it was longer hours and, in some ways, more intense. But it was also more rewarding, and she didn't feel like she had to hide who she was anymore. No more worrying about being late, or jumping the gun on anything. And definitely no more desk duty.

Conrad opened the front door and ushered them into the living room. He was wearing tracksuit bottoms and a T-shirt. The bristles on his chin suggested he hadn't shaved in a few days.

'I take it you've got news.'

'We do. Is Tina here?' Birdie asked.

'No, I'm on my own. She's taken on an extra cleaning shift to help cover the mortgage, and the girls are at school. Sit down.'

Birdie took a seat on the sofa next to a pile of CVs and some envelopes. Most job applications were made via email. Was he door-knocking looking for work?

'Looks like you've been busy. Are there many jobs out there?' she asked. He sat on the edge of the recliner, his arms resting on his knees.

'There's nothing. Either I have too much experience, or not enough. It's like you reach a certain age and suddenly you become invisible. Anyway, let's cut to the chase. I take it you've found my real father.'

'We have. His name's Roy, and he wasn't aware of your existence. After we explained the situation, he agreed to see you.' Seb's voice was calm and didn't divulge Pappas's less-than-enthusiastic response to the news he had another child.

'At the same time as Angie? That was the deal, remember. I want to see both of them together. When they meet me, they'll realise I'm a person, not just a thing.' His voice broke and he looked away.

Birdie's heart went out to him. She knew only too well the thoughts that had probably been going through his mind since he'd discovered the truth about his birth.

'They certainly don't consider you to be a thing,' Birdie said, wanting to reassure him. 'But unfortunately, it's not possible for you to meet them at the same time. Your birth father's currently in Marshdown Prison. We can arrange for you to visit him there. Under the circumstances, I'm sure you agree, it would be better for you to meet with Angie separately.'

Conrad closed his eyes in contemplation. He was silent for a long time until eventually he stood up and began walking around the room. Finally, he stopped and stared at them.

'Prison, eh? My adopted dad was always worried that I had a wild streak. I guess we now know where it came from.'

'Except you haven't been in prison before,' Birdie reminded him. 'Unlike your birth father, who's been in and out many times since his early twenties.'

Conrad sat down. 'So, what's he like? Actually... no, don't tell me. Probably better if I find out for myself.'

'That's a good idea,' Seb said quickly.

Birdie let out a sigh of relief. They hadn't wanted to lie about Pappas, but if they'd told Conrad the reality of the situation, the chances of him wanting to visit might diminish greatly.

'Is it okay for you to meet Angie separately?' Birdie asked, wanting to confirm.

'Yes. But I'm still not going to decide whether I'll be tested until I've met them both. Did you tell Angie that?'

'We did, and she's eager to meet you as soon as possible,' Seb said. 'If you consent, it could be arranged for tomorrow. Birdie and I will collect you from here and take you to her.'

'What about my father?'

'We're waiting to hear back from the governor of the prison regarding a time for your visit.'

'Okay.' Conrad walked over to the other side of the room and picked up an old photo album. 'By the way, I visited Mum – Maggie – yesterday and we talked about it.'

'You did?' Birdie's chest tightened. It would have been, no doubt, a tricky conversation; she had spent days agonising over her decision to find her birth mother and telling her parents about it. 'How did it go? Did she explain why they'd kept it a secret?'

'Not exactly.' He shook his head and stared at the book in his hands. 'When I brought it up, she seemed to think I already knew. I didn't have the heart to tell her the truth. The main thing was that she still remembered me. She gave me this album. She'd actually taken it with her to the care home and not left it with the things we've stored in our attic. In it are loads of photos that they'd taken of me over the years. She said they'd kept it for my real mother in case she ever got in touch. They wanted her to know how grateful they were to have had me.'

A lump formed in her throat as she pictured Margaret and Colin Olsen carefully collating the album on the off-chance someone turned up on the doorstep wanting to find the child she'd given birth to. It was very thoughtful of them.

'Will you give it to her?' she asked, her voice soft.

Conrad shrugged. 'Honestly? I don't know. I'll wait to see how I feel when we meet.' He rose to standing. 'I'm sorry, you'll have to leave now. I've got an interview this afternoon and Tina will slay me alive if I don't shave first.'

They said their goodbyes and stepped outside.

Birdie rubbed her hands together as they walked back towards where they'd parked. 'There's a pub a down the road. Let's grab some lunch and make the necessary arrangements for Conrad to see his parents. It will make a nice change from using your car as our second office.'

'It has been a busy few days,' Seb agreed as they continued past his car.

The pub was on the corner and appeared to have recently been done up. There were a couple of old men propping up the bar who had the easy familiarity of locals, but most of the tables were filled with a mix of people.

'Why don't I grab a table and you order lunch?' She scanned the menu before giving him her order and headed to a booth at the side of the room.

By the time Seb joined her, holding two lemonades, she'd updated her notebook and was studying it.

'Problem?' he asked as he placed the drinks and cutlery on the table.

'No. I'm making sure we haven't missed anything.' She closed the book and picked up her phone. 'We need to arrange the visits. I'll call Lady Angelica, and you can contact Rogers again to find out how soon we can get back into the prison.'

'I'll leave the prison governor until later. It was less than two hours ago that I spoke to him.'

'Okay, I suppose you're right.' She called Lady Angelica, who answered on the second ring. 'It's Birdie.'

'What did the police say? Are they looking into the case? Is everything still going ahead?' There was an edge of panic to her voice. Hardly surprising considering Devon's diminishing health.

'They are. It's too soon to say what will happen. *But*, if they do find something, they will need to interview you.' Birdie didn't bother to mince her words.

'I'm aware of the risks,' the other woman replied in a tight voice. 'I hope it's going to be worth it.'

Birdie felt the same. She rolled her shoulders, trying to shake off some of the heavy burden. 'We'd like you to meet your son tomorrow. Is that okay?'

There was silence, as if Lady Angelica was reminding herself what was at stake and how painful the meeting might be.

'Yes. I'm free at midday.'

'Great. We'll let him know. He has no idea who you are. We've only told him that your name is Angie. So, I suggest we meet at a café. It might be less intimidating for him... and for you.'

'Whatever you think is best. There is a nice café in Fleckney. I'll book a table for us... And Birdie, thank you for everything you and Sebastian have done so far.'

'You're most welcome.'

She ended the call and tried not to think of all the things that still needed doing for the case to be resolved.

Seb was staring at his phone. 'I've received a text message from Rogers. Conrad can visit Pappas on Saturday.'

'Excellent. Lady Angelica will meet Conrad tomorrow. I'll

contact him later and let him know logistics. You know, doing all this work makes me realise how great it would be to have someone like Keira to help us with general admin, appointment arranging, stuff like that.'

'We'll discuss it with her. Certainly during the school holidays we could make use of her. Also, if she really is interested in a doing a criminology degree, it would add to her CV and might assist in her university application.'

'And she'll get to see what the working in the field is really like. By that I mean the good, the bad, and the boring,' she quipped as one of the bar staff brought over two plates of bangers and mash. 'Let's eat. It's already been a long day.'

TWENTY-FOUR

Thursday, 14 December

The A45 was down to a single lane, with every car nose to tail, and Birdie let out an impatient groan as the cars heading back towards Coventry whizzed past. There was nothing worse than being stuck in traffic when the scenery was a flat expanse of fields and trees. She drummed her fingers against her leg.

'It appears there's been an accident up ahead,' Seb said, his voice as unflustered as ever.

Didn't he ever get mad? It wasn't natural. Sighing, she craned her neck and realised he was right. 'Good. Hopefully, once we get past, we can do more than five miles an hour. Because—'

Buzz.

Her mood instantly brightened as she glanced at her phone and saw Sparkle's name flash up on the screen. Before answering, she reached for her notepad, which was sitting on the car's console.

'Birdie, hey. Where are you? I've heard from the forensic anthropologist. She's on the way to Rolton Hall right now, along with her team. If you want to tag along, get here soon. I'm already here.'

'That's great.' She instantly sat up straight and glanced over to the satnav screen embedded in the dashboard. 'We're on our way back from Warwick. The traffic's been a nightmare, but we're actually not far. It won't take us too long to reach you.'

'Warwick? This case is taking you all over the place.'

'You don't know the half of it. Thanks for keeping us in the loop. We'll see you soon.' She finished the call and twisted in her seat. 'I'm sure you got all that. The forensic anthropologist and her team are heading there, now. Thank goodness we stopped for lunch instead of going straight back home.'

'It couldn't have worked out better, even if we'd planned it,' Seb said in a dry voice, as they finally passed a couple of tow trucks, and the traffic thinned out.

Ten minutes later, they'd reached Rolton Hall. As well as the unmarked pool car Sparkle had been driving earlier, there were two Land Rovers and a Transit van. Once Seb had found a spot to park, they pulled on their wellies and headed along the path leading to the summer house, which had once again turned to mud thanks to the foot traffic.

When they reached the clearing, Sparkle was in deep conversation with a tall woman dressed elegantly in a Barbour jacket and green wellies. Was she the forensic anthropologist? She was very stylish. A stark contrast to Birdie's jeans and hoodie.

The holly bush was gone, leaving behind an expanse of sodden soil. Several people were crouched down, carefully clearing away the dirt. A makeshift marquee had been set up to protect them from the light rain that was falling.

'Have you been to a dig like this before?' Seb asked.

'No. It was the one of the reasons I asked if we could come. I wanted to see them in action. How about you?'

'I've seen a couple in progress. While they're fascinating,

they can take a long time. Don't expect instant results,' he cautioned.

'Is that your way of telling me not to tap my fingers or mumble anything rude under my breath when I'm bored?' Birdie retorted.

But contrary to what Seb thought, she didn't get bored. Instead, she silently watched the team while they carefully brushed away the layers of soil. To one side, an older man was taking photographs of the team's progress, stopping regularly to make notes on a clipboard. Someone else was sifting through the soil that had already been extracted. It was almost like a dance. Birdie kept moving her focus from one member of the team to the next as they all shared the same look of intensity while they worked.

The tall forensic anthropologist rejoined the other technicians and spent several minutes inspecting something in the now open hole in the ground. She straightened up and beckoned for a man with a metal detector to get closer. Birdie unconsciously leant forward, and Seb seemed to do the same thing. Had they discovered something?

The man swept the detector back and forth several times before the machine suddenly let out a series of pings, which resulted in renewed digging.

'What's going on? What do you think it is?' she whispered to Seb.

'It could be metal from a belt buckle, or from a watch the deceased was wearing at the time. But don't get too excited. It could easily be a discarded beer can that had been buried in the undergrowth.'

'Or a beer can belonging to the dead man,' Birdie mused as the team continued to work.

To the left of them stood Jim. His mouth was set in a guilty frown and his hands were clasped together, as if he regretted his decision to hold on to such a secret for so long.

Good. Birdie still wasn't sure how she felt about the fact
he'd seen something so clearly dodgy and had chosen to
ignore it.

'I believe they might have found something,' Seb said,
breaking into her thoughts with a nudge on her arm.

The forensic anthropologist was kneeling down to inspect
something in the dirt.

Birdie sucked in a breath as the woman stood up and
nodded over to Sparkle.

'We have two bones, which appear to be human. One from
a hand and the other from a leg. I will organise for floodlights to
be brought in and the team will continue working.'

'Thank you, Dr Wilkes.' Sparkle swiped her phone screen
and made a call. Birdie's throat tightened. So it was true. The
body really had been buried. Next to her, Seb's jaw was tight.
The ripple effects could be very damaging not just for Pappas,
but for their client as well. And the fact it could posthumously
implicate Lady Angelica's father, too.

Once Sparkle finished her call, she joined them on the other
side of the cordon.

'What's going to happen now?' Birdie asked.

'As and when they're found, the bones will be taken to the
morgue, and Dr Wilkes will work with the pathologist to establish cause of death and identify the victim. I'll be speaking to
Lord Montague to see if he can help.'

'Good luck with that,' Birdie said. 'I believe staff records
dating back to the time Fred disappeared were destroyed in a
flood in 19...' She glanced at Seb.

'1982,' he said.

'This is why I work with him. Nothing escapes his memory,
as you may remember.'

'I do.' Sparkle grinned. 'You're very lucky to have that skill,
Seb.'

'Don't start that,' Birdie said, shaking her head. 'He'll start telling you it's not what it's cracked up to be, blah, blah, blah.'

'I'd rather you didn't malign me when I'm present,' Seb said.

'You know we don't mean it.' She turned back to Sparkle. 'What are you going to do next?'

'I've got a team door-knocking in the area, but it's a long shot. I expect we'll have more luck with dental records.'

'Will you be charging Pappas and Lady Angelica?' Seb asked.

'It's too early to say. We need to interview Lady Charing first. It's possible that she'll be charged as an accessory, although it will be hard to prove. Pappas, according to the gardener's statement, was more involved and had been there that night. He'd been instructed to dig the grave. It will be down to the Crown Prosecution Service and whether they can build a case. We will know more when – or if – we can identify the victim.'

'Okay. Keep us posted, and thanks, Sparkle.'

'Same to you. When your case is over, we'll have to catch up for a drink and you can fill me in properly. It sounds like you've had your hands full.'

Birdie gave her a reluctant smile. 'Remember I was worried life might get boring if I left the force? Well, I was wrong.'

'Wait? You just admitted you were wrong?' Sparkle raised an eyebrow and turned to Seb. 'I hope you were recording that.'

'I won't let her forget.' He tapped his head, and Birdie groaned.

Sparkle slipped back under the cordon to talk to Jim.

Birdie turned to Seb. 'We need to head back to Fleckney House to give Lady Angelica an update on what's happened, before the police visit.'

Seb agreed and they walked silently back through the mud towards the car. They were so close now, but there were still so many things that could go wrong, it was hard to celebrate.

TWENTY-FIVE

Friday, 15 December

The café Lady Angelica had directed them to was in a rustic repurposed barn that also served as a garden centre and gift shop. Judging by the way Conrad's eyes widened at the collection of late-model cars in the gravel car park to one side of the barn, along with the general affluence the place gave off, it had been a good decision not to take him directly to Fleckney House, because it would have been totally overwhelming.

'How are you feeling?' Seb checked in.

The man gave a quick nod of his head, though his continued look of awe and the tightness of his jaw told a different story.

Not that Birdie could blame him. She knew from her own recent meeting with her birth mother how confronting it was to face the past head on. Part of her wanted to share that with Conrad. But she didn't want to diminish his own experience, or make him feel he should talk about it, if he didn't want to.

Instead, she followed them both inside. They'd had a long conversation with Lady Angelica yesterday, and while she'd been deeply saddened to hear that Fred had been killed that night, she'd taken the news about the possible repercussions very well.

'I realised this all came with a risk,' she'd simply told them. 'And I'm willing to pay the price if it means saving my son... and... meeting my other son.'

Lady Angelica had already arrived and was sitting at a long wooden table in the corner of the café. At the sight of them, she stood up and gave Seb and Birdie a brief nod, though her gaze was fixed firmly on Conrad, who had come to an abrupt halt.

Birdie lightly touched Seb's arm and they both stood back, letting the mother and son take their time. Lady Angelica's mouth opened, no doubt seeing in Conrad's dark hair and eyes the man she'd had an affair with all those years ago.

As for Conrad, his eyes were filled with the same awe and confusion as when he'd seen the expensive cars outside. He stared at Lady Angelica's casually expensive attire and the plain gold chains around her neck that spoke of wealth.

'Thank you for agreeing to meet me, Conrad. I realise it's been a lot for you to deal with. Please take a seat.' She gestured to one opposite her. 'I promise to answer any questions you have. Providing I'm able.'

'Okay.' Conrad's shoulders were stiff and his hands were fisted into balls, as if unsure what to do with them.

'Coffee all round?' Seb asked.

Once everyone had agreed, he left them and headed to the long wooden counter that was laden with glass cake stands. Birdie had a feeling that neither Lady Angelica nor Conrad would even notice food or drink, but she was dying for a coffee, and whatever else Seb brought back.

Conrad sat opposite Lady Angelica, as requested, and Birdie positioned herself further down the table. She was within earshot but sufficiently out of the way that they wouldn't feel she was a part of the conversation.

Conrad reached for the napkin on the table, his fingers

twisting it into a small ball. Then he looked up, staring directly at his mother.

'First thing I want to know is who you are. I take it you're not really called Angie.'

'You're right. I'm sorry for the deception. My name is Angelica Charing.' She paused a moment, as if contemplating what to say next. 'Lady Angelica Charing. I live at Fleckney, which is only a few miles from here. But I grew up in Dunchurch at Rolton Hall. My family name was Montague.'

'Rolton Hall. I know that place. I helped do some electrical work on it a few years ago...' Conrad's voice trailed off, his Adam's apple bobbing in his throat.

Lady Angelica's honesty surprised Birdie. Considering the level of secrecy with this case, she hadn't been sure how much their client would tell her son. But, clearly, she'd decided to be frank.

'After my father died, my uncle struggled to maintain it, although my cousin, Darcy, has done much to improve it... But that's not why you're here. Rolton Hall is where I met your father.'

'Tell me,' Conrad said, his voice gruff.

Before Lady Angelica could answer, Seb rejoined them, closely followed by a waitress who deposited a large tray with coffee and several slices of cake on it. Not that Lady Angelica or Conrad noticed.

Instead, their client falteringly told her son everything about the summer with Pappas; being sent away to Norfolk during her pregnancy; giving birth; and having him taken away.

As she talked, Conrad was silent, and Birdie and Seb quietly drank their drinks.

'Giving you up was the worst thing I've ever been through. There hasn't been a day since that time when you weren't in my thoughts.' She dabbed her eyes with a handkerchief and then held his gaze. 'This might seem odd to you, but at the time, I was so used to obeying my parents that I didn't question them. In my mind, I had no choice. My parents certainly didn't give me one, and at that age, I couldn't have managed on my own.' She let out a long sigh. 'I'm sorry. Very sorry.'

'I-I don't know what to say.' Conrad leant back and ran a hand through his thick hair. Judging by the shock in his eyes, what she'd told him wasn't what he'd been expecting. 'Thank you for you telling me. It's a lot to take in.'

'I know. I've always longed to find you, but it wasn't right. I always feared that you wouldn't want to know me after I'd given you away,' she added, her voice thick with raw pain.

'So, why now?' Conrad said, pain in his voice. 'Aren't you worried about the scandal? I could go to the papers, or, or, or... anything.'

Birdie tensed and peered over at Seb, whose gaze was fixed on Conrad. Was he thinking about Tina and the Olsens' money troubles?

'You could,' Lady Angelica agreed. 'I hope you won't, but it's out of my control. You have a right to know your heritage. I am past worrying about what people think. It's not a good enough reason to hide anything from you.'

The answer seemed to satisfy Conrad and he nodded. 'Okay, so what's this test?'

The question hung in the air and Lady Angelica was motionless, as if suddenly remembering the terrible dilemma she was facing.

'After I married Lord Charing, I had three other sons. Your half-brothers. Devon, my youngest, is ill. His kidneys are failing and, without a transplant, the doctors give him six months to live. He's only thirty-four—' She broke off and took a shuddering breath.

'And because I'm your biological child, you want to see if I'd be a match? You want me to give him one of my kidneys? That's... I mean... How would it work?'

Lady Angelica's face was stricken and she glanced at Birdie, who dragged her chair closer until she was facing Conrad. 'If you agree, and the tests show you're compatible, you'll meet with Devon's medical team. They'll explain the entire process, including the risks. We've already spoken to them. A person's body can survive with one kidney, as long as it's healthy.'

'The risks are minimal, but, as with all medical procedures, there are some,' Seb added. 'The recovery time is two to three months. The team will discuss it with you before you make a decision.'

'I see.' Conrad closed his eyes, deep grooves running down each side of his mouth.

Lady Angelica winced, as if feeling his deliberations. 'Conrad... Whatever you decide, I'd like for us to remain in contact. Only if you agree, of course. I love my son, Devon, very much but his life is no more important than yours.'

Conrad finally met his mother's gaze. 'Okay. Is there anything else?'

Lady Angelica's mouth twitched with indecision. 'Actually, there is. I'd like to know more about you. If you don't mind.'

'Me?' The question seemed to catch him off guard and he flushed. 'There's not much to tell. Mum and Dad were great. Our house wasn't like your mansion but it was nice. I never wanted for anything. Dad died a few years ago and Mum's in a care home. She's got dementia and has good and bad days.'

'I'm sorry to hear that,' Lady Angelica said, moving her hand closer to Conrad's, as if wanting to comfort him. But she pulled it back. Did she think it was too soon?

Conrad gave a gruff shrug. 'She's ninety-two, so I guess it's to be expected. I'm married to Tina and we have two girls.' He pulled out his phone and dragged his finger across the screen. 'Here is a photo... if you'd like to see them.'

'I would. Very much.' Lady Angelica leant forwards and studied the photograph before swallowing. 'What a beautiful family. Thank you for telling me about your childhood and your parents. I'd always hoped they'd love you and give you a good upbringing.'

'They did.' Conrad suddenly got to his feet and looked at Seb and Birdie. 'Let's go. I've got another interview this afternoon, with a manufacturing company, and I need time to get myself together and prepare for it.'

'Of course.' Birdie got to her feet, soon followed by Seb and Lady Angelica.

'Thank you again, Conrad,' Lady Angelica said. 'I hope you'll consider my request. My whole— No, I should say, *our* whole family would be grateful.'

'I'm speaking to Roy tomorrow. Once I've seen him, I'll make my decision,' Conrad said, nodding.

'I understand,' Lady Angelica said.

Seb and Conrad walked on ahead, and once they were out of earshot, Birdie turned to Lady Angelica and put her hand on her arm. 'Are you okay?'

'Yes, I am, thank you. I appreciate your help. Meeting my son for the first time... It was...' Her voice trailed off.

'I know from my own experience of being adopted how overwhelming it can be,' Birdie assured her. 'It changes everything.'

'It's certainly emotional,' Lady Angelica agreed.

They said their goodbyes and Birdie jogged out of the café and across the car park to where Seb and Conrad were waiting in the car. The cool weather stung at her cheeks as she clambered in, and was pleased that the heater was already going.

Conrad was seated in the back seat, his dark eyes distant, as if he was reliving the whole conversation over in his mind. He hardly spoke on the return journey, giving them no indication of his feelings. Since he'd never been backwards in coming forwards on how he'd felt about everything, Birdie suspected that Lady Angelica's honesty had gone a long way to convincing him she was genuine.

Of course, he still had to meet Pappas, and from everything Seb had told her, she wasn't confident that meeting would go nearly as well.

TWENTY-SIX

Saturday, 16 December

Seb's phone beeped with a text message as he parked his car close to Conrad's house. It was from Keira, who'd gone to Market Harborough with Birdie to buy some toiletries and other essentials for her stay, because she'd only packed for a couple of days when she left London a few days ago.

He swiped the screen to see a photo of Keira about to bite into a huge piece of chocolate cake. He suppressed a smile. Clearly, his daughter and his business partner had been cut from the same cloth when it came to their sweet tooth.

He texted back, forcing himself to use a laughing emoji. It felt wrong on so many levels. Keira had teased him about not using them so he'd decided to make an effort. He pocketed his phone and flicked up his coat collar as he locked his car and walked along the road.

Yesterday had been gruelling for both Conrad and Lady Angelica, and it made Seb realise that Keira would doubtless have many unanswered questions as well. After their dinner, they'd sat down and he'd brought out some of the family albums that Sarah kept in the study. They'd looked through them together and then she showed him photos of her and Melanie.

Tina answered the door to the red-brick house, and Conrad was behind her.

'Good morning. How are you feeling after yesterday?' Seb asked.

'Like everything's gone crazy,' he admitted.

Tina's eyes were bright. 'We looked up Lady Angelica Charing. Bloody hell. There were photos of her wedding. It was in all the papers.'

'It was a huge affair at the time.'

'What do you reckon Conrad's life would have been like if he'd been brought up there?'

'I might not have met you,' Conrad pointed out and rubbed a hand across his brow.

'Oh, yeah... good point,' Tina said, with a shrug.

Seb checked his watch. 'We're due at eleven, so I suggest we leave now, in case there are any traffic hold-ups.'

'I'm ready. I'll see you later, love.' Conrad kissed Tina on the cheek as he left.

Conrad was quiet for most of the journey and Seb didn't attempt to engage him in conversation. It wasn't until they reached Marshdown and Seb had turned off the ignition that Conrad finally spoke.

'This whole business still seems surreal. Like it's happening to someone else. It's not what I ever expected. How am I meant to know what to think?'

'Give yourself time and don't try to force it to make sense. Have you told your daughters yet?'

'No. They know something's going on, but until it's straight in my own mind, I don't want to tell them. Though, as you might have noticed, Tina's beside herself over it all. She thinks we're suddenly going to be rich.'

'Do you believe the same?'

Conrad shook his head and stared up at the depressing prison block. 'No. Okay, so my birth mother's posh. But that's only half the story.'

It was hard to disagree. Lady Angelica might have been plagued with guilt regarding what had happened to her son over the years. But Pappas was only concerned with turning it to his own advantage.

Although Seb hoped that now Pappas had been given time to reflect, his attitude might have changed. If not, Conrad may well be facing a confronting interview.

'Have you ever visited anyone in a prison before?'

The question seemed to snap Conrad out of his brooding. 'Yeah. But only once. A friend got six months for not paying his speeding tickets. It was pretty relaxed. He even got to do work experience. A good job really, because he couldn't go back to driving buses after he'd lost his licence.'

'You'll find Marshdown very different,' Seb explained. 'It's category A and high security because the prisoners are considered dangerous.'

'Will we be searched before we go in?'

'Yes. That's routine procedure when visiting a prison.'

'I see.' Conrad scratched his right eye with his finger, as if piecing together what Seb was telling him.

At the entrance was a queue of people waiting to be admitted. A mix of young and old. Some in a group and others alone.

Conrad was silent as they waited in the queue until it was their turn. They didn't speak as they went through the security protocol and handed over their phones, before being checked for contraband items. A guard led them back through the same series of corridors Seb had been taken through at his previous visit and ushered them into the same room. Seb made a mental note to thank Rogers for, once again, allowing them some privacy.

'I'll bring the inmate through in a few minutes,' the guard said before disappearing out of the door.

Next to him, Conrad tapped his fingers nervously against the table.

Seb's concerns, however, weren't so much in respect of the meeting between father and son, but how Pappas would take the news that he could very well be implicated in a death.

Sparkle had informed them yesterday that, thanks to the silver hip flask found, the body belonged to a Frederick Timpson who had been seventy-two when he died. It had also been established that damage to the bones was consistent with being hit by a moving vehicle.

The door opened and Pappas appeared, followed by the guard, who led him to the other side of the table and waited until he was seated.

'Behave yourself,' the guard warned before glancing over to Seb and raising an eyebrow. 'Let us know when you're done.'

Conrad's lips were pressed together as he stared at his father.

Was he taking in the similarity in their dark eyes and hair?

Or was it the angry scar that ran down Pappas's weather-beaten face?

Pappas didn't appear at all curious. Instead, his arms were folded across his barrel chest.

He raised an eyebrow. 'So, you wanted to meet me, did you? What's your name, boy?'

'Conrad,' he answered as their eyes locked.

'Is that so?' Pappas's mouth twitched with amusement. 'I can see you got the Pappas jaw. Good for taking a hit, that's what my old man always said. Now, what's this about?'

The question seemed to throw Conrad and he blanched. 'I wanted to meet you. According to Lady Angelica, you didn't know about me.'

'Nope. Didn't have a clue, until this one' – he nodded towards Seb – 'came along and told me.'

'Do you have any other children?'

'Two. Well... two that I know of.' He shrugged and again his mouth turned up with a smirk, as if he found it amusing. 'I haven't seen them in years. Too big for their boots to visit their old fella now he's locked up.'

'What about your wife?'

'I've been long shot of her. Last I heard, she was in Scotland running some kind of bar.'

Conrad frowned. Whatever he'd been hoping for, it clearly hadn't been this.

'What about your parents?' Seb asked Pappas, wanting to give Conrad some time to pull himself together.

'Both dead, and good riddance to them.' He narrowed his eyes at Seb. 'Now, what news have you got for me? What's going to happen to my sentence? The guv told me that they found Old Fred.'

'That's correct. The body was located and identified. I am not involved in the next step. That decision will be made by the police and the CPS.'

'What are you talking about?' Conrad's brows knitted together as he gave Seb a questioning look. Pappas grinned.

'Ah, so our posh detective didn't tell you, then? Back when I knew your mother, we had a wild night out and hit someone while we were driving on her family's estate. Her old man wouldn't let us call an ambulance to take the body away to be buried properly. Instead he then made sure the death was covered up. Didn't want the scandal of knowing their precious daughter was dating the likes of me. Or that she was involved in someone's death.'

'Is that true?' Conrad demanded, his attention going back to Seb. 'Lady Angelica knew about this?'

'Not at the time. She knew that the man had been injured

but wasn't aware that he'd died. The following day, after her parents had discovered she was pregnant, she was sent away. By the time she returned, it was considered to be in the past and wasn't mentioned again.'

'Oh, is that what Her Ladyship says, is it?' Pappas let out a nasty laugh.

'It is. You omitted to mention that you went with Lord Montague and another person to find Fred. *And* that you were the one who dug the grave.'

'Who's been blabbing?' Pappas's voice had taken on a menacing tone. 'The old lord is long gone.'

'There's a witness. You lied when you informed me that you didn't know where the body was buried.'

'Witness? Who the hell's that?' Pappas demanded, leaning forward, his large hands thumping down on the table between them.

'I'm not at liberty to say,' Seb said, beckoning at the guard who was staring at them through the glass window to indicate that their conversation was over.

The door opened and the guard marched over to Pappas, hauling him to his feet. 'Right. I think we're done here. Unless you have any more questions?'

Seb glanced over to Conrad, who gave a quick shake of his head.

'No, we don't,' Seb said.

'Okay, come on, let's get you back to the hole where you belong.'

They didn't speak until they were outside the prison, where the sun had made a welcome appearance, turning the frosty ground into a glittering blanket of icy steam.

Conrad rubbed his hands together. 'Whoa. That was intense. And not what I expected. It's hard to imagine that Lady Angelica ever had anything to do with him.'

'They're both products of their family backgrounds. The

choices your father made set him on a very different path. I'm sorry it wasn't what you expected.' Seb unlocked the car and they both climbed in.

'Don't be. It's not your fault. At least now I know. I don't understand about this accident. Why did he ask you about it?'

Seb and Birdie had been unsure whether to tell Conrad about Pappas's demands, not wanting to colour his view of his father. But Pappas hadn't been shy about his true nature moments ago.

'Your father would only agree to meet you if we agreed to investigate the accident,' Seb said. 'He was hoping it would give him a reduced sentence. In addition, it's possible that he wanted to cause some damage to Lady Angelica and her cousin, Lord Darcy Montague, who inherited Rolton Hall and the title. I don't believe he expected us to discover he'd been involved in the cover-up, and that he'd been paid off to keep it quiet.'

'You mean that he might be charged?'

'That's correct.'

Conrad considered this, before frowning. 'What about Lady Angelica? If she was in the car at the same time, could she be charged as an accessory?'

'Yes. When we informed her that Pappas would only agree to meet you if we could convince the police to look into the accident, she knew that it was a possibility. But she was happy to accept it. She wasn't aware that anyone had been killed. More than anything, she wanted to do whatever she could to save Devon and to meet you. She was aware of the risks and made that decision.'

'I see. This tells me more about my birth parents than anything else.' Conrad swallowed, staring directly out the window.

'Yes, that is exactly right. I would like to add that although Lady Angelica is our client, if we hadn't believed in her integrity, we wouldn't have continued with the case,' Seb said, wanting to be honest with the man. 'Have you made a decision regarding your next steps?'

'I'd like to continue getting to know Lady Angelica. But I won't be having any more contact with *him*.' He nodded in the direction of the bleak prison building that was disappearing as Seb drove towards the motorway.

'Have you considered the testing?'

There was silence as Conrad continued staring ahead. Finally he let out a long breath.

'Yes. I'm prepared to be tested and we'll take it from there. Will you let her know?'

'I will.' Seb's fingers tightened around the steering wheel. 'Thank you. I realise it wasn't an easy choice.'

'You're wrong. My mother could have kept it to herself. But she was prepared to risk everything to protect one of her own. And that includes me now. I might never have known the truth about myself. It's the least I can do for my family.'

TWENTY-SEVEN

Doctor Indira Desai's office was on the second floor of a modern building in Leicester, and judging by the many framed certificates behind her desk, she was extremely well qualified. More importantly, she seemed very nice, and not at all patronising, like some doctors Birdie had spoken to. Dr Desai was talking to Conrad in a soft but direct voice while she went through the results of his blood test, which they'd rushed through over the weekend because of the urgency.

They'd already been there for half an hour, and while she and Seb would usually have waited outside, Conrad had requested they attend the appointment with him.

Before the appointment, Lady Angelica had told them that Devon's condition was deteriorating by the day and if he didn't receive a transplant soon, he might become too ill to go through with the operation.

Birdie chewed on her lip, willing Dr Desai to go faster and put an end to the waiting.

Finally, Dr Desai put down the file on the desk and leant back in her chair.

'Now, for the good news. We've checked your ABO compatibility, and because your blood group is O, which is what we sometimes call a universal donor, it means you're compatible with Devon.'

Birdie closed her eyes and let it wash over her. Even Seb nodded his head in approval.

Conrad sucked in a breath. 'Y-you mean I can be a donor?'

The doctor gave him a rueful smile. 'It's not quite so simple. We still need to do more blood tests to see if your tissue – or your human leukocyte antigen – is a match. The closer the HLA match is, the less chance there is of the kidney being rejected, and the longer the new kidney is likely to last.'

'You mean, it might not last very long?' There was a hint of alarm in his voice, which Birdie could totally relate to.

It was a huge thing to consider, especially if the transplant wasn't a permanent fix. It also made Birdie remember that despite the blood test, there was still a long way to go. The worst part was that it was no longer in her or Seb's hands. They'd done their part and all they could do was sit back and cross their fingers. Like everyone else.

'Again, it comes down to the match. Furthermore, when a living donation is considered, the chances of how long the new organ will last improve again. We'll talk further once we've done the HLA matching.'

'I understand. What about the risks if we do go ahead?'

She gave him a reassuring smile. 'Like all major surgeries, there are risks, but they're not high. I do hundreds of these operations each year. If your kidneys are in good condition, then your body can function perfectly well on just one, so there should be little or no physical impact on your own health and well-being.'

'I understand.' Conrad was silent for a moment. 'Tell me honestly. Do you think it's worth it? For Devon, I mean.'

Dr Desai swivelled around on her chair to face a wall that was covered in framed photographs of people. They were all different ages but each one was smiling broadly.

'Short answer is yes, absolutely. These are some of my patients who have received kidney transplants and are now living lives that would have been impossible eighty years ago. As I said, there are always risks when it comes to surgery, but being a living donor can give someone else a chance to live a full life. I can't think of anything more rewarding.'

Conrad nodded. 'Okay, let's go ahead with the other testing. At my next appointment, I'll bring my wife and daughters so you can answer their questions as well, if that's okay?'

'Absolutely. It's important to include your whole family in this decision.' Dr Desai got to her feet. 'First, let's take you through to the nurse for a biopsy, which will be sent to the lab for testing. Seb and Birdie, if you'd like to sit in the waiting room, I'll send Conrad through when we've finished.'

The waiting room wasn't busy and they found seats together. Birdie picked up a magazine and then put it down again before turning to Seb.

'Do you think he'll agree if the tissue stuff is a match?'

'I think he'll give it careful consideration. When we were at Marshdown, he appeared to understand that Lady Angelica was genuine in her request, and that she wasn't using him to save Devon. Nevertheless, it's a big step. I'm pleased he's going to discuss it properly with Tina and his daughters.'

'I keep thinking about how I'd feel if I was in his situation. It's such a big deal. All credit to him for being willing to consider it.'

'We never know what we're capable of until we're thrown into such a situation.'

'Like finding out you're suddenly father to a teenage girl?' Birdie teased, though, as always, he took it in his stride.

'In many respects, it's almost as life-changing as donating an organ. We're yet to see how I'm going to perform in this new role.'

'Judging by the way Keira's constantly smiling, I think you're doing okay,' Birdie said before studying him. 'Had you ever thought about having kids before?'

'When Annabelle and I dated, I'd assumed we'd marry and have at least two children, but there was always something holding me back. Initially, I'd wondered if I wasn't ready to have a family. Then I decided it was because I wasn't sure what that family would look like. I didn't want to totally replicate the family I'd grown up in, but couldn't see another way of doing things. Now, we'll have to see how it develops.'

'I'm happy for you,' Birdie told him truthfully, before grinning at him. 'By the way, did you and Keira have a nice day, yesterday?'

After she'd taken Keira shopping on Saturday, they'd gone back to Birdie's house for lunch with her parents, and her mum had mentioned there was a fashion and make-up expo taking place in Leicester on Sunday. Keira had immediately declared that she wanted to go and had convinced Seb to take her.

'It was... interesting,' he replied, though his lips were twitching with a hint of a smile. 'So many eyeshadows to choose from. Did you know that you should spend as much on your brushes as you do on the make-up itself? I promised Keira that next time you'd come with us. I hated the idea of you missing out on all the fun.'

'Seriously, if you think—'

She was cut off by Conrad's reappearance. His face was pale, from the blood tests, and he was holding a small lollipop in his hands, which he waved at them.

'Apparently I have good veins. Even if I do feel like a pincushion.'

Birdie got to her feet while Seb crossed over to the reception counter and had a quiet word with the receptionist before they all headed out to the lift. Birdie gave them both a wave.

'You lot are welcome to go in that square box, but I'm taking the stairs. I'll see you at the bottom.'

She took the stairs two at a time, pleased for the exercise after having to sit still for so long.

They were waiting for her on the ground floor and they made their way to the car park together. Seb started the engine and turned left down the busy road. Then Birdie twisted around from the front seat to face Conrad.

'How are you feeling? Do you have any more questions for Lady Angelica?'

'Actually, I do. Before we find out if I'm compatible, I'd like to meet Devon and talk with him. After all, it's not just my guts that they'll be cutting into, it's his as well.'

'Fair enough,' Birdie said, inwardly grinning at what Dr Desai would think if she'd heard her surgery described in that way. 'We'll take you home so you can get some rest and talk to Tina and the girls, and we'll get back in touch once it's arranged.'

The traffic was light and the rest of the journey passed quickly enough. Conrad was lost in his own thoughts and Seb was focused on the road ahead, so Birdie caught up on her emails and sent Keira a couple of text messages, checking in on her.

You and Dad seem to think I can't amuse myself. He sent me a message before as well.

Birdie peered over at Seb's profile.

He didn't always show his emotions, but it was clear he'd already started to take his role as a father seriously. Unlike

Pappas, who, from what Seb had told her, had all but ignored the fact Conrad was his child by birth. She swallowed and peered out the window. Now she'd met Kim, she'd always planned to start searching for her birth father. But this whole case had made her realise she wasn't ready for that yet. One step at a time, as her old cricket coach liked to say.

After they'd dropped Conrad off, Seb turned to her. 'You're quiet, everything okay?'

'Yes. I was thinking how different Conrad's experience with Pappas was, compared with Keira's experience of meeting her father. Which is you, by the way.'

'Yes, thank you. I am aware of that.' He seemed to be suppressing a smile. 'I agree, it's been strange to be going through it at the same time as Conrad and his parents. Speaking of which, do you want to call Lady Angelica and give her an update? After all, it's still a big decision for her to let her two sons meet.'

'It will mean her secret will be well and truly out of the bag,' Birdie said as she opened her phone and made the call. 'Let's see how she takes the news.'

TWENTY-EIGHT

Seb climbed out of the car and stretched his legs. He couldn't remember a case that had involved quite so much driving. Still, if it could save Devon's life, the miles would be worth it. Yet, despite all the obstacles, there was a long way to go. Even Birdie, who was more optimistic than him, had faint worry lines running down the sides of her mouth.

Conrad had been quiet during the drive from Coventry to Fleckney to meet his half-brother, but as Lady Angelica's home came into view, his mouth fell open. 'Bloody hell.' He let out a long whistle and tightened his grip on the photo album Maggie had recently given him. 'Tina found loads of photographs on the internet, but none of them do this place justice. Do they actually live here? It's massive.'

Seb nodded. 'Yes, Lady Angelica and her husband live here. We'll let them know we're here and then walk around the estate to the cottage where Devon and his wife, Celia, live.'

'Don't worry, you'll get used to it. Kind of,' Birdie said as

they approached the front entrance, where the butler was
waiting for them.

If he was aware of who Conrad was, he didn't let it show.

'Good morning, Mr Clifford and Miss Bird. Lady Angelica
is on her way down,' he announced as their client appeared.

The shadows that had been haunting her eyes had lessened,
but her shoulders remained tense. 'Good morning. Thank you,
Gibbs. I'll take it from here. We're visiting Devon, if anyone
wishes to know where I am.'

'Very good, madam.' He gave a slight nod and silently disappeared into the house.

There was no sign of Lord Edgar. Was that intentional?

'It's so good to see you again,' Lady Angelica said, genuine
affection showing in her blue eyes when she looked at
Conrad.

'You too. I... er, have something. When I visited my mum,
after finding out about everything, she gave me this. It's for you.
Photos of me growing up. She'd kept it for... well... you know.'
He awkwardly held out the album.

Lady Angelica stared at it, as if unsure how to react. Then
she took it from him, tears glistening in her eyes. 'That's most
kind. Please, thank your mother for me. Do you mind if I look at
it later? When I'm alone and not in the company of others.'

Conrad nodded. 'Yes. That's a good idea.'

'I'll take it into my study. I'll be back in a tick.' When Lady
Angelica reappeared, she was followed by one of the dogs, who
raced over to Conrad. Two more dogs quickly followed,
although they stayed by her side.

'Behave, Trixie, or our guests will think you have no
manners,' she chided. Conrad laughed and put his hand out for
the dog to sniff.

'Our last dog was the same. Right little princess, she was.'

Trixie licked his outstretched hand, and Lady Angelica
picked up the lead that had been placed on the marble hall

table. She led them outside and onto the wide path that overlooked the sweeping gardens.

Trixie trotted at Conrad's side.

'I'm glad you like dogs. We always seem to have a pack of them. It's easy for me to forget that not everyone feels relaxed in their presence. While we're heading to Devon's cottage, I'll show you some of the grounds and when we return, we'll take a tour of the house...' She paused. 'Only if you'd like to, of course.'

'Yes. Definitely,' Conrad said, his eyes wide as if he was trying to take in everything at once. 'This place is huge. It must cost a fortune in electricity. I've worked on several big properties over the years, and the wiring can be a nightmare.'

'This is no different. It's not helped by the fact that with every new generation, a wing or extension has been added. It's an absolute rabbit warren when it comes to the electrics and plumbing. We're undertaking a programme of replacement. But it takes time. And money.'

'You might want to consider solar arrays,' Conrad said. 'You could have them installed away from the building so they don't take away from the aesthetics.'

'Devon's mentioned the same thing, more than once,' Lady Angelica admitted as they walked past the front of the house and along the access road. 'Over to the right are several fields in which we keep a dairy herd during spring and summer. This time of year, the cows are housed.' At the mention of cows, Trixie barked and trotted to the fence line. 'Behind that redbrick wall is the market garden.'

'I read about it on your website. It looked very impressive. I grow a few tomatoes and courgettes every year in my back garden, but that's about it.'

'Tomatoes can be tricky,' Lady Angelica assured him, as they walked on ahead, leaving Seb and Birdie a few paces behind.

'It's good to see them becoming more comfortable with each

other,' Birdie said. 'Though I wonder what will happen when he meets Devon? Do you think Lady Angelica's told him the truth?'

'If she hasn't yet, I'm sure she will at some point,' Seb said. 'Considering what she's asking of Conrad, it would be unfair for him not to be acknowledged. Then again...'

'Well, I guess we're about to find out,' Birdie replied as they reached Devon's cottage.

At the sight of the simpler cottage Devon lived in, Conrad appeared to recover some of his equilibrium. Trixie raced on ahead and gave a series of barks before Celia appeared in the doorway.

'Hello, girl.' Celia patted the dog and then studied them. It was clear by the surprise in her eyes that she'd hadn't known about the visit.

'Angelica, Seb and Birdie, it's good to see you.' The woman turned towards Conrad and offered a polite smile. 'I don't think we've met. I'm Celia.'

'This is Conrad.' Lady Angelica finished off the introductions and gave her daughter-in-law a hug. 'I hope you don't mind us popping by unannounced. I want to talk to you both together, and it's not something I can do over the phone.'

'Oh.' Celia gave her mother-in-law a searching look, no doubt remembering the reason Seb and Birdie had been hired. 'Of course, come in. Devon's had a good morning.'

After she'd ushered them inside, she closed the door behind them. The house was warm, and Seb shrugged off his coat as they stepped into the sitting room.

It was much the same as the last time they'd been there, although Devon wasn't in his recliner. Instead, he was stretched out on one of the sofas. At the sight of them, he struggled into a sitting position. His breathing was shallow and the dark rings under his eyes seemed deeper than the last time.

'Take a seat,' Celia said. 'I was about to make tea. I'll be back shortly.'

'Thank you, my dear.' Lady Angelica sat on the edge of the sofa and nodded for Conrad to join her. Seb elected for the window seat, while Birdie placed herself at the other end of the sofa, making sure to leave room for Celia when she returned.

Devon didn't seem to notice what they were doing, as he stared directly at Conrad, before finally turning to his mother.

'Don't tell me you've found a long-lost relative?'

'Sort of. Devon, this is Conrad. Conrad, this is my son Devon.'

'Nice to meet you,' Devon said immediately.

Conrad, on the other hand, seemed unsure what to do and ended up giving a mumbled nod. An awkward silence settled between them until Celia appeared with a tray carrying a large teapot and several cups and saucers. Her hands were shaking so badly that the delicate china rattled.

Seb quickly stood and took it from her. 'Allow me,' he said with a smile.

'Thank you.' She retreated to the seat next to her husband and laced her fingers through his.

Devon's breathing had become heavier. 'Mother, cut to the chase. What's this about, and who is Conrad?'

Lady Angelica took a shuddering breath. 'When I told you that I'd hired Sebastian and Birdie to look for a long-lost relative, I wasn't entirely honest. The real person I'd wanted them to find was Conrad. I'd hoped he might be a match with you because you're closely related.'

Devon frowned. 'I don't understand. *Closely* related? Why is this the first I'm learning of this?'

'Conrad... is my son.' Lady Angelica shifted in her seat, her hands tightly fisted in her lap. 'Which makes him your half-brother.'

'Your son? But how?' Celia asked, speaking first. She

clasped her hand across her mouth, colour mounting her cheeks. 'Sorry, please excuse me for being rude.'

'Nonsense, don't be silly,' Lady Angelica told her abruptly, sounding more like her usual self. 'It's me who should be apologising. It's a secret I've kept to myself for a very long time. When I was sixteen, I became pregnant. My parents insisted that the baby should be adopted and that's what happened. I've always told myself it was the right thing to do... But deep down, I'd always had reservations. I accepted that it was a situation that couldn't be reversed. However hard it was. Then, when you got sick...'

She broke off, her eyes filling with tears as she stared at Devon and then back to Conrad.

'You hired investigators to find him in the hopes he would give me a kidney?' Devon stared at his mother, as if trying to comprehend the thought pattern behind it. 'But you don't even know him. Nor does he know me.'

'That's right.' Conrad spoke for the first time, looking directly at Devon. 'My parents never told me I was adopted, let alone that I might have another family. So, we're in the same boat.'

Devon frowned. 'This is crazy.'

'You're not wrong there,' Conrad told him, shaking his head.

'Why are you here? Do you want to help?' Celia whispered as her fingers tightened around her husband's hand.

'I don't know.' Conrad returned her gaze before rubbing the back of his neck. Seb gave him a nod of approval. Despite how difficult it was, the man was being honest, which was the only way this could have a positive outcome. 'My blood type's a match, but they're running some other tests. Something to do with tissues.'

'HLA. Do you have the results?' Celia sucked in a breath.

'No. But before I get them, I wanted to talk to you both. It's a big decision, especially to be asked to help someone I've never met before.'

'Does Father know about this?' Devon asked his mother, his eyes still clouded with confusion. Lady Angelica gave a sharp shake of her head.

'No. Not yet. Nor do your brothers. There's too much happening at the moment. I would ask that you keep it between us for now.'

'If that is what you wish,' Devon said before turning to Conrad. 'How do you feel about being asked to help me?'

'Honestly, it's like I've woken up in someone else's life. I grew up in a regular house that's nothing like where you lived.' He nodded in the direction of the hall. 'But having all that privilege doesn't protect you from getting sick, does it?'

'You're right there. I can't quite believe that you're willing to consider helping.'

'You and me both.' Conrad gave him a half smile and some of the tension eased. 'I've never even been in hospital before except as a visitor. The closest I ever got was when my missus was having our firstborn. I fainted in the delivery room and they had to carry me out of there.'

'Were you okay?' Celia's eyes were wide.

'Yeah. There was a *lot* of blood, not helped by me suddenly realising that I was going to be a dad. It hit me all at once what a big deal it was. Remembering that is what got me thinking about the whole family thing. After I met, umm' – he turned towards Lady Angelica, as if unsure what to call her – 'my birth mother, at first I thought she only wanted to find me to save you. But—'

'Mother's not like that,' Devon finished off, giving a weak smile. 'Underneath the tough-old-bird exterior, there isn't anything she wouldn't do for the people she loves.'

Lady Angelica's cheeks brightened as she stared silently at both of her sons.

'I figured that before I made up my mind, I'd better meet you. See what kind of person you are.'

'I'm pretty normal. I work here on the estate. But it does takes a *lot* of work to maintain. And money. I'd always wanted to help keep it going, which is why I studied horticulture at college and took over the running of the market garden.'

'Correction. Devon set it up from scratch.' Lady Angelica's eyes were full of pride. 'He's done a marvellous job and turned a profit after only two years. Remarkable.'

Devon simply shrugged. 'I've done okay. But there's still so much more in the pipeline. And there's only me to do it. My brothers weren't interested in working on the estate; they chose other careers. This year, we'd intended to start on the orchard. In spring, we've got the—' He broke off and leant back, his face a waxy colour. Celia squeezed his hand.

'There's plenty of time for that, sweetie,' she assured her husband before turning to Conrad. 'He gets tired very quickly.'

'I'm fine. I just stayed up too late.' Devon gasped, his breath still tight.

Lady Angelica made a tutting noise. 'Let me guess, you were working on the 5208 again, weren't you?'

'Guilty. I've almost finished it.' Devon nodded to the small table by his recliner where the tiny model train was sitting, alongside tiny tins of enamel paint and a collection of brushes.

'Wait.' Conrad turned to him. 'Are you talking about the *Llantilio Castle*?'

'One and the same.' Devon's eyes brightened. 'You know it?'

'Too right,' Conrad said, staring at the wall opposite on which was a collection of black-and-white photographs of old engines with the huge columns of steam trailing out behind them like a veil. He got to his feet and walked over to them. 'This is the *Flying Scotsman*.'

'It is. My father took that photograph when he was a boy. It's a beauty, isn't it?'

'Sure is. I did a couple of years working as a line engineer on the railways. Totally loved it.' Conrad headed over to the table where the small model was sitting. 'Mind if I have a look?'

'Be my guest. If you bring it over here, I'll show you what I'm planning to do next.'

As they spoke, Lady Angelica stood and picked up the tea tray. She glanced over to Seb and Birdie. 'I'm going to make a fresh pot. Perhaps you could both help me?'

The pair of them immediately did as she'd suggested. As they reached the kitchen, Lady Angelica's phone buzzed and Seb took the tray from her and placed it on the bench.

'Leave this to us,' he said.

'Thank you.' Lady Angelica disappeared from the room.

'I think it's going well. Considering what an awkward situation it is,' Birdie said as she peered around the kitchen.

'I wouldn't have picked Conrad as a trainspotter,' Seb said, filling the kettle with water and carrying it to the old Aga in the corner.

'Takes all types, I guess. I've never seen one of those cookers in real life. Do you know how to work it?'

'I do,' he assured her, lifting back the cover protecting one of the hot plates and placing the kettle on it. 'Though the beauty of them is that they're foolproof.'

'Aren't you a font of all knowledge?' Birdie teased.

Lady Angelica reappeared, and it didn't take them long to make a fresh pot of tea and return to the cosy sitting room, where Devon and Conrad were both examining a catalogue of model engines while Celia sat on the window seat, watching them.

The visit only lasted a further fifteen minutes because Devon's energy waned. The two men shook hands, and once they'd left the cottage, Lady Angelica gave Conrad a quick tour of the kitchen garden that her son had created before catching sight of a builder who was walking towards them.

'Damn. I forgot he was visiting. I need to speak to him urgently about some dry rot. Can I give you a tour of the hall another time?'

'Of course. Dry rot waits for no one,' Conrad said.

Lady Angelica smiled. 'You have my sense of humour. Thank you for agreeing to meet Devon. As I said before, whatever you decide, I'd like for us to meet regularly... You don't have to decide about that immediately.'

She turned and marched towards the builder.

Birdie patted Conrad on the arm. 'You okay?'

'Yeah, I am. It's weird. Growing up as an only kid, I'd always wanted some brothers and sisters, but, of course, my parents were in their forties by the time they had – well – adopted me. So it was never an option. To have a whole new family at my time of life, it's... But, you know, Devon seems like a good guy. Celia, too.'

'Does that mean you've made your decision?' Birdie probed in her straightforward manner, as they reached the car.

'Not yet. For now, I want to get my head straight and talk to Tina. I'll let you all know soon. I promise. He's not in a good way, is he?'

'No,' Seb said as they climbed into the car.

Devon Charing was definitely not in a good way.

TWENTY-NINE

Wednesday, 20 December

'Elsa, come here. Good girl.' Keira clapped as the dog trotted across the grass, the sodden tennis ball gripped firmly in her jaw, before depositing it at Keira's feet. 'Aren't you clever?'

'She's clever enough to know a willing subject when she meets one.' Seb smiled at them both. Keira's cheeks were bright, despite the cool weather, and she bounced from foot to foot, as if trying to burn off energy. 'Have you heard from your school yet?'

She let out a dramatic sigh. 'Yes. They've arranged for my teachers to email me all the work I've missed. You do realise that means I'll have to stay inside the whole of the Christmas holiday studying, which seems pointless when I'm starting a new school in January.'

'Your new school will expect you to have completed the work, and it will go in your favour at the interview,' Seb reminded her.

They'd spent the previous evening discussing her schooling

options. There was an excellent school in the area and he'd approached them regarding Keira. They had agreed, based on her previous exam results, but wanted to interview her in the new year, before the new term began. He'd expected more resistance in respect of her catching up on missed work, but after a few eye rolls and comments on how dumb the education system was in general, Keira had agreed to the plan.

'I want some time off for good behaviour. Birdie promised to take me Christmas shopping. Of course, I could go myself if you'd let me drive your car. Or even let me have one of my own. I have passed my test, you know.' She gave him a hopeful look.

'I suggest you go with Birdie for the time being and we'll discuss cars before term starts.'

'Deal.' Keira grinned.

Had persuading him to buy her a car been her plan the entire time? Was he out of his league, trying to navigate parenting a teen girl?

Keira appeared to have picked up on his self-doubt and patted his arm.

'Don't worry. I don't need anything fancy and I've got some savings to put towards it. Come on, Elsa, I'll give you a race.'

As she darted to the other side of the garden, closely followed by Elsa, Birdie appeared from the house and beckoned to him.

'I've finished returning emails,' she told him as he stepped into the hallway and shrugged off his coat. 'I was going to call you, but I could see Operation Car was underway.'

Seb raised his eyebrows. He'd been right. 'You knew about it?'

'Don't worry, it wasn't a conspiracy. Keira actually asked me if I knew a good place for her to buy a second-hand car because she didn't want to rely on other people. I told her to ask you first.'

'That does make sense. I don't want her driving anything unreliable. It took long enough to convince you to upgrade.'

'Yeah, well, when I was working for the police, it didn't matter, but now we're in business, I can see the benefits.' Her phone buzzed and she glanced at the screen. 'It's Conrad.' She answered and put it on speaker. 'Hey, we're both here. How's it going?'

'I wanted to let you both know that if I'm compatible, I'll be a kidney donor for Devon.'

Seb swallowed, the small knot in his stomach easing. This case, with its emotional toil, had been far more challenging than those they had undertaken in the past.

'Conrad, that's fantastic news. I know it's been a huge decision,' Birdie said.

'You know what? It wasn't hard. I imagined if it was one of my girls and what it would mean to me and Tina if someone said they'd help. Also, I really like Devon.'

'Have you thought about payment?' Seb asked.

Conrad had avoided discussing it with them, despite being asked several times the figure he had in mind. It had crossed Seb's mind that it might have increased after discovering the background of his birth mother.

There was silence.

Seb frowned, while Birdie tapped her foot, unable to hide her nerves.

'I've given it a lot of thought. I don't want any payment. It's not why I'm agreeing to do it. My parents might not have had as much money as Lady Angelica, but they always taught me that family is important and so is doing what's right.'

'But doing what's right isn't going to pay the mortgage and the bloody bills,' Tina's voice came through in the background.

'That's enough. The decision's made.' Conrad's voice was muffled. He returned to the call. 'Sorry about that.'

'Don't be,' Birdie assured him, her brow furrowed. 'Are you sure about the money? Because if you're compatible, and the surgery goes ahead, you'll be out of action for at least two or three months according to Dr Desai. What if it stops you from getting a job?'

'Then it does. Most of the jobs I've been applying for have been crap anyway. This is the way I want it done,' Conrad said firmly.

'Stubborn idiot,' Tina grumbled in the background, although there was an element of pride in her voice.

Seb agreed. There was much to admire in Conrad and how he'd dealt with such a challenging situation.

'Have you let Lady Angelica know?' Seb asked.

'No. Will you tell her, please? I'll speak to her directly after that. It's been a big day and we're out tonight with the girls. It's our family tradition to drive around looking at the Christmas lights. The girls complain they're too old, but last year, when we tried to cancel it, they kicked off.'

'Sounds like a great tradition. Enjoy yourselves.' Birdie ended the call and let out a sigh. 'Well, somehow we've managed to navigate our way through this case. I wasn't sure it was ever going to happen.'

Seb agreed. Although they couldn't be sure of the outcome, they'd done as much as they could. It was now out of their hands. 'We'll contact Lady Angelica with the news. Let's go through to the study instead of standing in the hallway.'

Nodding, Birdie followed him and they sat down on the armchairs in the corner of the room. Seb called the number and then placed the phone on the table between them.

The call was answered on the first ring. 'Sebastian? Do you have news?'

'Conrad has agreed to be a donor, providing the tests show he's compatible.'

There was a long gasp and a bang, as if the phone had been dropped. Seb glanced at Birdie, whose were eyes watering.

'I-I'm sorry about that,' their client said after a few seconds, her voice shaky. 'I hadn't wanted to allow myself to believe it could happen. Tell me everything.'

'Of course.' Birdie filled her in on the short conversation, before adding, 'And he wants you to know that he doesn't want any payment.'

'He must accept something. His living expenses, at least, while he can't work. Otherwise it isn't right,' Lady Angelica protested.

'It's something you can discuss with him, but he sounded adamant. He said his adopted parents always taught him that family isn't about money,' Birdie told her.

'What an extraordinary person he is.'

'He is. Though it's not something he's doing lightly. I doubt he would have agreed if he believed that you or Devon were disingenuous,' Seb said.

'Congratulations, Lady C— I mean, Lady Angelica,' Birdie said, glancing across at Seb and wincing. 'You must be so relieved. Such awesome news to get just before Christmas.'

'Yes. Although, please don't call me Lady C – it reminds me of my mother-in-law when she was alive.' Lady Angelica laughed.

'Noted,' Birdie said. 'But you're still excited about it, aren't you?'

'Yes, Birdie. I am. I'd been dreading Christmas. Leo, Charles, and their families are arriving on Friday, and I had no idea how we were all going to get through it knowing it could be our last one with... Well, let's just say, this will make it a little brighter.'

'What are you going to tell them about Conrad? Will you say he's a long-lost relative?' Birdie asked.

'No.' It was a firm answer, suggesting she wouldn't be changing her mind. 'Tonight I'll explain everything to Edgar and then tell the boys once they arrive. If Conrad can do this wonderful thing for our family, it's the very least I can do for him. After years of hiding the truth about my past, and my son, I owe him that.'

'There's every chance this will become public knowledge and be in the media,' Seb felt obliged to remind her.

While having an illegitimate child wasn't frowned upon in the way it once was, the circles that both Lady Angelica and her husband were a part of might view it differently. There could potentially be serious implications for the family.

'I'm tired of keeping this a secret. I'm not my parents, who believed that reputation mattered more than family. I don't blame them for their actions, but it's not something I want to continue.'

'What about the accident and your involvement in it?' Birdie asked.

'I will tell my family everything. I had a phone call from DS Litton earlier, and she wants to interview me tomorrow.'

Seb and Birdie exchanged glances. They'd warned their client about this possibility so she wouldn't be caught off guard. Despite the fact the car accident happened over fifty years ago, the serious nature of the crime meant there was a possibility that she could be charged.

'Are you going to the station at Rugby?' Seb asked.

'No, she's kindly agreed to come here. Sebastian, I do have another request. Until I've explained it all to the boys, I don't wish to involve our family solicitor in case it comes out sooner. He's an old friend and our children grew up together. I was hoping you'd be present during the interview, instead.'

Seb swallowed. Interviewing suspects and witnesses was always easier without a solicitor present and could put Lady

Angelica at a disadvantage. On the other hand, he understood her reasoning.

'Not having your solicitor with you isn't ideal; however, if you're determined not to, then I will attend. I won't be able to contribute or give you any legal advice. My role is as your support person.'

'Thank you.' Lady Angelica let out a shuddering sigh.

It appeared that she'd taken their warning seriously, and while it had been her decision to put Conrad and Devon before herself, and to let the truth come out, it didn't lessen the real danger of her being prosecuted.

'Up until last year, I worked with DS Litton and she's excellent at her job,' Birdie added, obviously picking up on their client's distress. 'If you like, I can be there, too. You might find it less threatening that way.'

'I'd appreciate that. Thank you. She'll be arriving at nine. If you arrive any earlier, we can have a coffee first. Now I'd best tell Devon the good news.'

Seb ended the call and leant back in the chair. 'Have you spoken to Sparkle today? Do you have any idea whether they're planning to press charges?'

Birdie shook her head. 'No. She won't want to put us in a compromising position by telling us anything that might affect our client, so we're just as in the dark as Lady Angelica. Do you think she's regretting it? After all, there's still a chance that Conrad won't come back as a viable match, and then all this will have been for nothing.'

As she spoke, Keira walked past the large French doors that opened out onto the terrace. Elsa walked next to her, stopping every now and then to nudge her new friend's leg. On seeing them both in the office, Keira stopped and mimed that she was heading to the kitchen to make a hot drink. Seb smiled and gave her a thumbs up, to which she pulled a face.

'I think she's telling you that you look like an out-of-touch dad,' Birdie told him bluntly. He sighed; she was probably right. He'd need to find out what kind of hand signals an *in touch* dad did. He watched his daughter hurry past before turning to Birdie.

'In answer to your question, no. I don't think Lady Angelica will be regretting that her son is now in her life. Not one bit.'

THIRTY

'Gibbs, we meet again,' Birdie said to the now familiar butler, as she stepped into the hall the following day.

'We do indeed, Miss Birdie,' he replied, though his mouth twitched into a hint of a smile. Birdie grinned. There *was* a sense of humour buried under there somewhere. 'Let me take you through to the drawing room. Lady Angelica and Lord Edgar are expecting you.'

'Thank you.' Seb and Birdie passed over their coats and they waited until Gibbs had carefully hung them up on one of the hooks before leading them through to a large room on the right.

Woah.

The other visits had either been in the family room or in Lady Angelica's study, so Birdie hadn't been prepared for the vastness of the drawing room. It had two huge chandeliers and a fireplace that was almost as tall as she was. The wooden floors were covered with thick Turkish rugs and there were several sofas dotted around the room.

Lady Angelica was sitting on one sofa, while her husband was in a wingback chair set at a right angle to her. It was an intimidating sight and Birdie suddenly wondered if it was Sparkle who would need a support person, not their client.

Lady Angelica rose and gave them a warm smile. The worry lines that had marred her face were still there, but there was also a calmness about her.

'Thank you both for coming. Gibbs, some coffee please?'

'Of course.' He slipped out of the room as quietly as he'd entered.

Birdie should ask him how he did that. It would be a good trick for when she was doing surveillance.

'How are you, sir?' Seb sat down on the long sofa opposite Lady Angelica, and Birdie joined him.

'Fair to middling. We had much to discuss last night.'

Lady Angelica patted his outstretched hand. 'You bore it very well, my dear.' She pushed up her chin and settled her gaze on them both. 'I explained it to Edgar over dinner last night and we decided to call the boys straight away rather than wait until tomorrow. The whole family knows everything.'

'I won't lie. It wasn't easy to hear. But we all understand. And the fact it might give Devon a chance... well... that's got to be a good thing.' Lord Edgar reached for the dog, Trixie, who'd woken up from a nap and was nudging his knee to get his attention.

'The boys were of the same opinion,' Lady Angelica told them as Gibbs arrived with a tray of freshly brewed coffee. Birdie inhaled deeply as he handed her a cup, the rich caffeine already making her feel more alert.

'That's good. I'm so pleased for you. I hope you don't mind me saying, but are you going to speak to DS Litton in here?'

Lady Angelica frowned. 'Yes. Is that a problem?'

'I think we might be better in the family room. This room... it's... well, very intimidating. If you don't mind me saying.'

'You're right, of course.' Lady Angelica picked up the bell on the table and rang it.

How on earth would Gibbs hear that?

Birdie needn't have worried, because the man appeared within seconds.

'Madam?'

'We're adjourning to the family room. Please bring Detective Sergeant Litton there when she arrives.'

The four of them headed to the family room, and Gibbs appeared a short time later, leading Sparkle and another officer.

Lady Angelica's face immediately paled, but Lord Edgar grasped her hand as the introductions were made.

'Thank you for agreeing to see us,' Sparkle said, turning to Birdie and Seb and raising an enquiring eyebrow.

'Don't worry, we're not here to interfere. We're giving moral support,' Birdie assured her.

'Okay, let's get started. Lady Charing, please could you tell us everything you remember from the night when Frederick Timpson was knocked over.'

'Yes.' Lady Angelica nodded. 'I'd arrived home from school for the Christmas break. I was a boarder and hadn't been home during term time. I'd been dreading seeing my parents because I was fairly certain I was pregnant. My mother and father were fierce and had no tolerance for mishaps like that. I felt like I'd messed up my entire life. I worried that they'd disown me.'

'The baby's father?' Sparkle asked.

'Roy. He was so different from my friends and family. I think that's what drew me to him in the first place. He was dangerous and, at the time, it seemed very exciting.'

'When did you first meet him?' Sparkle asked.

'It was during the summer, and while I knew it wouldn't last, it was intoxicating. He was the first person I could talk to about things that didn't revolve around my family name and background. We didn't stay in touch when I went back to school. I wasn't even sure if he'd still be working on the estate when I arrived home.'

'But he was there. What happened then?'

'I knew my parents had to be told about the pregnancy because I was already showing slightly. But I was scared. When I saw Roy, I arranged to meet him after he finished work. I wanted to see if there was a different option for us. Except I didn't get around to telling him. He had some beers, and instead, we both got drunk. I know it was stupid, but I was only sixteen, and at the time it seemed like a good way to stop thinking about what a mess I'd made of my life.'

'Whose idea was it to steal the car?'

'His. He wanted to go into town to buy some more beer and said we should use one of the estate cars. After all, the keys were kept in the house and it wouldn't be hard for me to get them. I was drunk and thought it would be funny...' She broke off and closed her eyes, as if reliving the scene in her mind. 'Before we'd even left the estate grounds we'd hit someone. Roy said the man was hurt. Not dead. I made Roy come back to the house with me to phone for an ambulance. My parents were waiting for us. Our butler had seen us in the car and had informed them. They were extremely angry that I was with Roy... and that we were both drunk. I was sent to my room while they called the emergency services.'

'Did you ask what had happened to the man you'd hit?'

Lady Angelica's face paled. 'The next day, my mother told me he'd been taken to the local hospital and had since been released. I didn't ask anything else, because after that, I told them about my relationship with Roy, and the pregnancy. I was sent to Norfolk the same day to be with my aunt. They were more concerned with me bringing shame on the family name. But it was a wake-up call. I realised how stupid I'd been spending time with Roy. That our worlds were completely opposite and there was no future for us, even if I'd wanted there to be.'

'And did you?' Sparkle asked.

'No. Not really. It was the excitement that drew me in, that's all. What will happen now? Are the police going to press charges?' Lady Angelica asked. Lord Edgar put a supportive hand on his wife's shoulder.

'I'll be recommending that no further action is taken against you.' Sparkle said. 'It seems clear that while you were a passenger and, by implication, involved in the accident, you had no idea what had happened to the victim. Considering the circumstances of your pregnancy, and the fact most of the other people involved are now dead, it would be difficult to disprove.'

Birdie let out her breath. It was no longer her job to make police decisions, but she was pleased with the outcome.

Lady Angelica nodded, her eyes filled with sadness. 'Thank you.'

It was understandable why the woman appeared sad. A man had died that night, and her affair with Roy had almost led her down a path from which she might not have returned. Not to mention her parents had sent her away, worried of the shame she might bring the family name.

Birdie hoped that with everything out in the open, it might make things easier for her.

Lady Angelica escorted Sparkle and DC Harris from the room and returned a few minutes later. Her gaze swept over Birdie and Seb.

'That went better than expected. Was it because you worked together, Birdie?'

'Definitely not. DS Litton is an excellent detective and would never drop a case unless she believed it to be the right course of action. Her decision would have been made based on the evidence and where it was pointing. She will still need the approval of her superior officer.'

'I believe it was the correct decision based on the facts,' Seb said.

'And just in time for Christmas,' Birdie added. 'Hopefully you can enjoy it now and spend time with your family.'

At this, she gave them both a rueful smile. 'This is the least organised I've been for this time of year. With so much going on, I've let a few things slip. Despite worrying about Devon, I'm actually looking forward to it more.'

'With no turkey.' Lord Edgar let out a relieved chuckle. 'Can't stand the meat. Never been so happy as when Angie told me she'd forgotten to order them in time.'

'Doesn't your cook do that for you?' Birdie asked with a frown.

'No. I've always chosen the turkey. I haven't yet informed Cook. She won't be happy.'

'Unlike me,' Lord Edgar said.

Lady Angelica gave him a stern glare but it was followed with a smile. 'There are a few other traditions we'll be changing as well. Conrad, Tina and the girls are all joining us on Boxing Day. I had thought of asking them for Christmas Day, but didn't want to overstep in case they had other family obligations or plans.'

'It sounds like you're going to have good fun.' Birdie beamed at them, the niggle she'd had that Lady Angelica was simply using Conrad well and truly buried. 'And speaking of Christmas, we'd better go. You're not the only one to let a few things slip. I haven't finished my shopping yet.'

THIRTY-ONE

Friday, 22 December

'You're absolutely sure I don't need to curtsey?' Keira smoothed down the new winter coat she'd spent the previous night debating whether or not to wear as Seb pulled up outside his parents' home in London.

'Definitely no curtseying required. They're not royalty. Take a deep breath. You have nothing to worry about. I'll be with you, and so will Elsa.'

'You say that now but look at this place. It's huge.' Keira stared up at Ovington House. It was a four-storey white stone Georgian building, with long windows and decorative wrought-iron balconies. 'I should have worn the red coat. It was stupid to think I should meet your parents in this horrible old thing.'

'You bought the coat a few days ago. It's hardly old. And it's perfect. If you're ready, we'll go inside. I promise your grandparents won't eat you. How bad can it be?'

Keira returned his gaze, her expression thoughtful. Then she let out a small laugh and climbed out of the car before unclipping Elsa from her harness.

'Good point. How bad can it be? That will be my new motto.' As they walked towards the front door Keira slowed down. 'What about Elsa? Does she need a walk before we go inside?'

'There's a back garden if need be. Don't worry, Elsa considers this her second home. She's even managed to convince my mother to let her sleep on the sofa.'

The news seemed to give Keira more courage. 'You didn't mention that your mum likes dogs. You should have led with that.'

'I'll remember for next time,' Seb assured her, barely managing to keep a straight face as they climbed the steps to the front door.

He rang the bell and after only a few seconds, Bates appeared. 'Good evening, sir and Miss Keira. Your parents are expecting you.'

'Thank you, Bates,' Seb said before realising Keira was staring at their long-time butler.

Bates didn't appear to be at all put out as he led them through to the sitting room, where Seb knew his mother would be sitting at her writing desk, pretending that she hadn't been checking the time, while his father would be reading a business magazine, nursing the one drink his mother allowed him before lunch.

Sure enough, his mother was at the table, but at the sight of him, she stood up, her smile wide. Next to him, Keira let out a tiny gasp. 'She's almost as tall as me,' she murmured, awe in her voice.

'I think you have a couple of inches on her,' Seb replied in a low voice before turning to his parents. 'Mother, Father, it's good to see you both. I'd like you to meet your granddaughter, Keira.'

'We're delighted you're here.' His mother walked towards them, a little faster than usual, her eyes full of love. 'I hope the drive was okay. Did Sebastian remember to stop at one of the services for a break? He can be a little impatient sometimes and forgets that not everyone has his stamina.'

Sebastian raised an eyebrow at his mother, but the gentle scold had the desired effect of making Keira laugh. 'I think he would have stopped, but I'd already packed loads of snacks. Thank you for inviting me. It's nice to meet you both.'

'You too, my dear,' Sebastian's father said, joining them. He shook Keira's hand and gave her an approving nod. 'I can see you have the Clifford nose.'

'Phillip, please. No young lady wants to be told they have a Clifford nose,' his wife scolded him.

Keira grinned. 'I don't mind. I like that I share it with Sebastian's great-grandmother, Mary Brighton Clifford. She seemed feisty, and set up a charity to help support widows whose husbands were killed in the war.'

'You have been doing your homework. My mother was indeed considered... feisty.' Seb's father looked at her more carefully. 'She was also committed to preserving historical buildings.'

'Like the greenhouse at Saffron Gardens,' Keira agreed. 'It's really gorgeous. I'd love to see it one day.'

Sebastian's mother's eyes were wide. 'How do you know all this?'

'I was looking for something to read at Rendall Hall, and there was a family tree in Sarah's study. Sebastian showed me all the research that had been done, so I figured it would be fun to learn about everyone.' Then she frowned. 'Was that bad? I didn't mean to be nosey.'

'Of course it's not bad. I'm shocked you can remember it all,' his mother said before letting out a little gasp. 'Goodness. Don't tell me you've also got a super memory like Sebastian?'

'Guilty.' Keira turned to Seb, sharing with him a shy smile. 'It's been kind of awesome to know where I got it from. In the past, it's always made me feel, you know, a bit weird. Especially some of the things my teachers used to say about it.'

'We had the same problem. Sebastian was accused of cheating by one of his school masters. Dreadful man. I made sure he didn't make those accusations again.' She took Keira's hand in hers and gave it a gentle squeeze. 'Come and sit down. I want you to tell me all about yourself. We have years of catching up to do.'

Sebastian watched as Keira followed his mother over to the sofa, along with Elsa – who, true to his prediction, climbed up next to Keira, her nose resting in his daughter's lap. While they were speaking, his father patted him on the shoulder.

'Your mother's been staring out of that damn window since nine this morning waiting for you to arrive. She thinks I didn't notice. She's terribly excited herself at having a granddaughter.'

'What about you, Father? What are your feelings?' Seb's father had always been concerned about appearances and the family name, and while times had certainly moved on, his father still had one foot in the past.

'I won't lie to you. I was shocked at first. My preference would have been for you to marry someone like Annabelle. But you've always been determined to march to the beat of your own drum.' His voice was gruff, but there was no admonition there. It had taken his father quite some time to accept Seb's decision not to be involved in the estate, and he would hate for their relationship to revert to how it was.

'Once you get to know Keira, you'll like her even more.'

'I'm sure I will. Extraordinary that she can also remember everything she reads or hears. I'll have to watch myself.'

'Now you're sounding like Birdie,' Seb said in a lightly teasing voice, which was as close as he ever got to joking with his father.

'How is that business partner of yours? Your mother mentioned you've been very busy recently.'

'That's correct.' Seb never went into details about his cases. If Lady Angelica wanted to tell his parents, that would be her decision. 'The case is over and now Birdie's taking a few days off to relax with her friends and family.'

'Speaking of Christmas, your mother has charged me with convincing you and Keira to change your minds and join us at the estate for Christmas Day. Hubert and the family would love to see you. We're travelling down there tomorrow.'

'Sorry, it's not possible. I did explain to mother that Sarah's boys will be there from university. We're having Christmas Day together and will catch up with Sarah on a Zoom call. It's already planned.'

'Yes, that's the right thing to do, considering you've been living at Rendall Hall.' His father gave a grudging nod. 'Hubert was looking forward to seeing you. The estate has been certified organic. Feeling jolly pleased with himself about it.'

'We'll visit in the new year. Keira can meet everyone then,' he promised.

Bates appeared, announcing that lunch was ready. By the time dessert was served, Keira's nerves had disappeared and her eyes sparkled with excitement as Seb's mother regaled her with far too many stories about his childhood.

'That is so hilarious. Why didn't you tell me about that?' she demanded at the end of a particularly embarrassing anecdote involving a bead being lodged up his nose.

'I can't think how it slipped my mind,' he said as the grand-father clock in the hall chimed. 'We need to leave if we're to beat the traffic,' Seb said, getting to his feet. 'Plus, I know you have a cocktail party to attend this evening.'

His mother gave them both a reluctant smile. 'Yes, but it will be such a bore compared to this. Phillip told me you've promised to visit in the new year. I will hold you to that. I want to show Keira some of my old ball dresses.'

'They sound amazing,' Keira agreed before standing up and smiling at them both. 'Thank you for today. It's been lovely.'

The goodbyes took longer than usual, but finally Seb pulled out away from the house and joined the procession of cars heading towards the M1.

Initially, Keira was quiet although a contented smile clung to her lips. Finally, she turned to him.

'Your parents are so cool.'

He smiled. 'I can't say I've heard that description of them before.'

'Well, it's true. They are. I thought they were going to be stuffy and full of "thou shalt do this" or "it's off to the gallows with you, my girl", but they weren't like that at all. They're just regular people.'

'I'm glad you think so. Speaking of grandparents, I spoke to your other set before they left for Cornwall, and they suggested we join them for lunch in two weeks, once they've returned.'

Keira frowned. 'Do you promise this isn't a trick to make me go back and live with them?'

'It's not a trick. Besides, we've already arranged your interview at Churchill School. You'll be living at Rendall Hall for the foreseeable future, but I hope you'll agree that your grandparents will still be part of your life. Remember, this will be their first Christmas without your mother.'

'I know,' Keira said softly. 'I keep thinking about Mum, and then I feel guilty, because compared to a few weeks ago, I feel so much happier. Like I suddenly have this new life. Then I remember she's not here to see it, and that sucks.'

'It does,' he agreed in a low voice. 'It's okay for you to feel like that. Your mother would be pleased to know you're feeling happy for at least some of the time. If you are sad, tell me about it. Don't hide it. I'm here to listen.'

'You're pretty cool as well.' Keira gave him a half smile. 'Thanks, Dad.'

THIRTY-TWO

'Don't even think of offering me one of those,' Birdie announced to Keira, who was standing in the doorway to the office, holding a tray of brownies that she'd baked. 'I'll burst if another thing passes my lips. You must have a bottomless stomach.'

'Am I hearing correctly?' Seb retorted, thinking of the vast quantities of food his business partner regularly ate.

'I'm no match for your daughter,' Birdie said, with a grin.

Keira waved the tray in front of him and he shook his head. 'Maybe later... for afternoon tea.'

'Lightweights,' Keira informed them both, before returning to the kitchen, where she was experimenting with making sourdough bread in preparation for her New Year's resolution to be able to feed herself.

Seb enjoyed spending time in the kitchen and loved seeing how fearlessly his daughter dived into any challenge.

'Lightweight?' Birdie said. 'That's a joke. Between the Bird Family Christmas Day Extravaganza and then catching up with all my friends over the last couple of days, I've eaten my body-weight in mince pies and fruit cake. You still haven't told me about your Christmas. Where are the twins, by the way?'

'They're visiting some old school friends in Leicester. They'll be back this afternoon. It was a surprisingly loud occasion. Or maybe not so surprising. The boys appear to have adopted Keira as the younger sister they never had.'

Seb wasn't the only one surprised at how well it had gone. When his cousin Sarah had called, he could see the delight in her face when she saw how happy her sons were. He'd spoken privately with Sarah on Boxing Day, and she'd mentioned returning to the UK sometime next year. He was looking forward to seeing her and discussing her plans for the future. Not least because he had his own future to consider. He wouldn't contemplate leaving the area until Keira had completed her schooling.

'Good to hear. It will be nice to see them both. Oh, and—' She was cut off by Seb's mobile ringing. She gave him a hopeful look. 'New case?'

He picked it up to see Lady Angelica's name flash up on the screen. 'No. Old case.' He answered and put the phone on speaker. 'Lady Angelica, how are you?'

'Very well, thank you. I wanted to let you know that DS Litton called to confirm that I won't be prosecuted.'

'That's great news,' Birdie said, raising her hand for a high five, which Seb ignored.

High fives, like emoticons, were for others... Most of the time.

'Did she mention Pappas?' Seb hadn't been in contact with the man, but John Rogers mentioned that the police had interviewed him several times.

'Yes. Despite him confessing to running over the man and helping cover it up, he's not being charged. He gave them the name of the other estate worker who was present at the burial, but he's no longer alive. Furthermore, the police were unable to trace Frederick Timpson's family. The case is now closed. DS Litton did say that they weren't going to speak on behalf of Roy when he asks for a sentence reduction.'

Birdie let out a whistle. 'I wonder how he took *that* news? I can't imagine he'd be best pleased, since he seemed to think it was his ticket out of there.'

'Once he'd discovered there was a witness, I suspect he expected it,' Seb said. 'I take it he hasn't asked to see Conrad again?'

'Not as far as I'm aware,' Lady Angelica said. 'Conrad told me he doesn't wish to establish a relationship with him. There's another reason for this call. We've spoken to Dr Desai, and Conrad's HLA type is a match. The operation's going ahead.'

'Excellent news.' Seb leant back in his chair and exchanged a look with Birdie, who was punching the air, in her usual fashion. He didn't blame her. Usually when a case was over, there was a sense of completion. In this instance, with so much else at play, it had been hard to feel they'd been successful.

Until now.

'Tell Conrad and Devon how happy we are. Do you have a date yet?' Bird asked, still smiling broadly.

'February. Conrad will undergo counselling prior to the op and Devon's required to pass a health check. But for the first time in a long time, we're hopeful. It's thanks to you both.'

'We're pleased it's all worked out. How are the rest of the family? Did your Boxing Day meal go well?' Birdie asked.

There was a slight pause. 'It went as well as could be expected. Conrad and Tina were overawed to begin with, and Edgar was frostier than I would have liked. But once Devon's two brothers realised Conrad wasn't a conman attempting to disinherit them, they relaxed.'

'Their reticence is only to be expected,' Seb said in agreement. 'It will take time, but you're heading in the right direction.'

'You're absolutely right. When I gave Conrad a tour of the house, he spent most of the time inspecting the wiring, and has taken it upon himself to do all the remaining work. Edgar, who's a great believer in one rolling up one's sleeves, was most impressed. I've offered for the family to live on the estate in one of the empty cottages until after the operation. Not only will it give him time to recover, but they can rent out their own house. It will relieve some of their financial pressures.'

'That is a big step. What about the girls' schooling?' Seb asked.

'When I suggested attending the local school, the oldest girl burst into tears. From happiness, not because she didn't want to move. She was being bullied but hadn't wanted to tell her parents for fear of adding to their worries. It's only short term for now, but I do like the idea of them being close. It means we can continue getting to know each other. I'd better go. Thank you both, once again, for your work and for your discretion.'

'You're welcome. Please let us know how the operation goes,' Seb said.

'I will.'

Seb ended the call and Birdie turned to him.

'So, neither of us were kidnapped, threatened, or attacked this time. That's what I call a win.' She headed to her desk and opened her laptop. 'Now, I'd better do my least favourite job: compiling the receipts so we can send Lady C the invoice.'

'I'm one step ahead of you,' Seb told her as Keira reappeared, this time clutching a large tray with pot of tea, three cups and yet more brownies. 'I pulled everything together last night and was waiting for you to check I haven't missed anything. Once you've approved it, you can press send.'

'Brilliant. Less boring work for me. And, more importantly, another case over.' Birdie closed her laptop and joined Keira. 'Maybe I can squeeze in a brownie after all.'

EPILOGUE

'Damn.' Birdie checked the time on her phone and grabbed her laptop before scrambling out of the car. She'd promised to be back in the office by two, so they could go over their client notes before a conference call. Except it was now almost three in the afternoon, which meant she was late.

It wasn't even her fault. She'd been stuck behind some stupid van that was obviously trying to set a new Guinness World Record for being the slowest vehicle on Earth. And it had taken her longer than she'd expected to get the surveillance photographs she needed for a tenant who suspected their landlord was entering the property without informing them. Had he ever? Birdie had even got a shot of him eating food from the fridge.

She opened the door and ran down the hallway, before bursting into the office.

'Sorry, sorry, sorry,' she said, her voice breathless, before realising Seb wasn't there. Bloody typical. She'd panicked for nothing.

However, he appeared a moment later, holding a collection of books under one arm and didn't appear at all fazed to see her.

'How did it go with the Mulligan Avenue property?'

'Very good.' She put her laptop down on the desk and pulled out the digital camera from its padded bag. 'I have some damning shots which need uploading for the client. I went over the case notes while sitting in the car, so I'm prepared for the call.'

'Birdie, relax. I realised that the job had taken longer than anticipated and rearranged our meeting.'

She gave him a grateful smile. 'Does that mean I've got time to make a cup of tea? I'm desperate for one.'

'You do. In the meantime, I'll get the computer ready.'

The call only lasted thirty minutes and once it was over, Birdie returned to her desk to begin working on the photographs. She was just uploading the last one when Seb's phone rang. He glanced at the screen and held it up for her to see Lady Angelica's name.

Birdie's heart pounded. The transplant operation had taken place ten days ago, and while they'd been kept updated with text messages to confirm that Devon's body hadn't rejected the kidney, he was still in the hospital.

She waved her arms at Seb to signal for him to answer.

'Good news. Devon's home, and his new kidney is working,' Lady Angelica said without preamble. 'I've just left the cottage. It's the happiest I've seen my son and his wife since he was first diagnosed.'

Yes!

Birdie grinned at Seb, whose smile was as wide as her own.

'We're delighted for you. How's Conrad?' Seb asked.

'He's come through the whole thing like a trooper and seems to be thriving. He's already talking about starting to strip out the old wiring in the house. It's been a full-time job persuading him to rest.'

'It must be a big change for him, Tina, and the girls,' Birdie said.

'Initially, yes. In particular for Tina, who admitted she was resentful that Conrad wasn't being paid, considering they were struggling. But once they'd moved into the cottage at the beginning of January, it changed. They all seem very happy. Having them close by has made it much easier for us all to get to know them.'

'That's awesome. Will they move back to Warwick once Conrad's recovered?' Birdie asked.

'There's been an update there as well. The people who are renting their house are desperate to buy it, and so they're considering moving out here permanently. Conrad and Devon have become very close and have been discussing other ways to improve the estate. There's work here for Tina as well. I'm hopeful about the future.'

'We're pleased to hear it,' Birdie said.

'I have one other thing to tell you. I drove to Norfolk last week and visited Edith. So silly, but I burst out crying when I saw the place. Much of my life was tied up in that single event, which was probably why I'd avoided contacting her. But it was lovely to become reacquainted, and she was very forgiving. I'm arranging for her to visit once the weather improves.'

'I'm sure Edith will enjoy that,' Birdie said, thinking of how Edith spent so much time alone, staring out of the window at the sea below.

'I hope so,' Lady Angelica said.

They talked for several more minutes before ending the call.

'It's all turned out well,' Seb said.

'Thank goodness. Though, I'm struggling to imagine Tina working there. Can you imagine her and Gibbs together?' Birdie said, wincing at the thought.

'He might have met his match with her. Then again, it

might be a refreshing change for her, and for him. It's good to know that Devon might soon be well enough to be involved in running the estate.'

As he spoke, the sound of a car engine caused Elsa to sit up from her bed, her brows scrunching together the way they always did when Keira came home. Moments later, the front door opened and Keira's footsteps echoed in the hallway before she appeared in the doorway.

Birdie watched the way Seb's face brightened at the sight of his daughter. Keira returned the smile and then walked into the room and collapsed onto the small couch, her long legs stretched out in front of her. She was wearing jeans and an over-sized hoodie but her backpack had the Churchill School crest embroidered onto it – the only sign that she wasn't attending the local comprehensive that Birdie and her brothers had gone to.

In the past, Birdie had thought the private school was full of snobs and kids who thought they were too good for the likes of her, but since Keira had started attending, she realised it was just like any other secondary school.

'How was the test?' Seb asked.

'Oh, that? It was fine. I nailed it.' She shrugged, as if it was no big deal. Then again, with her memory, most standardised tests weren't a challenge. 'But in more exciting news, today we learnt about cognitive psychology. Do you know that our brains store and interpret information depending on our environment and what's happened to us in the past?'

'Sure do,' Birdie agreed. 'It's why people act differently, even when they've had a similar upbringing.'

Keira nodded, her eyes gleaming. 'Exactly. It means that when Dad acts all calm, even when I accidently break a crystal vase, like I did last week, it's because he's never had to worry about money. But... say if when he was a kid, he drew a mous-tache on the big portrait of Granny and Grandad, and he got grounded for a week, well, that might have caused him to act differently.'

Over at his desk, Seb's mouth twitched with amusement. 'Indeed. Of course, it could be that the vase you broke wasn't crystal. It was cut glass and I was able to replace it for less than the cost of a takeaway meal.'

Keira stared at him before grinning. 'Interesting. The fact you didn't mention this could mean that when you were a kid, you learnt it was safer to conceal things rather than tell anyone.'

Birdie burst out laughing as she turned to Seb. 'She's got you there.'

'Thank you, Birdie, for recognising my brilliance.' Keira did a mock wave of her hand. 'But seriously, this stuff is so cool. I've been looking into it and instead of doing criminology, and I'm going to read forensic psychology. That way I get to combine both things at once. There are some great courses. Especially at Oxford. Unfortunately, I missed their open day, but there's another one in a couple of months. I was thinking we could go together and find out more about it.'

Seb and Birdie exchanged an amused glance. He stood up and joined his daughter on the couch. 'A friend of ours lectures in forensic psychology. Dr George Cavendish.'

'You mean Dr *Georgina* Cavendish?' Keira said, her eyes huge. 'She's referenced all the time in everything I've read. Like she's really famous. And you know her?'

'Yes, I do. Would you like to meet her?' Seb asked.

'For real?' Keira's gaze went from Seb to Birdie and back again.

Seb returned the smile and nodded. 'Absolutely.'

A LETTER FROM THE AUTHOR

Dear reader,

Huge thanks for reading *Wake the Past*. I hope you were hooked on the Detective Sebastian Clifford series. If you want to join other readers in hearing all about my new releases and bonus content, you can sign up for my newsletter.

www.stormpublishing.co/sally-rigby

If you enjoyed this book and could spare a few moments to leave a review that would be hugely appreciated. Even a short review can make all the difference in encouraging a reader to discover my books for the first time. Thank you so much!

Thanks again for being part of this amazing journey with me and I hope you'll stay in touch – I have so many more stories and ideas to entertain you with!

Sally Rigby

www.sallyrigby.com

facebook.com/Sally-Rigby-131414630527848
instagram.com/sally.rigby.author

ACKNOWLEDGMENTS

I'd like to say a huge thank you to everyone who helped with this book. In particular, my good friend and author Amanda Ashby who was a great sounding board during the planning stages – it was also a great deal of fun.

I'd like to thank my editor Rebecca Millar for her fantastic edits; my proof reader Becca Allen for picking up all those things I'd missed; and my cover designer the incredible Stuart Bache for yet another amazing cover.

To my advanced reader team, once again you stepped up to the plate and gave some tremendous feedback. Thanks so much. I could never manage without you.

Finally, thanks to all my family for the continued support, it's very much appreciated.